THE SOULKEEPERS SERIES BOOK THREE

RETURN TO EDEN

USA TODAY BESTSELLING AUTHOR

G.P. CHING

CONTENTS

SOUL CATCHER

BOOKS BY G.P. CHING

The Soulkeepers Series

The Soulkeepers, Book 1

Weaving Destiny, Book 2

Return to Eden, Book 3

Soul Catcher, Book 4

Lost Eden, Book 5

The Last Soulkeeper, Book 6

Soulkeepers Reborn

Wager's Price, Book 1

Hope's Promise, Book 2

Lucifer's Pride, Book 3

The Grounded Trilogy

Grounded, Book 1

Charged, Book 2

Wired, Book 3

GLOSSARY OF TERMS

Healer (pr. n.) A rare type of Soulkeeper who has the power to heal people and situations. Healers can tell right from wrong even in the most confusing of circumstances.

Helper (pr. n.) A type of Soulkeeper specialized in the art of equipping Horsemen for their work.

Horseman (pr. n.) A type of Soulkeeper who acts as a warrior, battling Watchers when all other tactics have failed.

influence (v.) Act of placing a human under the spell of a Watcher. Usually, Watchers will lure their victims to drink an addictive elixir that subjects the person to the Watcher's will.

red stone (n.) An enchanted gem given to another Soulkeeper by a Healer that allows the Soulkeeper a window into the Healer's abilities. It is given when the Horseman or Helper needs guidance over an extended period of time away from the Healer.

Soulkeeper (pr. n.) A person with a recessive genetic abnormality that gives them power to fight Watchers. Each Soulkeeper's gift is as unique and individual as a fingerprint but their purpose falls into three categories: Helper, Horseman, or Healer. A Soulkeeper's power is triggered by a stressful event and is only fully realized when the person accepts their true purpose.

soulkeeper's staff (n.) A branch of the tree that grew out of Oswald Silva's buried corpse. Used by a Soulkeeper, the staff acts as a portal, transporting the user from one place to another. Makes a sound like a firecracker when activated. Also known as an _enchanted staff_.

Watcher (**pr. n.**) Angels who defected with Lucifer from God's grace. Also called fallen angels or demons, these beings have the skin and eyes of a snake, and wings like a bat. They are skilled in illusion and sorcery, appearing as model-perfect human beings most of the time. They are notoriously lazy, preferring to wait until their victims are physically or emotionally weak to attack. They live below ground in a place called Nod because the sun drains their powers. They gain strength by eating human flesh obtained by abducting people and keeping them as slaves.

ONE

FORBIDDEN FRUIT

Abigail Silva knew she was dreaming, the kind of bittersweet dream that could float away on the current of a waking breath. Clue one was the June snow. It drifted down around her as she walked into her garden, the delicate plants unbothered by the winter storm. The lush foliage harkened back to the days when Oswald's soul still warmed the air.

Gideon waited for her, closer than usual, close enough to cause her skin to prickle from the heat in real life. A lock of wild auburn hair cut across his forehead and his pearl-white wings folded against his back.

Holding her breath, she reached for him. Slow. Tentative. Would her imagination allow her this one sweet experience? Or, would her touch fill them both with scorching pain as it did in the waking world?

Soft ecstasy. There was no pain, no burn. Her shaky exhale ruffled the feathers where her hand made contact. Gentle but eager, she stroked his wing downward, moving her caress to his upper arm. The light from within him shimmered between her fingers. Touching Gideon was touching heaven. She inhaled the smell of sandalwood, orange blossoms, warmth, and light.

A smile spread lazily across Gideon's face, reaching all the way to his emerald-green eyes. He raised one rugged palm. She pressed her cheek into his hand. Those pearly wings enveloped her body, protecting her from the snow, a thoughtful but unnecessary gesture considering her Watcher skin couldn't feel the cold.

Abigail decided as long as she was dreaming, she'd make the most of it. For centuries she'd wondered what it would feel like to kiss Gideon. His lips were full, parted, waiting. Tilting her chin, she pressed her mouth to his. She closed her eyes, desperate to cling to every detail of the honey-sweet kiss. How long could she remain here in this fantasy? She vowed to fight waking with everything she had.

Pain. Abigail opened her eyes. Gideon was gone, replaced with the cold, blond illusion that the devil preferred to use. She might have screamed but there was something in her mouth. What had tasted like honey now moved bitter and rough on her tongue. She gagged, pitching forward. A cock-roach crawled from her bottom lip and dropped to the dirt.

"Lucifer!" she spat.

"You remember me, Abigail? So glad I made an impression the last time we were together. Have ten thousand years of absence made the heart grow fonder?"

She scrambled away from him. "Am I still dreaming or is this real?"

"Both, my dear. You are still asleep, and this is very much real."

Pulse racing, she tried to turn for the gate but her legs refused to obey. When Lucifer wanted an audience he got one. "Why are you here? I thought we agreed to go our separate ways after the fall?"

"Separate ways, yes. But I hadn't counted on you going the opposite way. You've crawled straight back to God. The list of Soulkeepers I stole from you—I believe you had no intention of sharing it with me. You're helping Him now. Unfair, Abigail. You were supposed to be mine."

"We had an agreement."

"I've never had a problem breaking an agreement." Lucifer rolled his eyes and spread his hands.

"What do you want, Lucifer?"

"I want you, Abigail. I need your help with something, help only you can give me. Join me and we will conquer this Earth, and I will make you a queen over it."

"Not interested," she said, crossing her arms over her chest. "I know how your promises work. Sure, you'll make me a queen—Queen of the Damned. Queen of the Broken. The most sorrowful of the sorrowful. No thanks. You forget I have free will. I choose not to help you."

Lucifer stepped closer, smoothing his blond hair with his hand. "Oh, but I can give you something God can't. I can give you Gideon."

As dangerous as it was, she leaned toward his face, her teeth coming together in an audible snap. "You've been breathing too many sulfur fumes. Gideon is not yours to give. God has promised us humanity. Gideon and I *will* be together."

"When? Pity about God's promises. He's always sketchy on the details. You never thought it would take this long, did you? For all you know, it could be another thousand years." Lucifer picked at something under his nail, then held his hand to the light, admiring his manicure.

"God always keeps His promises," she said softly.

"Yes, eventually. Like Moses reaching the promised land." Lucifer turned his attention back toward her and pressed his finger into his bottom lip. "Oh wait, that didn't work out so well for him, did it? What did He promise you, exactly? Did He say He'd make you human when evil is vanquished from the Earth? Clearly that's never going to happen. Must be easy for Him to make promises He never has to keep. And they call *me* the Lord of Lies."

"I'm not talking to you about this. I'm not helping you." She shook her head and backed away.

"If I ran things, Abigail, Gideon could fall. I could make him like us. If you were both Watchers, you could touch. You could kiss. And you could be together, forever. Human bodies age and die. What I offer you is permanent."

"Gideon would never fall. He's too good. He's not like me and he's definitely not like you."

"You underestimate your influence over him. He'd fall for you. You know he'd do it for you. He's already left heaven for you. It's not that much farther to go."

Abigail squared her shoulders and did a very stupid thing. She met Lucifer's eyes directly. There was a reason the name Lucifer meant morning star. With his bright blond hair, golden skin, and aqua blue eyes, he was attractive by human standards. But the way he glowed was like looking into the sun. Everything about him pulled her under, a deceivingly bright undercurrent that promised safety but delivered death. Only, somehow, Lucifer made her thoughts twist until she believed she wanted to die. She was desperate to die.

She tried to remember what she planned to say to him. Even when she looked away, she couldn't shake his hold on her. He smelled just like Gideon. He gave off light like Gideon. She buried her face in her hands and began to weep.

"There, there, Abigail. I know my presence is overwhelming. Take some time. Think about my offer. I'll be around." Where his hand touched her shoulder, Abigail's skin squirmed like it was covered in maggots. "I'm *always* around."

In the time it took her to lower her hands, he was gone. The darkness swallowed her, suffocating her under ten thousand pounds of weight, as if she were buried alive in her own subconscious. She struggled against the pressure, flailing her arms and kicking into the blackness. With a scream, she awoke tangled in her sheets. Black snakeskin fingers gripped her pillow. Her fingers. She'd lost her human illusion.

With a few deep breaths, she extended her hand and focused her energy. The scales transformed into smooth alabaster skin. A perfect French manicure took the place of her talons.

"Another nightmare?" Gideon asked, approaching from the corner of the room where he slept standing up. His light spilled over her.

"Yes."

"I don't suppose you're going to tell me about it."

"Don't be like that, Gideon." Abigail swept her platinum hair behind her shoulders. The blade-straight coif, her preferred illusion, cascaded elegantly down her back. She hugged her knees to her chest.

Gideon climbed onto the bed, kneeling beside her carefully. "Abigail, you've been secretive and obviously tortured since Lucifer stole the list of Soulkeepers. These nightmares, they mean something. You're feeling guilty. You should talk about it."

As well meaning as the sentiment was, Abigail felt the edge of his words. It was as much an accusation as a suggestion. "I've told you, Gideon. I don't feel guilty about what happened. I conjured the list of Soulkeepers for a good reason. Who knows how many lives I saved by calling Mara here to help slay those Watchers in Chicago? We needed help and I got it. There's no way I could have foreseen Lucifer would get the list."

Two fists came down on the bed in front of her, so hard it bounced her backward on the mattress. "No, Abigail. The Healer told you to wait. You should have waited. Don't you get it? You acted in your own will. You invited this mess."

"No, *you* don't get it, Gideon. We have free will for a reason. We're supposed to think for ourselves, to do what we know is right even when it means breaking the rules. And let's not forget that I was smart enough to place a spell on the list to keep Lucifer out. He can't read the list because of me."

"He wouldn't have the list at all, if it wasn't for you."

Abigail crawled forward, until she was so close to Gideon her face burned. "I don't feel guilty for what I've done. But let's be honest, you feel ashamed. Right now you are wondering whether your choice to join me on Earth was worth it. You are wondering if I am worth it."

Gideon lowered his eyes.

"That's all the confirmation I needed." Abigail bounded off the bed.

Gideon reached for her, the muscles in his shoulder

bunching with the effort. "I know you are worth it, Abigail. You've always been worth it. But I wonder if we will ever be in the same place at the same time. I can't understand what you did because I don't think like you." He narrowed his eyes and his reaching hand formed a fist. "We are together, every day, but still worlds apart. Lately, it feels like galaxies apart."

Abigail folded her arms over her chest and turned toward the stained-glass window. "Maybe we are."

"I do not regret coming to Earth for you, but this is hell. Having you but not having you is *hell*. No, I don't understand how you stay as strong as you do, or how you have the courage to risk our future on what you *feel* is the right thing to do." He crawled off the bed and took a step toward her. "I don't have that kind of courage."

With a deep sigh, Abigail pivoted to face him. "I'm not ready to give up."

Gideon shook his head. "I won't give up. Ever."

Silence wedged itself between them, but it wasn't because there was nothing left to say. The words that waited in the corners had sharp edges. Words like that could do permanent damage if flung too hard at the one you loved.

"Do you want to watch the sunrise from the tower?" Gideon asked.

"Can you still hear it?"

"No, not really. Sometimes, when it breaks the horizon, I think, maybe. There's a smell like citrus and seawater. But it only lasts a second and then it's gone. I'm beginning to think it's more memory than reality."

"I can't even remember it anymore. All I can see is the light."

Gideon's face twisted and he looked away from her.

"It's still worth seeing." She spread her arms. "It's worth seeing with you."

He ran toward her and leaped, transforming into the red cat before landing in her embrace. She scratched him behind the ears and sank her lips into his plush red fur. "Don't worry, my love. I can fix this. If we keep believing, if we keep moving forward..."

Gideon purred.

"Trust me. Trust me and I promise I'll do whatever it takes to keep us together."

TWO

THE LAUDNERS

Behind the kitchen window of their cheery yellow home, John and Carolyn Laudner did what they always did on lazy mornings. John read the paper from front to back while Carolyn gossiped to the rafters about anything and everything she'd heard that week. With Lillian opening the shop, Katrina away at summer school, and Jacob spending the day with Malini, Carolyn had plenty of time to speculate about everyone else's business and didn't spare John a single thought.

"Did you know they still haven't found Stephanie West-cott?" she asked. "Every time Fran comes to book club, it's like the pink elephant in the room. No one knows how to comfort her."

John grunted, flipping to the sports section.

"Well, Fran Westcott is just beside herself. She insists the police aren't doing anything, but I heard from Rosanne that her husband has exhausted all of Paris' resources on searching for the girl. Even as captain, there's only so much he can do. You know what people think, John?"

"Hmm."

"They think she ran off with a boy. She's the oldest and Fran always treated her like the baby of the family. People think she just had enough of her mother and took off." Carolyn took a sip of her coffee. "You know what I think?"

John grunted.

"I think that Fran Westcott needs to let it go."

This made John look up from his paper. "Her daughter is missing, Carolyn. She could be dead, or worse. A person doesn't just let that go. A person shouldn't just let that go. How would you feel if it was Katrina?"

Carolyn pursed her lips and took another sip of coffee. "I suppose you're right. It's just so darn sad. And now, with the bombing at the school and Dane Michaels still missing, I wonder what this world is coming to. A body doesn't know what to do to help."

John mumbled something that sounded like "stop blabbing about it."

"What, John?" Carolyn asked, sure she misheard him.

He looked her in the eyes. His lips parted.

"Oh wait, John, look!" Carolyn pointed out the bay window. "Abigail is headed for our door. I wonder what's going on?"

"I'm sure you'll find out," John said, folding his paper and pushing back his chair.

When the doorbell rang, Carolyn motioned frantically with her hand. John slowly walked to her side before she opened the door.

"Why hello, Abigail! How nice of you to stop by."

"Carolyn," Abigail said, tipping her head forward. "How are you and John doing today?"

"Us?" Carolyn glanced toward John, who smiled stiffly over her shoulder. "Oh we are just fabulous! Enjoying all of this time together now that Katrina is out of the house." She bobbed her head.

"Good to hear." Abigail smiled and handed her an envelope. "Looks like Pete accidentally put one of your letters in my mailbox."

Carolyn accepted the envelope and ran her finger over her name and address on the label. Her eyes narrowed and her mouth pulled into a straight line. "Thank you. So unlike Pete. I wonder if something's going on at home?"

"I wouldn't know," Abigail said. "Well, I'll let you get back to your morning." She turned to leave.

"Wait, Abigail," Carolyn called, her voice rising in pitch. "Can I ask you about something?"

"Of course. What?"

"I thought I saw a man through your window the other day." Carolyn lowered her chin and raised her eyebrows. "A very attractive man. Are you seeing someone?"

Abigail's face was unreadable. She was so still Carolyn thought she was having a stroke or something. After a few awkward moments of silence, Abigail glanced at the yard and smiled sheepishly. "Nothing gets by you, Carolyn. Yes, I am."

Carolyn bounced up and down clapping her hands. "Is it someone from town? Someone I know?"

"Nope. He works at the University of Illinois with me."

"How exciting! Well, tell us his name." Carolyn slapped back the nudge of John's knuckle.

Abigail opened her mouth and tilted her head. "Gideon. His name is Gideon."

"Ah, a biblical name. A man can't go wrong with a name like that," Carolyn said.

"Unless he's one of the many murderers named Matthew, Mark, Luke, or Moses," John chimed in. "Notice I left off John. Johns are good people."

Abigail laughed. Carolyn elbowed her husband in the ribs.

"So, do I hear wedding bells in your future? I've always told John that it's amazing a man hasn't already snatched up a beautiful woman like you, and smart, too."

Abigail's eyes shifted toward the hem of her long skirt.

"Please excuse my wife, Abigail," John said. "She has a terrible time minding her own business."

Carolyn shot him an appalled stare.

"No, John, it's okay. Carolyn, to be honest, I'm not really the marrying type. I like being on my own. I'm not sure you'll see Gideon around much anymore."

"Oh?" Carolyn's lips pressed together. She wondered what must be wrong with a woman to not have any desire to be married.

"Well, I've got to get back to my research. Nice to see you again, John, Carolyn." Abigail gave a small wave and retreated to her home across the street.

Carolyn backed into the house, sliding her finger into the envelope flap and ripping it open. There was an official-looking form inside. She read it over as John returned to his paper.

"John. John!"

"What is it now, Carolyn?"

Her hand pressed into her sternum, a smile dimpling her full cheeks. "We've won a cruise to the Caribbean!"

"What?" John returned to her side, lifting the paper from her hands.

"I entered that Crispy Crepes contest that came on the box. We won! We won the cruise!"

John read the letter twice over Carolyn's shoulder, then slapped his upper thigh. "Well, I'll be damned! Wait, it says we leave from New Orleans the day after tomorrow. If we're going to do this, we've got to hustle."

Carolyn shook her head. "We can't just leave? What about Jacob? What about the store?"

"Jacob has his mom now, and I'm sure Lillian wouldn't mind watching the store for a couple of weeks."

Nodding her head, Carolyn moved toward the stairs. "Ooh, I've got to get packing. There's so much to do." She jogged up the steps, anxious to get started. *Wait until my book club hears about this.*

THREE

JACOB AND MALINI

With Malini's hand pressed over Jacob's eyes, he tried to use his other senses to figure out their location. Wherever they were, it was sunny. Light broke through between her fingers and warmed his skin. The roll of ocean waves mingled with the unmistakable smell of saltwater. He slipped off his shoe and was rewarded with sand beneath his toes.

"The beach," he said.

"Which beach?" Her lips grazed his ear and the warm whisper made his skin tingle.

"Malini, I can't possibly guess. It could be any beach in the world." He tugged at her fingers.

"Ah, ah, ah. You're smarter than that, Jacob. Guess again."

Jacob took a deep breath and tried to concentrate, not an easy task with Malini's cheek pressed into the side of his neck, and her body against his. He'd play along. After all, he didn't actually have to sort through all the beaches of the world, just the ones Malini might take him to for his seventeenth birthday.

Since they'd arrived by way of enchanted staff, they had to be somewhere Malini could picture clearly in her mind. That meant she'd either been here before or seen pictures.

It had to be Hawaii. Not only had Jacob shown her pictures of his favorite beaches, but for months he'd been begging her to go. Since the day he'd met her, he'd longed to show her where he grew up.

"Hawaii," Jacob said. "Oahu for sure. But which beach?"

Malini sighed but didn't say anything.

"I think ... Waimea Bay," he said.

Malini groaned and dropped her hand. "How did you know? I thought I had you."

"Lucky guess." He smiled. Content, his attention drifted to the blue-green waves. "Thank you, Malini. I've wanted to come back here since my first day in Paris."

"Why didn't you come back before this? I mean, with the staff you could've come any time you wanted."

Jacob took off his other shoe and sat down on the beach, tugging Malini down next to him. Sifting handfuls of sand through his fingers, he tried to put his feelings into words. "I guess I was afraid to come alone. It's hard to explain. Before I found Mom in Nod, I wanted to come back here because I thought of it as home. But now, all the family I have left is in Paris. Sure, I like the weather here better, but every time I thought about leaving, I wondered if that would be the day Lucifer would launch an attack on Paris." He leaned back on the heels of his palms. "Last year, I thought I lost everything, and then I met you and found Mom. Coming here alone would feel like tempting fate. You know?"

Malini slid herself between Jacob's knees and leaned her back against his chest. He wrapped his arms around her shoulders, breathing in the familiar scent of coconut that lingered in her hair from her particular brand of shampoo.

"I think I get it," she said. "We can't go backward in life. Your memories here were important but returning alone would feel like you weren't grateful for your new life. Only with me here, it's okay because we're building new memories."

A warm breeze wafted through his hair and Jacob watched a pair of pigeons fight over a French fry at the water's edge. "Yeah," he said. "Anyway, I love it. Thank you for coming here with me." He kissed her on the cheek.

Turning her head, she met his lips. He dipped her over his leg to position her for a deeper kiss, but stopped when the father of a family with small children cleared his throat accusingly behind them. Self-conscious, he sat up and put some space between their bodies.

"What do you want to do first?" he asked. "I'd teach you to surf but no surfboard."

"Sorry. Surfboards and enchanted staffs don't mix."

"We could get shave ice from Matsumotos? Or pop over to my old apartment building."

Malini shrugged. "Both. Unfortunately, we have an errand to run first."

"Nooooo," Jacob said. "Are you telling me that my birthday trip isn't just celebratory?"

"It's time to start gathering the Soulkeepers. Master Lee is here, as is a Horseman named Jesse that he's training. We need to persuade them to come with us to Eden. They're not safe here. Not anymore."

"And you know this because?"

"Because it's my job to know this."

"Seriously, Malini, prom was three weeks ago. Why now? Couldn't it wait one more day?"

"Jacob, I'm sorry but you know how this works. I see it in the fabric and I have to act. When I go to the In Between, it's like finding a needle in a haystack. The details jump out to me when the time is right."

Pushing himself up onto his feet, he sighed. "Fine. Soul-keeper stuff first, but you owe me a shave ice."

"Absolutely."

"And, Malini, please tell me you brought cab fare because Red Door Martial Arts is across the island from here and no way can we use the staff in that part of town."

She reached into the pocket of her shorts and pulled out a wad of cash. "I got it covered."

"Let's go. The sooner we get this over with, the sooner we can do something important, like celebrate the day of my birth."

Smiling, she took his hand and led him toward the street.

⌣

THROUGH THE PLATE-GLASS WINDOW OF RED DOOR Martial Arts, Jacob watched a class of elementary school kids dressed in karate uniforms. A Filipino man with a Mohawk demonstrated a series of kicks and punches at the front of the dojo. The far wall was decorated with a display of weapons. Beside them, a ginormous red door with a clunky metal ring for a knob spanned the building.

"I guess we're in the right place," Malini said to him, eyeing the door.

"This is where it all started for my mom," Jacob said. "She

told me she saw the weapons and wanted to know if she could use them. It was before she knew she was a Horseman."

"I'm sure she raised some eyebrows. Overnight Ninja." Malini threaded her fingers into his.

"Yeah, they should have a special belt for that." Jacob tugged the door open and slid quietly along the windows, past the place where a group of parents watched the lesson. The instructor eyed them suspiciously as they made their way toward the door labeled *Office* in gold press-on letters. One *f*, half-peeled from the wood, hung precariously by a corner. Jacob knocked twice.

"Come in." Jacob recognized the man's voice. It had been a long time since their phone conversation about his mom but the deep, accented tone was not one he could forget easily.

Inside, a small Chinese man with a shaved head and one milky eye sat, hands folded, behind a desk. For a moment, Jacob questioned whether he was mistaken about the man's identity. The frail body in front of him couldn't be the great Master Lee. But when the man saw Malini, he leapt over the desk and bowed at the waist in a series of unnaturally lithe movements.

"Master Lee?" Malini asked.

"At your service, Healer."

"Please, call me Malini, and this is Jacob." She extended her hand to the elderly man.

"To what do we owe the pleasure of your visit?"

Malini sighed. "Something's happened. We need to talk with you and Jesse."

"Your timing is perfect. He's here practicing now. I'll introduce you," Master Lee said.

Jacob was confused. The office was small and the only

door led out to the dojo. But if he'd learned anything during his time as a Soulkeeper, it was to expect the impossible. Master Lee walked to a tall file cabinet with a keypad lock in the upper left corner. After punching in a series of numbers, the front of the drawers swung open to reveal a narrow passageway.

"After you." Master Lee pointed his hand toward the opening.

Jacob followed Malini through the cabinet, down a hallway lit by bare incandescent bulbs, to a dojo behind the office. Unlike the area up front, this one had no windows. Painted cinderblock walls and fluorescent lights were the extent of the decor. At the center of the room, a boy knelt on the sanded wood floor. He wasn't wearing a uniform like the students out front. Instead, he was clothed in sweats and a T-shirt with a logo too faded to read. With dark-blond hair, long for a boy, and a scrawny build reminiscent of high school band geeks everywhere, he was unremarkable, like he might blend into the floor and disappear. His eyes were closed.

"Jesse, we have guests," Master Lee said softly.

The boy opened his eyes and instantly went from unre-markable to spooky. His irises glowed electric violet. Malini gasped.

"Yeah, I get that sometimes. I usually wear special glasses or contacts when I'm with the general population." His soft voice barely carried across the empty room.

Curiosity got the best of Jacob. He stepped toward Jesse. "Excuse me, not to be rude, but what can you, um, do?"

"Geez, Jacob. Forward much? Don't you think we should introduce ourselves first?" Malini elbowed his side.

"Sorry. I'm Jacob. I'm a Horseman, too, and this is Malini." He stared at Jesse expectantly.

Malini sighed deeply. "Patience isn't high on Jacob's list of virtues. We're sorry to disturb your practice."

"It's okay," Jesse said. "If Master Lee brought you back here, he must trust you, and I so rarely have an audience when I practice." He rolled onto his back and flipped up onto his feet. "I'm a ghost."

"A ghost." Jacob furrowed his brow. "Like you're dead?"

He chuckled. "No. I'm very much alive, but have perfected the art of making others forget that particular flaw when I want them to."

Jacob rotated his head toward Master Lee and raised his eyebrows. The old man nodded. There was a bottle of water against the wall behind Jesse. Jacob reached out with his power, keeping his hands folded innocently in front of him. He willed the water to pop open and then sent four razor-sharp needles of ice hurtling toward Jesse's back.

Jesse didn't flinch. For a moment Jacob worried he'd shred the new Soulkeeper. But the ice passed right through the guy, as if he were an illusion. The needles hit the opposite wall and melted down the cinderblocks. Floored, Jacob stepped forward and grabbed Jesse's forearm, as solid and human as Jacob's.

"You owe me a new water," Jesse murmured. His arm dissolved from between Jacob's fingers. In the blink of an eye, he'd completely disappeared and reappeared next to Master Lee.

"Wow," Jacob said.

Master Lee beamed with pride. "When he came to me, he could only shift the molecules in his arms. Now he can disperse his entire body and bring it back together. We've had him in the air for as long as five minutes."

Malini cleared her throat. "Your gift is amazing, Jesse. Unfortunately, we need to talk about something serious and I don't think we should wait. Master Lee, here or in your office?"

"I believe the chairs in my office will be more comfortable." Master Lee led the group through the corridor and keyed the code to open the cabinet. They emerged into the small office. Malini and Jesse slid into the two chairs in front of the desk. Jacob pulled over a stack of boxes with Chinese characters written in permanent marker on the front and got comfortable.

"As you both know, Watcher activity has been increasing steadily over the last several months," Malini began.

Jesse shifted in his chair. "We noticed. We can hardly keep up."

"We have reason to believe that Lucifer is planning an attack. We're not sure of all of the details but we do know that he's obtained a list of active Soulkeepers. Your names are on that list."

Master Lee cleared his throat. "He knows who we are?"

"Not yet. The list is guarded by a spell but it's only a matter of time before he finds a way to read it. You're not safe here anymore. We believe Lucifer is planning to kill the Soulkeepers. Everyone on that list."

"How do we stop him? What do we need to do?" Lee rubbed his milky eye with his fingers.

"We need to move you to a safe house. We have a place where we can train together and prepare a coordinated defense."

Jesse's head snapped around. "Malini, is it? I don't understand. I'm a Horseman. It's my job to protect people from

Watchers. If they come, I'll kill them. Not the other way around."

Placing her hand on Jesse's, Malini turned her full attention to the boy's purple eyes. "If it were one or two, I'd know you could handle it. Lucifer is raising an army and he's collected hundreds of humans to feed them. If you are able to fight off the ones who come for you, you'll be distracted from the real attack, the battle for humanity."

Master Lee leaned forward. "Are you saying Lucifer is attempting to reclaim the earthly realm?"

"Exactly. We don't know how he's planning to do it but we know translating the list is a major step in his plan. Our only hope to stop him is to convene the remaining Soulkeepers. He'll expect us to be scattered. We need to unite and have a coordinated defense of our own."

"Remaining?" Jesse pushed forward to the edge of his seat. "You said, 'remaining Soulkeepers.'"

"There may be others, in other countries, or who haven't come into power yet, but we have reason to believe that the names on the list are key to thwarting Lucifer's plan. The list has thirteen names: nine Horsemen, three Helpers, and me, the Healer."

Jesse's hand went to his mouth. "You're the Healer?" he said between his fingers. "I didn't know."

Malini smiled and shook her head. "It's okay. I wouldn't expect you to. I was surprised Master Lee recognized me." She squinted eyes at Lee. "How did you know?"

The old man pointed at his milky blue eye. "My gift. The supernatural have an aura. Horsemen carry a ruby glow, Helpers a cool azure, but you, Malini, sparkle an intense green. I've only seen that color once before, the last Healer."

"Can you see Watchers?"

He nodded. "Their aura is black as tar."

"I think that ability will come in very useful. As I was saying, there were thirteen on the list but one of our Horsemen, Mara, died a few weeks ago. Twelve remain. Besides myself and Jacob, we have another, Jacob's mother, Lillian."

"One of my students! How is Lillian?" Lee asked.

"She's wonderful. She's getting our new facility ready. There is a place, a school where we can train safely. I need you both to come with me and stay there while Jacob and I gather the other seven."

Jesse shook his head. "I can't. I'm a freshman at the University of Hawaii. I'm halfway through the semester. I can't just leave. I'll fail all my classes."

"We have someone that helps us with situations like this," Jacob said. "She can alter records, make the school believe you've come down with a long-term illness. She'll make it work. You can go back to majoring in basket weaving when you're done saving the world."

"Elementary education, thank you very much. The children are our future." Jesse flashed a lopsided grin. "I get your point. I guess if Lucifer is running the planet it might curb the employment opportunities. If my Helper goes, I go."

Master Lee nodded and picked up the phone. "I will arrange for my assistant, Michael, to take over the dojo in my absence." A voice buzzed on the other end of the line and Master Lee rambled something in Chinese.

"I'll need to stop at my dorm and pack a few things," Jesse said.

"No problem." Malini rose and moved toward the door. Master Lee hung up the phone and stepped around the desk.

Jacob nudged Malini's hand out of the way. "Let me get that for you," he said, wiggling his eyebrows. Opening doors for her had become a kind of joke, a way to play the chivalrous male even though she was ten times more powerful than he was. He kept his eyes on hers as he swung open the pinewood door.

Silver flashed at the edge of Jacob's vision and searing pain ripped through his stomach. He crumpled in the doorframe. Beside him, Malini screamed. The man with a Mohawk, the one who'd been teaching class, tore the blade from Jacob, sending a spray of blood up Malini's side and across her face. Removing her glove, she thrust her skeletal hand at the man's chest, but he kept coming.

"He's possessed!" Lee yelled, dodging the man's slashing blade.

Malini clenched her healing hand, but before she could act, Jesse materialized behind the man. With a pair of nunchucks from the wall, he thwacked Mohawk in the head, sending his body tumbling to the ground. Thrusting his hand into the man's skull, Jesse's molecules broke apart as they entered the flesh, fishing for the Watcher inside. He pulled his fist back, latched onto the black ooze.

"Come on out and play," Jesse said through his teeth. He discarded the nunchucks and caught the knife Lee tossed him from the wall. Extracted from its host, he severed the Watcher's oily head from its body. The rest of the beast bubbled out of Mohawk and fried on the wood like hot tar.

From the place where Jacob watched from the doorway, he reached for Malini. Blood sprayed across the hand he brought to his mouth to cover a cough. His breath came in wet rattles.

Folding to her knees, Malini pressed her healing hand to

Jacob's stomach wound. The heat of her power poured into him. "It will be all right. I'm here. You're going to be okay," she said.

Her skin bubbled and blackened to the elbow and the smell of burning flesh filled the room. She grit her teeth and wept, but held her hand to him until he was able to push it away. Longer than necessary.

"You should have stopped sooner," Jacob said, eyeing the burnt skin on her arm. That was the price she paid for healing someone. Thankfully, he could fix it. He pulled Malini into his arms.

Jacob called the water. From within the walls the pipes groaned and dust and drywall snowed down around them. He focused on a fountain in the hall. The spout blew off, skipping across the dojo, and a wave crashed into the office, washing Malini's burns away.

"I had to make sure you were completely healed," Malini said. With her newly healthy arm, she slid her flesh-colored glove over her still-exposed skeletal hand. Jacob was relieved; the gift from Death was dangerous without the glove.

"Well, that's convenient," Jesse said, gawking at Malini.

Master Lee stepped over the man with the Mohawk and the Watcher that Jesse had extracted from his body. "Antonio has worked for me for years." His wrinkled face sagged, as if he'd aged a decade in the last five minutes. He spread his hands toward the empty dojo, covered in splatters of black blood.

Jesse pulled the blinds on the windows and locked the door.

"He must have been possessed recently. You would have seen it." Malini wiped a drop of Jacob's blood from under her eye and crawled over to the man. "He's alive, but knocked out. He'll need hospitalization. I think it's better if I don't heal him. Too hard to explain the gaps in his memory."

Lee groaned. "We'll have to drop him at the emergency room. No one can know this happened here."

"How did Lucifer know? How did he know we'd be here?" Jacob asked. "I didn't even know before today and he can't translate the list."

Malini's eyes darted over the body and then toward the slits of light that filtered through the windows. "I don't know. But one thing's for sure. The war has begun."

FOUR

MARA AND HENRY

Who would have thought Death slept? On the bed next to Mara, Henry's body lay like a corpse. With his arms crossed over his chest, she couldn't tell if he was breathing and his flawless white skin didn't twitch. He hadn't moved at all in, well, she wasn't sure how long. She couldn't find a clock in the room and was afraid to leave, mostly because she had no idea where she was.

"Henry?" she said.

His eyelids flipped open and his head turned toward her on the shiny red pillow. "Mara. You're here. I wasn't dreaming."

She couldn't stop a huge cheeser from blooming across her face. "Yeah, you were kind of dreamy though. I haven't made out like that in, um … I've never made out like that."

Henry hinged at the hips, sitting up in a way that defied gravity, slowly and with an abnormally straight back. He turned his torso to face her. "Mara, I died in 1349 when I was seventeen. Believe me, what little experience I had over six hundred years ago was dwarfed by what happened last night. You are absolutely enchanting."

"Thanks." She pushed herself to a seated position. "I ate the pastries. Sorry. I should have saved one for you."

A half smile lifted the corner of Henry's lips. "Not necessary. I don't have to eat."

"Right, because you're Death."

He nodded.

Mara played with the corner of the sheet. Hand stitching decorated the edges and the silky fabric draped heavily in her hand. The material felt expensive but she wouldn't know for sure. She'd never owned anything like it.

"So, Henry, can you take me home? I mean, back to Dr. Silva's. That's where I'm staying."

Henry's features hardened and he tipped his face away from her. Whether by levitation or propulsion, he rose from the bed and paced toward the window on the far stone wall. She noticed no glass in the frame but also no breeze, no birds, no dust.

He folded his hands, bowing his head slightly toward the sill. "I'm sorry, Mara, but you can never go back."

"What do you mean I can't go back?" She crawled from the tangle of sheets, tripping over her silver sandals as she closed the space between them. Grabbing his shoulders, she turned his stiff upper body toward her. She searched his face for answers but he was entirely closed off, locked away. If she wanted answers, she'd have to be direct. "Am I dead?"

"Not exactly." His eyes blinked robotically and his breath came out in a sigh. "You're In Between. When you kissed me, I was in a state to take Malini's soul. That part of me latched on to you instead. Normally when that happens, I usher the soul to either Heaven or Hell but, normally, the person is dead. Because you were not dead, your soul clung to your body. I found myself unwilling to kill you, and since I was attached, I brought you back here, to my home."

Back, back, back, she toppled away from him, only stopping her retreat when she bonked into the bed. Her breath came up short and she gripped the bedpost to hold herself up. Under her fingers, ornate carvings of skulls and twisted body parts decorated the wood. What the hell did she think would happen? She'd kissed Death. She wasn't going back.

"I thought I would die. When I kissed you, I expected it to be the end," she said breathlessly. "But I didn't know what that meant."

"It should have meant death. It should have meant Heaven or Hell. I broke the rules bringing you here."

Steadying herself, Mara folded her arms across her chest in an attempt to hold the emotions swirling through her torso inside her skin. The next logical question begged to be asked, but she was afraid of the answer. "What happens when you break the rules here?"

"It's never happened before, Mara, but if I had to guess, either God or Lucifer is going to notice they're missing a soul, and when they do, they will want an explanation."

"And they'll come to you to get it."

He bowed his head in agreement.

"I'm sorry, Henry. I'm so sorry I got you into this."

Henry appeared in front of her, his hands rubbing her shoulders and his face softening to a more human expression that could only be described as tortured.

"Do not be sorry for me. I wanted you here. I felt a connection to you from the moment I saw you. I can't explain it, but last night, for the first time in forever, I felt whole. I almost felt human again."

"I'm only nineteen. I'm not ready to die." As much as Mara wanted to hold it together, the knowledge that her future was gone, wiped out with one choice, hit her like a bulldozer. Eternity was a very long time to ponder a choice like that. The words broke on her tongue and she did something she rarely allowed herself to do. She cried.

"I am sorry you are only nineteen, but this was your choice. You kissed me." He backed away, a hand on his heart. "Do you regret your decision?"

Mara wiped under her eyes and tried to give him an honest answer. He deserved as much. "Yes ... No. I felt it, too. When we shook hands, it was like ... I can't describe it. I didn't want to let go." Her butt landed on the bed and she met his dark eyes. "It felt like I'd been underwater my entire life and you were my first breath of clean air."

The smile that Henry rewarded her with was worth any price she'd paid. It was a smile that said her feelings weren't one sided. They'd shared a connection, one she didn't entirely understand but an important one nonetheless.

He took a tentative step forward, then another. Kneeling down in front of her, he scooped her hands into his. "If that is true, then I have a proposal to make."

Mara's eyebrows shot skyward at the word proposal, given that Henry was on his knee. Her spine stiffened.

"Until they find you, maybe we should enjoy the time we have," Henry said.

Of course. She didn't really think he'd propose something more serious. Looking down at her wrinkled gray dress, Mara tucked a stray hair behind her ear. "This is awkward. It's like the walk of shame but without the actual walk. Can I borrow your shower? And maybe a toothbrush."

Henry stood, raising an eyebrow. "Allow me to introduce you to the pleasures of the In Between world." Henry focused his attention and a basket appeared on his dresser, overflowing with soaps, hair care products, and her requested toothbrush.

"How did you do that?"

Positioning himself behind her, he slid his hand down her arm, sending electric tingles through her skin to her belly-button and below. He reached her wrist and extended her hand, palm up.

"This realm is constructed from thought. If you can think it, you can create it. This castle, everything you see, is my creation. Let's see if you can create something. Start small. Something that can fit in your hand."

Mara concentrated. A silver swirl danced across her palm and disappeared. "It's not working."

"You must solely picture what you want. Block out all other thoughts and feelings. Think of it as analyzing the thing down to the atoms that make it up. Concentrate."

She closed her eyes and pictured the one thing she couldn't live without. It was her crutch and what made her different from everyone else. It was her history and maybe a piece of her soul. She thought of her bell.

It wove itself out of the air, not instantly as it had for Henry but chunk by chunk. First the wooden handle, then the crown, shoulders and waist, and finally the clapper. She opened her eyes and wrapped her fingers around the finished product. Perfect.

"I left it behind when I kissed you. I can't remember where. This one feels exactly the same."

"It won't work here." Henry frowned.

Mara gripped the bell tighter and brought it to her chest. "Why not?"

"Time doesn't exist here, not really. Nothing here ages. Nothing changes unless we want it to. There's nothing to stop."

"But that's impossible. Things happen here. I was in bed. Now, I'm not. Time has passed."

"But here it isn't measurable. On Earth, the planet is spinning. Hours, days, years are measured by its rotation. The In Between isn't a physical place. Things happen but time isn't measured in the same way."

"Oh," was all she could manage. She stared desperately at the bell, her soul sagging to that dark place that threatened to own her. The bed called to her. Maybe she could crawl into it and never come out.

"Do you like horses?" As if he could sense her despondency, Henry pulled her backward into his chest and kissed the top of her head.

"I think so. I mean, I've never met one in person."

"The bathroom is through that door." He pointed at a section of wall that transformed into a door at his will. "Clean up and change into the clothes inside, and I will take you on a date to meet my horses. We will worry about the rest when we have to."

She pivoted in his arms. With Henry's body pressed against her, he'd shed the stiff composure of Death. His chest rose and fell. His dark eyes searched hers from below long lashes. His full lips parted and a blush colored his cheeks in an expression Mara could only describe as longing. Forgetting everything else, she gave in to the beat of the drum whose rhythm had grown stronger in her chest. Lifting on her tiptoes, she met his lips with hers. It felt just as good as the night before. A walk in the moonlight. The flutter of raven wings. Dark water on a cold night. Thoughts that should have scared her filled her with wanting, a blazing fire beneath her sternum.

She wasn't sure how long the kiss lasted. It was as timeless as the In Between.

"I can't wait to spend the day with you," she said when she finally pulled away. She lifted the basket, pausing at the bathroom door. "Henry, can I tell you something?"

"Of course."

"Not one day of my life has felt normal. I've watched people through windows doing normal things: eating together, hugging their children, doing the damned laundry. But I've never had that. I've never been a part of what the world called normal. My life's been ... complicated. Kissing you here, in this place between places, it feels right. It feels like home."

He didn't respond with words but pressed his right hand over his heart and bowed slightly at the waist. She ducked inside the bathroom, swearing not to waste any more time feeling sorry for herself.

FIVE

DANE

Dane woke coughing. A sulfur stench burned in his nostrils. He turned on his side but repositioning didn't help his discomfort. Jagged stone cut into his shoulder and blistering heat scorched his lungs. He pried his eyes open against the pain. Wiping the sweat from his forehead, he blinked. Fire. He was too close to the fire. A wicked headache threatened to knock him over but he forced himself to his feet and turned in a circle, following the path of the flames that surrounded him.

Lucifer grinned on the other side of the blaze. "Careful." Fire shot up, forcing him back to the center of the circle. "I wouldn't want you to burn. Not yet anyway. I still need you alive."

The circle he was in was about twelve feet in diameter. Beyond the flames, pillars of dark stone marked a brutal landscape. There were things out there. Things he couldn't see clearly in the darkness beyond. Things that shifted unnaturally in the shadows.

"You brought me to Hell," Dane rasped.

"Yes. Home, sweet home. Do you like it? You don't think the brimstone makes it look small, do you?"

"Why? Why did you take me?" Dane focused on movement beyond the flames. A creature on the other side of the fire licked oily black lips and sniffed hungrily in Dane's direction. Shaped loosely like a dog, it was less human looking than a Watcher, without eyes or ears but with plenty of razor-sharp teeth and claws.

"Because you pissed me off. A petty human like you involving yourself so willingly in the battle between good and evil. You would give up your life to protect your friends." He gave a sinister chuckle. "I'm giving them the chance to return the favor."

Despite the oppressive heat, Dane shivered. "I don't belong here. I believe in God. You can't keep my soul in Hell forever."

"No. I can't." Lucifer rolled his blue eyes. "A tiny inconvenience. What I can do is torture you for as long as I can keep you alive and then kill you. Sure, you'll go to Heaven, and in the grand scheme of things, that's what matters, right?" Grinning, he circled Dane's fiery prison, the oily creature heeling to his side as he walked by. "But, fortunately for me, human hearts think life is precious, and your life could buy me something I want."

"I don't understand," Dane said.

"You wouldn't. Let me try to explain." He stroked the head of the creature at his side. "When I left the Great Oppressor's power—"

"You mean, God."

"*Don't* use that name in my presence."

The flames shot higher and Dane had to cover his face with his arm to protect it from the heat.

"As I was saying, when I left, certain realities came into being. You might call them laws or limitations, but think of them like the law of gravity. There was no agreement, only consequences."

Dane blinked at Lucifer's blond illusion.

"Let me put this in terms your underdeveloped psyche can comprehend. Think of the universe as a giant football field. Hell is the south goal post and Heaven is the north. The earthly realm exists at the fifty-yard line. Between here and there is Nod. Beautiful place. They'd love you there. You look very tasty." He raised an eyebrow and gave an evil grin.

Dane hugged his chest.

"The In Between exists on Heaven's side of the earthly realm and even though the immortals are supposed to be neutral, they've always favored their neighbor to the north. As such, Fate has played a cruel trick on me. Human souls like yours are easy for me to manipulate. I can feel each one of them swarming all over the planet. But Soulkeepers? Very hard to see. Very hard to find. Malini was almost impossible until my Watcher, Cord, captured an imprint of her soul." Lucifer pulled a circular object from his pocket. A hologram projected from the disc held in his palm, Malini covered in Watcher blood.

Stomach twisting, Dane covered his mouth to keep from throwing up.

"Such delicate sensibilities," Lucifer said. He collapsed the image and slid the disc back into his pocket. "As I was saying,

Soulkeepers exist to balance the power of my Watchers. Abigail is a Watcher, down to her very bones. I've tolerated her living in the earthly realm in the past because she's always remained neutral. But when she conjured the list of all the Soulkeepers' names, she shifted north of neutral. That list should have been mine, just as she is mine. I was able to retrieve the list itself but she placed a spell on the names so that I can't read them. Do you see the injustice? If Abigail crosses over to serve the Great Oppressor, then I should get something in return. I should get the Soulkeepers. You, Dane, are my guarantee that balance will be restored."

"Why are you telling me this?" Dane shook his head. "You're lying. It doesn't make sense. Abigail's been on our side for years. You're not interested in balance."

"Silence!"

Lucifer snapped his fingers and two pillars of light appeared on either side of him. Inside the pillars, Malini formed to the left and Dr. Silva formed to the right. Their bodies glowed, slightly transparent against the darkness.

For a moment, Malini examined her surroundings like a bee trapped under glass.

"Dane!" She banged her hands against the inside of the pillar.

In the other tube, Dr. Silva's expression turned stone cold, unreadable. She linked her hands behind her back.

"Welcome, ladies," Lucifer said.

"Let him go. Let him go!" Malini cried. The look on her face brought tears to Dane's eyes. She cared. She really cared about him.

"I will, Malini, but only if you give me what I want first.

Translate the list. Give me the Soulkeepers and I'll give you your friend."

Her eyes darted around her tube, then landed on Dane. Her face begged him for forgiveness. She shook her head. "Never. Never." The words came out broken, like an apology.

"And what about you, Abigail? Will you do what I need you to do, or does Dane die?"

"You can't keep him here. His soul isn't yours," she responded.

"Don't tell me what I can and cannot do," Lucifer hissed. "I've ruled for thousands of years, Abigail. You of all should know what I am capable of." The flames heightened around Dane. "Let me make this perfectly clear. For every day that you two refuse to help me, your friend's cell will shrink. One foot for one Earth day. At midnight on the eleventh day, if I don't have my list, Dane will *barbecue*."

Malini covered her face with her hands.

"Don't do it, Malini!" Dane cried.

"Shut up!" Lucifer snapped.

Dane's voice stopped working.

Lucifer approached Malini and whispered toward her light. "Malini, darling, don't think I won't find them anyway. I may not know who the other Soulkeepers are, but I know who you are. Where you go, I will go, and next time, you won't be fast enough to save the ones you love."

Dane saw the tears run down Malini's face, then watched as Dr. Silva turned her back on Lucifer. Seeing this, Malini did the same. Lucifer snapped his fingers and both Malini and Dr. Silva disappeared.

The devil turned toward Dane, his face red with fury.

"You'd better hope your friends change their minds, Dane, or it's going to get a whole lot hotter for you."

Lucifer stormed away. Whatever power he'd used to make Dane mute must have gone with him. Once he'd disappeared behind the brimstone, Dane was finally able to scream.

SIX

MALINI AND JACOB

Cruising at 30,000 feet, Malini snapped back into her body with a jolt. Jacob's hands pressed into her shoulders, holding her into her window seat. A nosy gawker stared across the aisle of the 747 in flight from Oahu to Chicago. Malini frowned pointedly in her direction and Jacob responded by positioning his body to block the woman's view.

"She probably thinks I had a seizure or something," Malini said, reaching for her bag.

"It looked like you did. What's going on?" Jacob whispered.

She found her phone and dialed Dr. Silva.

"I don't think you're supposed to use that on the plane," Jacob said.

"Let's just hope it works," Malini responded.

"Why? What's going on?"

"Lucifer."

Master Lee and Jesse glanced back from the seats in front of them. After the attack, they'd decided to fly home. With only one staff between them, the group would've had to split and take turns to get everyone back to Paris. But more Watchers could be out there. Everyone agreed splitting up would be playing into Lucifer's hands. One call to Dr. Silva and they had first-class tickets on the next outgoing flight. Only, now Malini wondered if being trapped together in a tin can, hurtling through the sky, was the best idea.

"What's going on?" Jacob asked again, a little louder.

"Malini? Are you okay?" Dr. Silva's voice came through the phone, high-pitched and unusually flustered.

"Yeah. Okay for now. But what was that? I didn't know Lucifer could do that."

"It's forced astral projection. He has an imprint of your soul and, of course, he has similar power over me. He can draw us to him for a time."

"For a time? Does that mean he can do that to me again?" Malini asked. She swallowed and placed her hand on Jacob's arm to quiet his prodding.

"Lucifer is not omnipotent like God. He can only be in one place at a time. Although he's powerful, keeping our souls in Hell is as restrictive for him as it is for us. Yes, he can do it again but I don't think he will. Not for a while."

"What do we do? How do we save Dane?"

"I'm sorry, Malini. I don't know if we can. We can't allow him to have the list. And if I go physically to Hell to rescue him, chances are I won't come out. You could say Hell is a one-way ticket."

The plane entered a bank of clouds and Malini watched the sun slip behind the foggy air. "Unless we give him what he wants," she said.

"Are you mad? He'll slaughter them all."

"Not if they're already in Eden. Two more Helpers and five more Horsemen in twelve days. We can do it, Abigail. We can collect them all, take them to Eden, then translate the list once they're safe."

"He'll know. He'll follow you."

"We'll split up. You said yourself he can't be in two places at once. Jacob and I fought off the Watchers this time, and we can do it again. With your help, we can have them out of his reach before he realizes they're gone. Then we give him the list." Malini bit her lip as she realized, if it hadn't been for Jesse, the Watcher might have succeeded at killing one or both of them. The plan was risky, but what choice did she have?

"It could work."

"It has to."

A flight attendant tapped Malini's shoulder. "Miss? You need to put that away."

"We're landing. We should be outside O'Hare in about forty minutes. We can talk more then," Malini stammered.

Tap. Tap. "Miss, now. Put the phone away."

"Lillian is meeting you. She can take the others to Eden. Gideon's returned to the university to check on Katrina. I've placed a protective spell on her room but that won't help her if they use her roommate. I'll meet you at the house to debrief. Then we'll find the others."

Tap. Tap. "Miss!" The flight attendant grimaced in Malini's direction.

"Gotta go." Malini powered off her phone. Thankfully, the flight attendant was satisfied and continued down the aisle.

Jacob narrowed his eyes and pursed his lips. "Tell me what's going on."

"Lucifer has Dane, and he's going to kill him in twelve days if Dr. Silva or I don't translate the list for him."

Jacob took a deep breath. "You saw him? Just now?"

"Yes. Apparently, since Cord captured an image of my soul, he can demand my astral projected presence any time he wants."

"Great."

"I know, right? But the worst part is Dane looks awful." Malini fought back tears. "Lucifer is torturing him, Jacob. I'm worried he won't survive until we can get him back."

"Can we rescue him?"

"Honestly, no. But we might be able to win him back if we give Lucifer what he wants without getting him what he needs."

"That doesn't make any sense."

Malini lowered her voice. "We get the other seven Soulkeepers, then give him the list when it's useless."

Jacob frowned. "Malini, it took three weeks for you to say it was the right time to get Master Lee and Jesse. You said the information comes to you when it comes to you. Can you force this?"

Turbulence shook the plane and she gripped the armrests hard enough to turn her knuckles white. A storm had moved in and they descended toward Chicago in a series of uncomfortable drops.

"I'll have to, Jacob. Somehow, I'll have to."

The plane touched down, whipping her head back against the seat. As they taxied down the runway, the rain and thunder rocked the plane. Lightning struck the tarmac outside her window. Malini hoped the weather wasn't an omen of the turbulence ahead.

SEVEN

KATRINA AND GIDEON

Katrina opened the window to her dorm room and placed a bowl of peaches on the windowsill. A large red cat jumped to her side and didn't waste any time sinking its whiskers into the offering.

"You're going to get in trouble for feeding that thing," Mallory said. At her desk on the other side of the room, she swiped electric-orange nail polish across her fingernails. "Not to mention you're probably giving it major intestinal problems with those cafeteria peaches."

"Nothing's happened so far. I think it's okay." Katrina folded her legs underneath her on her bunk and rested her elbow on the windowsill. The first drops of a summer rain danced on the awning above the window and a cool breeze broke the oppressive summer heat. From her nightstand, she retrieved her physics text and binder but didn't open them. She rested them in her lap as if she could absorb the contents by osmosis.

"I'm going to a Kappa party tonight. Do you want to go?"

Mallory asked. She'd finished her final coat and was waving her nails in the air to dry.

"No. I think I'll just hang out here. I've got a ton of studying to do. Summer sessions are so aggressive."

Mallory ran her pinky finger along the border of the lipstick on her bottom lip, careful not to ruin her polish. "You know what I think?" she said toward the mirror. "I think you're going to spend the night staring out the window and talking to a stray cat."

Katrina tilted her head to the side and shot Mallory her best death stare. The middle finger she flashed said what her eyes couldn't.

"Don't get all pissy with me, Katrina. Ever since that party before spring break, when there was all that weirdness with that guy, you've been a total killjoy. You've completely changed."

"Maybe I have changed, Mallory, but I think it's for the better. I don't need to drown my brain in alcohol every night to prove I fit some artificial definition of cool. I'm just done with partying. I'm serious about my life."

Mallory stood from her desk chair and placed her hands on her hips. "That speech would be so much better if it were true. You're nineteen years old, Katrina. A little young for the retirement home."

"I go out. I've just been really busy with school lately."

"Riiiiight. Not buying it. You're staying home because you're afraid. I don't know what happened that night, but I'm willing to bet it's more than you've told me." She pointed an orange fingernail in Katrina's direction. "Let me tell you something, living your life in fear is no way to live. If you stay in this dorm room for the rest of your college existence, you're going to regret that you let that guy steal your youth. Whatever happened, don't let him win."

Katrina turned her face toward the window, effectively shutting Mallory down. "Don't forget your umbrella."

The shuffle of Mallory snatching her bag from its hook was followed by the squeak of the door opening. "Don't wait up." The door clicked shut behind her.

"She thinks I'm either crazy or depressed," Katrina said to the cat.

The animal leaped into the room, transforming into an angel mid-flight. Katrina lowered the shade behind him. She didn't need anyone noticing Gideon's glow.

"I am sorry we need to be so careful," Gideon said. "But you are in danger, Katrina. You know too much about the Watchers."

"I know." Katrina played with the cover of her book.

Gideon sat down on Mallory's bed, across the small room from Katrina. His warm green eyes settled on her. "There's something else bothering you."

"Do you think she's right, Gideon? Am I living my life in fear? Am I letting Cord win?"

The angel leaned forward, clasping his hands together and resting his elbows on his knees. "Do you think a person who evacuates a burning building is letting the fire win?"

"Well, no."

"Mallory's advice might make sense with human problems, but you, Katrina, don't have a human problem. If Mallory knew there might be a Watcher waiting to eat her flesh around the next bend, she might appreciate a healthy dose of fear."

Katrina smiled. "You always know just what to say."

"I try." He stretched his wings, then tucked them behind his back. "So what are we supposed to be studying tonight?"

"Ugh, physics! Why did I take physics this summer? My brain cannot absorb these concepts." Katrina lifted her book from her desk and flipped through the pages.

"Sorry, physics isn't my strong suit." Gideon reached for her binder.

"They didn't offer a class in celestial beings," Katrina said. "Plus, you don't have to help me. I'm sure it's bad enough having to sit around here all night. You shouldn't have to study physics, too."

"I like learning human things. Someday, when I'm human, I might need to know about physics."

"No. Trust me on this. Physics is useless in everyday life. I recommend personal finance. Much more practical."

Shifting, Gideon crossed his feet at the ankle. "When I am human, I'll take that, too."

Katrina tore the corner of a piece of paper and began folding it into tiny squares. "I don't want to be rude, but how do you know you'll ever be human? I mean, I've heard you say that God promised when you and Abigail have served your purposes that he'll make you both human, but it's been almost a century. What if you're never done?"

Bowing his head, Gideon's wings tensed where they met his body, lifting from his back. Lit from within, the pearly white feathers were short and downy where they disappeared under his gray T-shirt, and long, like a swan's wing, where they swept toward the floor.

"I don't know," he said. "I have faith but I don't know for sure."

"That sucks." Katrina tossed the tiny square of paper

toward the trash. It hit the rim and landed on the floor. "I mean, it seems vague and one sided. No upfront contracts, no escape clause, just, 'Trust me. Someday I'll make you human.' I guess that's why God is doing it for you. You have faith."

Gideon's expression became distant, his body motionless. "Perhaps you are right, Katrina Laudner. It does, as you say, suck."

"At least you have Abigail. Even though you can't touch, you have each other."

The binder in his hands attracted his full attention. The pages flipped aggressively between his hands as he skimmed over her notes and handouts. He seemed agitated until something caught his eye and made him smile.

"I thought you said this class was not about celestial beings?"

"It isn't."

He turned the binder toward her. "Then what is the God particle?"

She giggled. "It has nothing to do with God. It's this theoretical particle that would explain why things have mass. Physicists say it exists but they've never actually found it. There are people who spend all day smashing particles together trying to make it happen."

Gideon's brow wrinkled. "Why do they call it the God particle?"

"For three reasons. One, like God, it might not exist—"

"God does exist!" Gideon's eyebrows shot to the ceiling.

"Yeah, but unlike you, most of the world doesn't know that for sure." She held up two fingers. "Two, if it does exist it will help us understand how God created the universe."

"How would discovering this particle explain creation?"

"It's part of the Big Bang theory. You know, people think that the universe was a mass of spinning particles that came together in just the right way and, BANG." She clapped her hands together. "The universe. If we could make the right particles hit each other at the right speed to make the God particle, then we could prove that's how it all started."

Gideon grunted and shook his head.

"And three, there are some people who think smashing particles together could create a black hole that swallows the Earth."

"Sounds frightening." Gideon handed the binder back to her.

Katrina shrugged. "They used to do experiments here in Illinois to try to make it happen, but my professor says they shut down the particle accelerator last year. The only place that can do it now is CERN in Europe. If they do create a black hole, I guess we'll have a few extra microseconds before it absorbs us."

"Nice." Gideon leaned back until his head hit the wall behind Mallory's bed and stared at the ceiling. "You know, it says in the Bible, 'You were made from dust and to dust you will return.' Particle is another word for dust."

"So do you think they're on the right track? Will they eventually find the God particle?" Katrina positioned her book and binder in front of her on the bed and began filling out note cards to study from.

"No," Gideon answered softly. "I think what they don't realize is that anyone can mix clay, but it takes a potter to make the vessel."

Katrina looked up from her note cards. "That's deep."

It was Gideon's turn to shrug. "You should study."

Returning to her notes, Katrina reviewed her materials in earnest but paused when she realized she'd been rude.

"Gideon," she said.

"Yes."

"I hope it all works out for you and Abigail. Regardless of what I said before, true love is always worth the risk. At least, I think it is. I can't say I've ever had it to know."

"Thanks," he said. "Now get some studying done. I'll be right outside the window."

He transformed into the red cat and bounded over her into the cool evening rain.

EIGHT

MARA AND HENRY

Mara emerged from the bathroom in the outfit that had magically appeared while she showered. Taupe riding pants hugged her legs and tucked into tall black boots. A white blouse and red riding jacket completed the ensemble. Her raven hair fell in a tight braid over her shoulder.

"You do know I've never been riding before," she said.

Henry broke from a trance-like state near the window and gave her his full attention. "I'm sorry, Mara. I was working. What did you say?"

"You were working?" Mara's mouth dropped open and she pointed a hand toward the window. "Just now? Ushering souls to the beyond?"

He nodded.

"But you're still here. I thought you had to be present with the, um, deceased." The word *deceased* weighed heavily on her tongue now that she met the definition.

"One of the benefits of being Death is that I can project

myself into the earthly realm without actually leaving the In Between. It's necessary. People die all over the world, every minute of every day."

Mara took a cautious step closer to him. Considering the level of intimacy they'd shared the night before, it seemed odd that she felt nervous now. "What's happening to the people who die now or who died when we were at prom?"

"Part of me is there with them, while another part of me is here with you."

She stepped closer, searching his eyes for any sign that he was joking. "How does that work? Isn't it confusing being in two places at once?"

Henry rubbed his chin. "I'm not sure how it works; it just does. Always has, since the time I won the job."

"You won this job? What, like in a poker game?" She'd moved in close enough to hook her fingers in the folds of his riding jacket. It was red wool, like hers, with gold-crested buttons down the front. The texture felt strangely familiar, as if she'd done this before, like they'd known each other longer than they had.

He slipped his hand into hers. "That is a story for another day. For now, we ride."

Mara stood her ground. "Wait, I want to know. How did you become Death?"

Henry frowned and shook his head. "I can't tell you. It's against the rules."

"You can't, or you won't?"

"Can't. I physically can't. It's a restriction on my station."

"Huh. Like vocal handcuffs?"

He nodded.

Searching his face, she didn't think he was lying. Why would he? "Okay," she said.

He led her from the bedroom, down a magnificent flight of stone steps, and through a marble foyer to the outdoors. Henry's castle was built on an English hillside. A well-manicured garden gave way to a rolling green landscape. Beyond, a variety of full-grown trees marked the edge of a dark wood.

A skeleton in a powdered wig and red uniform waited in the yard, a pale gray stallion on his left and a black mare on his right. Henry approached the gray, rubbing its muzzle.

"This is my stable boy, Tom," Henry said. The skeleton extended his hand to Mara, who shook it politely, aware of how the bones collapsed inside her grip.

"I should take the black one?" Mara asked nervously. She reached up to touch the mare but flinched when the horse shifted her feet.

"Necromancer is quite gentle. She won't fight you. Tom can assist you if you need help getting on."

Mara rolled her ankle and plugged her hands into her pockets. "I'm not sure this is such a good idea. Shouldn't I have a lesson or something first?"

Leaving his pale horse, Henry tilted his head and approached her. His hand shot out, passing through her chest as if she were a ghost. "What's going to happen, Mara?" he asked, retracting his hand. "None of this is physical."

She patted her sternum with her hand, solid enough.

"Remember what I showed you." He tapped his temple. "Build your reality."

Rubbing the spot where his hand had passed through her, Mara decided he was right. She had nothing to lose. She might as well make the most of it. She hooked her foot in Necromancer's stirrup and willed herself into the saddle. Effortlessly, she floated into place and lifted the reins.

"Very good," Henry said. "Now, we are going hunting, so you will need a weapon. I prefer a blade." A scythe appeared in his right hand. He folded the handle and hooked it to his back from a harness that conveniently appeared there.

"A scythe? How cliché." She laughed.

"And what will you be using?"

"What are we hunting?"

"A golden buck."

"A buck." Mara tapped her chin. "I think bow and arrow." She concentrated and the bow built itself within her hand. The arrows appeared one by one in a quiver she slung over her shoulder. "How come when you create something it's like poof and it's there, but when I create something it forms slowly, like my school's antique printer is churning it out line by line?"

"Centuries of practice." Henry grinned. He mounted his steed. Unlike Necromancer, Henry's horse danced under his weight, snorting and fighting against the tug of the reins.

"What's your horse's name?" Mara asked, rewarding Necromancer's patience with a pat on the neck.

Henry licked his lips. "Reaper."

Mara laughed. "You're kidding."

He shook his head.

Hooking her bow onto her back, she lifted the reins. "How do we begin?"

He flashed a wicked smile. "Follow me into the forest. Try to keep up. The first one to slay the golden buck wins."

"It's on like Donkey Kong." Mara raised an eyebrow in his direction.

"Hah!" Henry prodded Reaper forward. The stallion sprung into a gallop toward the forest.

Mara's heels slapped Necromancer, who flowed gracefully into a run, although not quite as fast as Reaper. She followed Henry to where the trees started. Quickly, the forest thickened, the canopy blocking out the light from above. Tendrils of mist curled through the underbrush.

"Henry!" Mara called. He was too far ahead to hear her. Kicking Necromancer harder, her eyes darted to the shadows between the pines. Pounding hooves. Snapping branches. Necromancer panted with exertion. Reaper banked left and disappeared behind the thick trunk of a sycamore. Mara reached the turn but couldn't find Henry anywhere. She slowed her horse to a walk, searching the gaps between the trees for signs of Henry's passing, a hoof print or broken twig.

Alone in the ever-darkening forest, Mara tried not to panic. She turned Necromancer in a half circle, thinking she'd return to the castle, but the forest looked the same in every direction. A cobweb-covered branch swept across her cheek and she jerked in the saddle. Necromancer pranced nervously at the shift in her weight.

She'd seen a movie once with a forest like this one. What was it called? *Fun and Games*. It was about a psycho carnie who went crazy and killed a bunch of teenagers in the woods with a chainsaw. Woods exactly like these.

Mara's heart pounded in her chest and her fingers grew strangely cold. Funny, her heart could still beat considering her body was dead, or undead as Henry had called it. She turned her horse in another circle, hoping to spot Henry. Instead, the grinding sound of a chainsaw made Necromancer shift right and bob her head. Mara screamed.

The man she remembered from the movie was a few yards away. In tattered clothing and a clown's mask, he advanced through the trees, the whirring metal of the chainsaw echoing through the woods. He raised the weapon above his head and charged her.

Quick as hummingbird wings, Mara snatched the bow from her back and sent an arrow cruising toward her attacker. It dropped harmlessly to his feet. She strung another one, concentrating on the arrow. Closer. Louder. The chainsaw's steel teeth revolved toward her. She released, guiding the arrow with her will, straight into the man's head.

Bull's-eye! The arrow sunk through the man's eye socket.

The stranger paused for a beat, then ripped the arrow out. Necromancer reared up, knocking Mara to the forest floor. The whinny the horse released ripped through the forest. Necromancer leapt into the woods, leaving Mara crawling backward beneath the whirling steel.

With everything she had, she screeched, "Henry! Henry!" Arrow after arrow flew from her bow until the man was covered in them. He kept coming. The chainsaw lowered toward her panicked body.

Pounding hooves distracted the masked man. Mara kicked the hand holding the chainsaw up and away from her, rolling out from under the blade. She jumped to her feet, ready to run. She didn't have to. Henry's scythe cut the clown in half, sending his bloody torso into the underbrush.

"Get rid of it, Mara!" Henry shouted.

"What do you expect me to do?"

"You created it. Unweave it. Send it away."

Mara froze. Was it possible that her memory of the movie had created the thing that almost killed her? She concentrated on the pieces, picturing them sinking into the earth, cotton candy caught in the rain. In moments, the clown and the chainsaw were gone.

"It almost killed me." Mara's hand pressed into her chest.

"You almost let it," Henry snapped. He looked disappointed.

It was too dark. The mist was creepy and the reaching branches reminded her too much of gripping hands. She turned her face toward the canopy and concentrated on a patch above her head. A ray of sunlight broke through, warming her skin.

"Better," Henry said.

She whistled and Necromancer came running. Mara bounded to her and leapt onto her back. More changes were in order. To find the golden buck, Mara was sure they needed a golden forest. With visions of Christmas in her head, she twisted the trees into gorgeous sculptures of gold and silver. Fluffy flakes of snow drifted from the sky at her will. In minutes, the forest became a magical world that sparkled like a winter wonderland.

Henry raised an eyebrow in her direction.

"Now this is a forest worthy of the golden buck."

"I'm impressed," Henry said. He opened his mouth, presumably to say more, but stopped when a huge gold deer bolted past them into the trees, its branched antlers glinting in the snow.

Henry launched Reaper after it, sweeping his scythe out and to the side so that the handle locked into place. Mara swerved Necromancer left, digging in her heels and hoping to cut the buck off up ahead. She loaded her bow from the quiver she'd refilled, tying off the reins and guiding the mare with her knees. At the first glint of gold, she fired, her arrow landing in a gold tree of her creation. Racing to the right, she heard Reaper's pounding feet and another set of scurrying hooves. Then he was ahead of her, his scythe swinging toward the buck's neck. Mara released her arrow. It cut between Henry's thigh and elbow and plowed into the buck's neck, only a second before the scythe sliced the deer's shoulder. The beast fell in a shower of blood to the snow-covered earth.

Stowing her bow, Mara snatched up the reins and pulled Necromancer to a halt. Reaper trotted up beside her, Henry straight-backed and exuberant in the saddle.

"You've won!" Henry said, motioning toward the carcass. "You really are a fabulous rider."

The golden buck's stately antlers poked awkwardly into the snow. Eyes glazed over, its blood flowed crimson against the collecting white.

Mara's chest felt heavy. "This sucks. Why did we have to kill it? He was so beautiful." She wiped a rogue tear from under her eye.

Henry shrugged. "If you don't want the buck to die, bring it back, Mara. This is your party." He smiled ruefully.

Mara startled at the thought, but didn't hesitate to picture the buck whole again. It was harder than with the trees, slower. After several minutes the proud buck raised its head and galloped into the forest.

"Next time we use paintballs," Mara said.

Henry folded the handle of his scythe, storing the weapon on his back. "Deal."

NINE

ABIGAIL

Abigail strode out her back door, passed her greenhouse and raised bed garden, and entered the maple orchard. In their late spring splendor, the trees spread bright-green branches above her but she didn't stop to enjoy them. She traversed the hill to the privet at the edge of the wood and ducked through the gate that now hung open on rusty hinges.

For June, the weather was unseasonably cool, but it wasn't the temperature that had her crossing her arms over her black slip dress. She rubbed her shoulders. The magnificent garden she'd planted, grown from the seeds she'd collected with her late husband, Oswald, was dead. One hundred years of work rotted brown at her feet, overgrown with native weeds.

"Such a shame," she said to no one. She climbed the sand dune and entered the maze of cacti, now reduced to sharp brown skeletons. At the center, the burnt branches of the tree that used to house Oswald's soul twisted like writhing black snakes. Burning the tree had been the only way to ensure

Oswald could never be used as a portal again. The enchanted staffs were all that remained of what the tree used to be.

She approached the charred trunk and waved her hand over the base. Green vines sprouted from the earth and wrapped themselves around the dead bark. Crimson roses bloomed between the leaves.

"I've come to visit, Oswald. I need to talk to someone. I know you can't answer me. Maybe you can't even hear me. That's okay. I'll do the talking."

With a flourish of her hand, a stump emerged from the sandy soil. She sat down, crossing her legs.

"I miss you, Oswald. I miss how simple it was when it was just you and me. You never knew what I was, but I loved you anyway." She turned her face toward the sun, closing her eyes against the light. "And I think you loved me, too. But as much as I loved you, you loved the illusion. Who I was when we were together, was a lie."

She stood and walked to the tree, cradling one of the roses in her hand. "When I was with you, a lie was a lie. Now that you're gone, everything is more complicated. I'm supposed to live like this illusion is the real thing." Thumping her chest with her palm, she paced the sand. "I've had serpent skin for thousands of years. How is a person supposed to change what they are, for any reward?

"I used to think that there was something left in me from what I was before, something deep inside that still glowed like Gideon, but now I wonder. I wonder if there's anything good or right in me at all. I wonder if my love for Gideon is really some sort of yearning for the innocence we once shared. I do love him, in a different way than I loved you, but just as real.

"Is love enough to change someone? It wasn't for you and

me. Love didn't make you immortal or change the evil in my flesh. Love doesn't make a person good. It doesn't transcend our reality. It wasn't enough to stop me from getting Dane into this mess or risking the lives of the remaining Soulkeepers.

"In the end, we are who we are, good or evil. If there is change, if you believe people can change, it's because we choose it. We choose it for our own reasons. People say we come into this world alone and we leave alone. You may have left this world alone, Oswald, but I was left alone. I am destined to always be alone. What is asked of me is impossible. God says He will make me human, but only if I am already as good as human."

She pounded her sternum with her fist as if she could make her heart start beating.

"This foul organ might as well be stone."

Blood red and fully open, one of the roses caught her eye. She plucked the flower from the vine. A thorn dug into her finger but she did not bleed. She could not bleed anything but black Watcher blood. It would take more than a thorn to draw it from beneath her scaly shell.

Resting in her hand, she held the bloom out toward Oswald's grave. "This rose has a better chance of turning into a butterfly and flying from my hand, than I do of making the right decision when the time comes."

She shook her head and tossed the rose on the sand. "Now you know, Oswald. Wherever you are, you know exactly what I am. It was good talking to you again, even if you couldn't hear it."

In the blink of an eye, she was gone, out of the maze and back up to the house. She moved too quickly to be sure, but out of the corner of her eye, she could've sworn a crimson red butterfly stretched its wings and fluttered toward the sky.

❦

FROM THE PORCH OF HER GOTHIC VICTORIAN HOME, Abigail watched the Laudner's Flowers and Gifts delivery van pull into her driveway. Malini and Jacob exited the vehicle and hurried toward her.

Lillian leaned out the driver's side window. "Jacob, I know this is important, but John isn't going to take any excuses for you missing dinner again. Malini, you need to check in at home, too, or things are going to get complicated."

Abigail grinned. "Don't worry. They'll be out of your hair soon enough. It seems both of your parents have won a two-week cruise to the Caribbean."

"That's convenient," Malini said, exchanging glances with Jacob.

As Lillian backed down the driveway, all Abigail could think of was how ridiculous it was for God to send a couple of teenagers to stop Lucifer and his army. They weren't ready. Not for this.

"Come in," she said, holding open the door. She led them into her parlor and took a seat in the leather recliner. "In light of Dane's impending death, I'll dispense with the formalities. Malini, who do we need to bring in first?"

"I'm not sure."

"What do you mean, you're not sure? You're the Healer. You have to know." Abigail grabbed Malini's wrist, shaking it as if the names would fall out like loose change. "You need to know. You need to know now."

Jacob pushed Dr. Silva's hand away. "Relax. Give her some air. We've been traveling for the last fourteen hours."

The look Abigail shot him made Jacob lean away from her. She'd looked at him like this once before, when she'd thought he'd left the gate open back when the enchanted garden was alive and dangerous. She knew her expression wasn't human and the message it sent was as clear as if she'd said the words out loud. *I could kill you.*

"She's right, Jacob. This is my job," Malini said, voice shaking. "When I say I'm not sure, I mean I don't have a clear vision of our outcome. What I am sure of is we have to move forward. We could have better timing but Lucifer has forced our hand. We can't afford to wait. We go tomorrow. I've decided we start with—"

"Stop, Malini. Don't say it." Abigail retrieved a piece of parchment from a box on the mantel. "Write mine on this. It's enchanted to only appear for me. You never know who might be listening."

Abigail slid the parchment across the table and offered Malini a pen. The Healer wrote the information on it, the ink disappearing into the parchment.

"Dr. Silva?" Jacob asked, tentatively. "I thought your house was enchanted. I thought Watchers couldn't come here without being invited. How could anyone be listening?"

Turning her face toward the window, Dr. Silva gave a deep sigh. "My home is safe from Watchers, Jacob, but we're not dealing with Watchers anymore. We're dealing with Lucifer. I wish we hadn't garnered his attention. Lucifer goes anywhere he wants to go, he looks any way he wants to look, and he listens and sees much more than you can imagine." She rubbed her eyes, feeling more exhausted than ever.

Malini's golden stare fixed on Abigail "Maybe so but he's not God. He may be able to do all of those things but he can't do them everywhere at once. If he's following me, he can't be following you. You taught me that. We can use that to our advantage."

Dr. Silva nodded. She held out the parchment and allowed her touch to pull the ink to the surface.

Tomorrow night, Ethan Walsh, Pauly's Nightclub, Los Angeles. Go exactly at 1:15 a.m. He'll be behind the bar. He doesn't know what he is. Horseman Bridget Snow and Helper August Ward, 2 p.m., The Bean Grinder, Hot Springs, Arkansas. They'll be expecting you.

She blinked several times, memorizing the names and locations, then crumpled the note and tossed it into the fire. The page ignited and turned to ash. "You're right, Malini. Lucifer has his limitations, although I wish he had more of them."

"The times I wrote on your parchment, stick to them," Malini said. "Even if it's not what you expected."

"Of course," Dr. Silva said toward the fire.

"Jacob and I will do our part. We'll check back in with you after your first mission," Malini said.

Abigail nodded.

Malini motioned for Jacob to follow her and the two headed for the door without saying goodbye. Abigail heard the click as it shut behind them. She leaned on the mantel and rested her forehead on her crossed arms.

Lucifer had his limitations. Malini was right about that. He couldn't be in two places at once, but he could make plenty of trouble for all of them. She pitied Ethan Walsh most of all. He had no idea what he was about to be pulled into.

TEN

MARA AND HENRY

Mara had never laughed so hard or from a place so deep within her soul. The conversation with Henry flowed easily. After the hunt, they'd roamed the forest talking about books and movies. Death was surprisingly up to date, although his knowledge ended with living artists. It made for an excellent discussion of the classics, and an interesting attempt by Mara to describe a recent blockbuster.

"So, the machines become people?" Henry asked, confused.

"No, they're still machines but they look like people."

"Why?"

"Because it's more exciting. They can take on human characteristics."

"Why don't they use people?"

"The machines are bigger and scarier."

"Use bigger and scarier people."

"You'll understand when you see it."

Henry mumbled something under his breath.

She shrugged. "It's not my favorite or anything."

"Are you ready for lunch?" Henry asked.

"Starving. Should we go back to the castle?"

"How about a picnic in the park."

"What park?"

The snow stopped. The sky became a bright blue. All of the trees Mara had created shed their foil leaves and grew a more deciduous variety.

"This way." Henry led her across the changing landscape. The trees gradually opened up to a rolling green hillside. Lapping water called to them. A lake stretched on the horizon, its stone beach blending into the soft expanse of grass. Henry dismounted Reaper at the edge, allowing the horse to lower its neck for a drink.

"This is beautiful," Mara said. She took her feet out of the stirrups and swung her legs to one side of Necromancer, dropping awkwardly. She lost her balance and landed on her backside in the grass.

Henry chuckled softly.

"I meant to do that," she said.

"Sorry, I shouldn't have laughed, but you are adorable." He dropped Reaper's reins and sauntered over to where she sat on the lawn. He didn't stop until his feet were between hers. Extending his hand, he offered to help.

"Adorable? More like adorkable." Mara accepted his help and he lifted her to her feet. With how close he was standing, she ended up losing her balance in an attempt to avoid falling into him. His hand pressed into the small of her back, steadying her by pulling her flush against his chest. She rested her gloved hands on the lapels of his riding jacket and raised her eyes to meet his.

For a moment, it didn't matter that there were layers of leather and wool between them. She felt naked and vulnerable, like he could see into her soul, and maybe he could. But the oddest part was she also felt safe. She trusted him with her soul, with her whole self. Maybe it was a silly thing to do, to give your heart and soul to someone you'd known such a short time. If it had been a friend, she'd most certainly suggest the person take it slow. But Mara couldn't help herself. Her insides fluttered like a butterfly trying to break from its cocoon. If she let this thing inside her fly, there would be no turning back.

His arm bent at the elbow and his fingers worked under her hand on his chest. At first she wondered if he was pushing her away. He'd stepped back slightly. Maybe the full eye contact was too stalkerish.

Plucking the leather upward, he slipped off her glove. He did the same with his own, then threaded his bare fingers into hers.

Mara had to stare at their melded palms. Were they really just holding hands? Electrically-charged honey oozed over her skin from that small place of contact. She wanted to keep going, to melt into him until she forgot where he ended and she began.

Henry cleared his throat. "Lunch is ready. You must be famished." He turned, lowering their coupled hands to his side.

Breaking eye contact, Mara gasped at the spread that had knitted itself out of the ether. A plush black velvet blanket spread across the grass, loaded down with silver trays of bite-sized canapés, bowls of fruit, and salads of all kinds.

"Are we expecting company?" Mara teased.

"I wasn't sure what you liked."

She walked to the edge and lowered herself to the velvet. The silver candelabra lit itself at the center of the blanket, and the china plates, so carefully set for her pleasure, reflected the sun.

"I love it. It's perfect." Mara's voice broke. Her eyes stung with welling tears.

"Why are you crying?" he asked softly.

She beamed at him, tilting her head up to where he stood behind her. "Because it's the nicest thing anyone has ever done for me."

Henry lowered himself beside her and handed her a plate. "How is that possible? Someone like you ... I would expect you've received your share of masculine attention."

Mara lowered her eyes.

Hooking his bare hand under her chin, he tipped her face to his. "I know this situation isn't ideal. We went from our first kiss to living together overnight. I'm not sure how long we'll have, but I want to know everything I can about you."

With a trembling hand, Mara lifted a small tart to her mouth, savoring the velvety chicken center. When she finished, Henry handed her a crystal goblet of lemonade.

"What I'm about to tell you isn't a happy story," Mara began. "Part of me wants to change the embarrassing parts. But it's my story. If you want to know me, you have to know the truth."

He nodded.

She began with her first memories: the trailer park she lived in, the way her mother would get drunk, the fights, and the knife that landed her in the mental institution. She told

Henry about finding her power when she was twelve, the bell she learned to rely on, and even the SpongeBob pajamas. The story ended with her life in Chicago, where she spent years believing she would always be alone, and then Jacob and Dr. Silva.

"You've had to be stronger than any person should have to be," Henry said, looking out across the lake. His face was distant, like his body was with her but his mind was in another world.

"It was too much too soon, wasn't it? You think differently of me? I mean, let's be honest and get it all out on the table. I was basically raised by white trash." She pointed at her chest. "I'm not exactly a fairy princess."

Henry raised his eyebrows at her. "I do think differently of you."

Mara's face fell.

Leaning toward her, his hands pressed into the velvet. "I think you are a rare diamond of a soul, as indestructible as you are beautiful, as transparent as you are a mystery, and inherently precious even if there are many who don't realize your value."

She thought her heart might leap out of her chest. What she did next took more courage than anything she'd ever done. More than the night before when her actions could be mistaken for passion independent of affection. Crawling across the velvet, she caressed the tops of his hands and met his offered lips.

ELEVEN

GIDEON

Gideon stopped watching Katrina's dorm once Mallory returned smelling strongly of alcohol but without the arsenic-sweet scent of Watcher. Katrina was as safe as she could be for now. There were ways around the spell on her room. Mallory could be possessed or another human might be influenced into killing Katrina. But the opportunistic nature of Watchers meant they'd be unlikely to strike in a way that called attention to what they were. Dragging a screaming girl from her bed in a crowded dorm in the middle of the night was definitely not their style.

He materialized inside the gothic Victorian, in the hallway near the parlor. If Abigail noticed he was home, she didn't show it. She was watching the fire, her forehead resting on her crossed arms braced against the mantel.

"What are you thinking about?" Gideon asked.

Abigail straightened and rubbed her eyes. "Lucifer has Dane in Hell. He's going to burn him alive if I don't help him."

"You know he'll do it anyway. No one makes it out of Hell." Gideon scowled and took a step toward her.

"I know. I didn't tell Malini though. She's already in over her head on this one without the guilt of her friend's slow death weighing her down. And we all know Jacob is useless if Malini isn't happy."

Gideon fluffed his wings defensively. "You don't give them enough credit. After what we've faced this year, you need to trust that God has given us the tools to succeed."

She glanced at him over her shoulder, her hands coming to rest on her hips. "What if this time God isn't in control? What if this is the beginning of the end?"

"You mean, the end of times?" Gideon shook his head.

"The great tribulation. The beginning of Satan's rule on Earth. What if this time is the one time he's supposed to get lucky?"

A fiery light washed across the floor, pouring off of Gideon in waves.

Abigail squinted to maintain eye contact. "The promise God made us seems impossible. Maybe it is. Maybe this was a battle He knew from the start we couldn't win."

"You think this was all a ploy to get us to serve God's purpose? That He had no intention of fulfilling his promise to us?" The muscles in Gideon's jaw flexed.

She shook her head. "I don't know. I just don't know."

"I don't believe it, Abigail. It's not true."

She turned back toward the fireplace, the light from the logs dim in comparison to Gideon.

"Abigail, instead of speculating about our promise, maybe you should ask yourself why the father of all lies gave you twelve days to do something you could do in a heartbeat. Why so much time?" He stepped closer to her.

Her head tilted to the right. "I don't know. Maybe he thought Dane's suffering would bring us to our knees."

"I think there is a reason Lucifer needs twelve days. We both know he intends to kill the boy no matter what. Challenging you and Malini is a distraction, a way to set you off your guard. He has something else up his sleeve. I can feel it." He stepped in as close as he dared, the itch of a heat rash breaking out across his chest.

"It's a good thing we have a Healer to sort this out for us," she said sarcastically, "because from where I stand, it looks like the devil has painted us into a corner and I, for one, don't see any way out." She turned around and shouldered past him, blistering where her skin touched his.

Gideon sprung forward, his wings extending, knocking the lamp on the end table to the floor. His hands grabbed her shoulders long enough to force her to face him. Sparks and the smell of burning flesh filled the room.

She dropped her illusion.

Releasing her, he stared into the slit pupils of her yellow eyes, sunk into a face of black serpent skin. Her leathery wings extended defensively.

"I think the real problem is you do see a way out," Gideon said. "Only, it is not our way out, it is your way out. You can't make a deal with the devil and expect to come out unscathed, Abigail."

Leaping backward onto the kitchen table, she pointed a talon in his direction. "Gideon, you of all should know better." She crawled off the other side of the table and bolted halfway down the hall. "Stay away from me. Stay far away from me."

Her illusion snapped back into place as she rounded the banister and ascended the staircase. Platinum-blonde hair cascaded down her back, hiding the place where her wings tucked away. Dark scales smoothed to alabaster skin and her yellow eyes became icy blue. She patted the edges of her burnt shoulders. The burns would take all night to heal and be impossible to cover up with any illusion. Gideon had known the consequences when he'd touched her. The two of them had learned the hard way early on.

Frowning at his burnt palms, Gideon returned to the parlor to clean up the lamp.

WHEN THE GLASS WAS CLEARED AWAY AND THE PARLOR was spotless, and every surface of the main floor was dusted, Gideon still couldn't forgive himself for attacking Abigail. That's what he'd done, attacked her. He'd known his touch would burn just as he knew his words would burn in an entirely different way.

This wasn't what he'd had in mind when he'd come here. The day he'd delivered her message of redemption, he saw something in her eyes, a glimpse into a soul at the brink of transcendence. She wasn't truly fallen, but she wasn't like him either. She was as close to human as any angel he'd ever known. That was what he fell in love with, the battle within, the freedom, the humanity in the divine. He always envied humans.

At first he'd returned to watch her, but when she'd discovered him in her garden, the visits became mutual. Long walks turned into entire days spent together. Abigail couldn't hear enough about Heaven, and Gideon couldn't stop asking about Earth. The day God told him he could stay was the happiest point in his existence. He'd fallen in love with Abigail, the way she saw the world and the heavens for what they were, accepted her role in the universe without blaming anyone but herself, and planted her garden every year the human way, with faith that the seeds would sprout and grow, even though she could have used magic.

Loving someone meant believing in them, and helping them to do the right thing. Tonight was an epic fail in that department.

From the candy dish on the coffee table, Gideon lifted the red stone necklace. Malini had left it with Abigail and him after their battle against Lucifer at the school, when she came into her own as a Healer. He never used it. But now he needed guidance and, although Abigail wasn't confident in the Healer's abilities, Gideon believed that the part of Malini that resided in the In Between was infinitely wise. He made himself comfortable in the armchair and raised the stone to the light.

The walls faded to red and then disappeared. The floor dropped out. Gideon was falling, falling, falling. He flapped his wings but there was no air to catch under his feathers. He landed softly in solid black nothingness. After only a moment, a room shingled itself around him. Squares of stainless steel, white, and red formed a mosaic that filled every corner of the darkness. The black-and-white checkerboard pattern of the floor spread toward a gleaming white counter edged in stainless steel. Red padded stools formed in front of the counter. A jukebox against the wall kicked on and *Johnny B. Goode* drifted across what Gideon now recognized as a '50s diner.

"Don't look so surprised. This came from your mind, Gideon," a heavyset black woman said from behind the counter.

Gideon looked down at himself then twisted to see better in the mirrored wall to the left of the counter. He was dressed in khaki pants and a button-down shirt. His hair was slicked back and his wings were ... gone.

"Why do you think my subconscious picked a '50s diner?" Gideon mumbled to the woman. After all, he'd been to Heaven. It seemed odd.

"'Cuz, Gideon, you have idealized being human. Look at me." She motioned toward her ample bosom. "You gave me this look. A black woman owning a diner in 1950s America. Believe me, this is an idealized version of human history." She loosed a heady laugh.

Gideon squinted at the woman's face. "Malini?"

"Not exactly. The stone is enchanted to be an echo of the Healer's power. I wouldn't exist without the Healer, but she's not here entirely."

The woman lifted a frosted glass from behind the counter, scooped vanilla ice cream into the bottom, then filled in the space with what looked like root beer. She inserted a straw and slid the float down the counter to Gideon.

"I think you'll like that," she said.

He took a sip and was rewarded with an ambrosia of flavors he'd never experienced before. It was so good he had to close his eyes.

"Now, I believe you wouldn't be here if you didn't have some questions." She leaned a brown elbow on the counter. I have some limitations though. I can only tell you the future as it stands today. But let me caution you, angel, knowing the future is a dangerous thing. It's always changing, shifting with every thought and decision we make."

Gideon stirred his drink. "I want to know if Abigail is thinking about joining Lucifer. I want to know if she's given up on us."

The black woman shook her head. "Neither of those are questions about the future, Gideon. Do I need to explain the rules again?" She rolled her brown eyes.

"I apologize." Gideon sipped from his drink and concentrated on how to ask what he needed to know. "Will Abigail make a deal with the devil?"

The woman pulled a piece of white bread from under the counter and slid it in the slot of a stainless steel toaster near the mirrored wall. She pushed down the lever and drummed her fingers on the counter. Accompanied by a loud ding, the toast popped out of the toaster and landed on the counter. The bread was browned except for a symbol in white at the center.

The woman ran her fingers over the grain. "Yes, she will."

The answer was a punch in the gut. "Will I be able to stop her?" Gideon whispered.

Another slice of bread lowered into the toaster. The woman caught it this time when it flew from the slot. "No."

Gideon buried his face in his hands and was surprised when they came away wet. "What is this?" He held his wet fingers out to the woman. "There's something wrong with me. My chest feels hollow and my throat aches. Am I coming apart?"

"You're crying," the woman said softly, placing a hand on his shoulder. "It's a human thing and here, in this reality, you are human."

"I've seen people cry. I've just never done it myself."

The woman nodded and patted his shoulder. "Being human isn't easy."

Gideon wiped under his eyes. "I have one more question."

"Go ahead."

"Will Abigail give up on us? On me?"

The bread slid into the toaster and sprung out almost as quickly as it went in. "No. No." The woman shook her curly black hair. "Abigail will never give up on you."

Gideon met her kind eyes. "Thank you."

The bell above the door rang and a girl walked in. Whatever clothes she'd had on transformed into a cardigan and a pink poodle skirt.

"You have got to be kidding me!" she said, looking down at herself and stomping her foot. "Whose idea was this?"

"Mara?" Gideon asked.

The girl looked up and a smile bloomed across her face. "Gideon?" Mara ran to him and tossed her arms around his neck, pressing her lips into his cheek. "What are you doing here?"

"I used the red stone to visit—" He turned back toward the counter with the intention of introducing the black woman, but she was gone. "She was just here. I was talking to her about Abigail."

"It's like that around here. You never know what to expect." Mara climbed onto the stool next to him, then realized he had an ice cream float and jumped down to make herself one.

"We all thought you were dead," Gideon said.

"I guess I am. Well, Henry says I'm *undead*. I don't know for sure. I'm the only one who's ever been here body and soul."

"Undead?" Gideon didn't like the sound of that. "So, what does that mean for us? The Soulkeepers need you."

"I can never go back. The way Henry talks, I'm some sort of a lost soul and as soon as the powers that be notice I'm missing, he and I are going to get our comeuppance." She scooped vanilla ice cream into a glass. "Of course, Henry is Death so what can they really do to him?" She pointed the ice cream scoop at Gideon and squinted her eyes. "I have a feeling I'm going to take the brunt of it."

"So, you are supposed to be dead but Death spared you by bringing you here."

"Yep." She poured in the root beer. "We're kind of an item. I mean he's never actually asked me to be his girlfriend but I think with the living together and the tonsil hockey, it's a sure thing."

Gideon's mouth fell open. He closed it again and cleared his throat. "Where's Henry now?"

She sighed. "He's working. We've been inseparable and he needed to give it his full attention for a while. I decided to explore and ended up here. Strange choice by the way. I suppose if I wasn't the one wearing the poodle skirt it would be cool."

"I wonder how long you'll be able to stay here?" Gideon asked because he couldn't think what else to say.

"Who knows? How's Dr. Silva?"

"I'm worried about her. She hasn't been herself lately."

"You mean she's been kind and cooperative."

"Very funny." Gideon frowned.

"Seriously, Gideon. When has Abigail ever been herself? She's a Watcher trying to be human or better. Her whole existence is an attempt to *not* be herself."

Straightening on his stool, the clouds in Gideon's mind parted. He stood up and hugged Mara. "Thank you. You are a brilliant girl. Thank you."

"Uh, no problem. What did I do?"

Gideon didn't answer her, but concentrated on backing out of the stone. "I'm sorry, Mara, I've got to go. I've got to go, now."

"What's going on?" she called.

The walls turned red then broke apart. He heard Mara swear as her drink disintegrated, and then he was in the chair in the parlor. He placed the stone back in the dish on the table and headed for Abigail's bedroom. Maybe the answer to all of this was for him to become like her. If he fell like she had, if he became like her, they could be together. It wasn't ideal and he'd be giving up the humanity he'd desired for as long as he could remember, but if it kept her from Lucifer, he would do it.

He hurried up the stairs, hoping they could watch the sunrise from the tower and talk about the future. It was a beautiful morning for a sunrise.

When he opened the door, the room was empty. Abigail was gone.

TWELVE

JACOB AND MALINI

"Why can't we go in now?" Jacob asked. They waited, parked outside a restaurant called Nowhere Oasis, somewhere in rural Nebraska. Jacob wasn't exactly sure where it was because he'd slept the last two hours of the journey while Malini drove. They'd made the long trip in her mother's Honda, and Jacob was anxious to get out and stretch his legs.

Malini leaned back against the seat and sighed. "It's not time. A little while longer."

"I'm hungry."

"How could you be hungry? You ate all the snacks."

"I don't know. I just am."

"It won't be much longer."

Jacob sighed and repositioned his knees against the glove compartment. "Okay. If you say so, but if we're going to keep doing this, we need to borrow a bigger car."

"Just wait until we put three more in the back."

"Three?"

Malini grinned. "Yep. You know that expression 'hit two birds with one stone?' Well, today we're going to hit three Soulkeepers with one trip."

"How did you manage that?"

"I didn't. Fate did. They're a family, like you and your mom."

Jacob raised an eyebrow. "Makes sense, since Soulkeeping is genetic. Who are they?"

She popped open the car door just as a couple with two small children exited the restaurant. "Come on. See for yourself."

Relieved, Jacob unfolded himself from the passenger seat, stretching his arms above his head. "After nine hours of driving, this better be good."

Rolling her eyes, Malini led the way into the restaurant. There was a tiny foyer with a dusty and outdated braided rug, brick walls decorated with the occasional hanging plant, and Formica tables set with paper placemats. The restaurant was completely deserted.

Malini took a seat at a booth by the windows and Jacob slid in across from her. He grabbed a menu from the stack wedged behind the napkins. A girl, maybe sixteen, sauntered from the kitchen, still chewing whatever she'd been eating, and pulled a pad of paper from the apron pocket of her tailored blue uniform.

"Hi, I'm Sam. I'll be your server. Can I get you something to drink while you're deciding?" She flipped her long, red hair behind her shoulder.

Jacob piped up. "I'll take a cheeseburger, fries, and a Coke. Do you have Coke?"

Malini gave him a sharp look, obviously annoyed that he interjected his order into their mission.

"Sure," Sam said, taking the menu from his hands and replacing it in the stack. "Do you know what you want?" Sam raised her eyes to Malini's.

With her left hand, her healing hand, Malini touched Sam's wrist. The girl's eyes widened. Jacob was familiar with the feeling, like waves of light from the inside out.

"I need to talk to your mom and your sister," Malini said.

Sam nodded and backed away.

"And I want a cheeseburger, too," she called after her.

Jacob chuckled. "Pot who calls the kettle black."

She shrugged. "I'm hungry. It was a long trip, and you hogged all the snacks."

Only seconds later, a heavyset woman with dark red curls fringed in gray ran from the kitchen. "Hello! I'm Grace, Grace Guillian." She eyed Malini suspiciously. "Can I have your name?"

Malini extended her left hand. "Malini Gupta, it's a pleasure to meet you."

The woman accepted her offered fingers. A moment's connection and she lit up like a Christmas tree. "Welcome, Healer." She bowed slightly at the waist.

"And this is Jacob Lau, a Horseman," Malini said. Jacob extended his hand and she accepted it eagerly.

"Girls! Come out here."

Samantha returned and so did another Samantha. Jacob tried not to stare but the two girls, obviously twins, looked exactly alike, down to their baby pink nail polish. He'd known twins before but these two were exceptionally the same. Every hair seemed to be trained to lie identically, like they were dolls manufactured in a factory.

"You've met Samantha. This is Bonnie." Grace flapped her fingers, calling the girls to come closer. They walked at the same pace with one arm tucked behind their backs in exactly the same way.

"Weird. You guys look *exactly* alike," Jacob said.

"Don't be rude," Malini whispered.

Jacob's head snapped toward Malini and then back toward the twins. "I'm not being rude. Look at them! They are the most identical identical twins I've ever seen."

Grace chuckled. "It's true! Except that they are even more rare. Samantha and Bonnie are mirror image twins. Look here." She pointed to a large freckle on the left side of Samantha's nose. The same freckle was on the right side of Bonnie's. "And believe me, that is only the beginning of what makes these two special."

"Will you show us?" Malini asked softly.

Grace nodded. "Of course, Healer."

"Please call me Malini, Mrs. Guillian."

"Only if you call me Grace. Besides, my husband, Burt, passed away five years ago, so I'm not exactly a Mrs. anymore."

"I'm sorry," Jacob said.

Malini nodded in agreement.

Grace smoothed her apron. "Water under the bridge." She turned toward Samantha and Bonnie. "Since we're on the subject, why don't you show Malini and Jacob what your father looked like when he was alive?"

"Sure, Mom." Samantha smiled and reached for Bonnie's hand. There was a silent exchange between them and then one twin melded into the other. Like two mounds of clay that were forced together, they blended and blurred, until one was a six-foot-tall man with brown hair in a police uniform, and the other was a four-foot-tall version of herself.

"This is what my father looked like," Bonnie said, in a man's voice. Samantha, whose new form made her look around nine, pointed her hands spokesmodel-like at her sister.

"The voice is off, but they've done a winning impression," Grace said.

Jacob couldn't speak. His mind tried to wrap around what he'd just seen.

The girls seemed to revel in his amazement. They nodded at each other, grabbed hands again, and transformed into Jacob and a very small version of Malini.

"So, they can share mass and look like anyone?" Malini asked.

The girls transformed into themselves. "Anyone, yes. But we can't weigh more than three hundred pounds," they said in unison.

Grace smiled proudly.

"Are you their Helper?" Jacob asked.

"Yes. My mother was a Soulkeeper before she died. I'm a black-belt in Shotokan." The woman squinted her eyes and made a karate chop in front of her round belly. The twins rolled their eyes.

"My mom's more of a behind-the-desk kind of Helper," Sam said.

"Sam! I have many underutilized talents."

"We've trained but we've never actually faced a Watcher," Bonnie said. "We took down a shoplifter at the IGA last fall though."

Malini frowned. "I'm sorry to have to be the bearer of bad

news but we've come to tell you, you're not safe here anymore. Your identities have been compromised."

"Compromised to whom?" Grace asked.

"Lucifer," Malini said, lowering her chin and closing her eyes as if it hurt to utter the word.

"Lucifer! My heavens! The girls aren't ready for that. Who could be ready for that?"

"We want you to come with us. There's a safe place. A place made for us by God where we can train until the attack. We want to take you to Eden," Malini said.

Grace scowled. "Eden? As in *the* Eden?"

"Yes. We want to organize the Soulkeepers so that we can face Lucifer with a united front. Will you come with us?"

Sam and Bonnie nodded but Grace didn't seem as enthusiastic. Rubbing her mouth, she shook her curly red head. "The girls have school, and I have the restaurant. It's just us running this place. We'd have to close the whole thing down. This is our livelihood!"

"I understand it's a difficult decision, but we're starting a school for Soulkeepers in Eden. The girls could continue their education there." Malini folded her hands. "To be honest, I'm not sure about your restaurant. I can't promise you any money or extra help if you need to close it down. But I can promise that you and the girls will be safer with us."

The corners of Grace's thin lips pulled ever downward. She thrust her hands into the pockets of her apron. "I need to think about this."

Bonnie rushed to her side and whispered something in her ear.

Grace nodded. "How about I make the two burgers you ordered? I always think better when I'm cooking."

"That sounds like an amazing plan," Jacob said enthusiastically.

"I agree." Malini slid out of the booth as Grace returned to the kitchen with Bonnie. "Jacob, I'm going to make use of the facilities. Be right back."

"Okay. I think I can handle things out here." He chuckled and glanced over the empty tables.

"So, you're a Horseman, like us?" Samantha asked, sliding into Malini's seat.

"Yeah."

"What's your gift?"

Jacob steadied the empty water glass on the table and reached out with his power. He sensed the faucet in the kitchen, the pipes that led to the bathroom, a pot of water boiling on the stove, and a pitcher behind the counter. He chose the pitcher.

The water arced into the air, circled over their heads, and filled the glass in his hand. Every drop of the remainder returned to the pitcher.

"Cool," Samantha said. "Can you do it with any liquid?"

"No. Just water. If it were, say, lemonade, I could move the water out of the lemon and the sugar. But I can't move that other stuff and the more mixed into the water it is, the harder it is for me to use it. Take a person, for example. Malini and I thought maybe I could control people's movements since the human body is mostly water, but it didn't work. I tried it on Malini's arm and she said it felt like needles were piercing her flesh, but she could still move her arm away. Plus, the skill would be useless on Watchers anyway, since they're made out of, um, evil, I guess."

"You don't know for sure what Watchers are made of?"

The front door opened and an attractive couple walked in.

"Go ahead and seat yourself, I'll be right there," Samantha called toward the door. She lowered her voice. "It's early for the dinner rush to start, and when I say rush, I mean the six people who come here on any given week night." Samantha stood and pulled her pad from her apron. She strolled toward the couple's table.

Jacob wasn't sure why, but he couldn't take his eyes off the couple. They looked like they belonged in Hollywood. The woman had flawless skin and sleek black hair, and wore a tailored black dress. The man was equally handsome, muscular but sophisticated. Jacob couldn't fathom what a couple like that was doing in rural Nebraska.

Samantha asked if she could get them something to drink. As before, her eyes were focused on her pad of paper, which was why she didn't see the man reach inside his jacket and wrap his fingers around the hilt of an obsidian blade.

"*Samantha, move!*" Jacob launched himself from his seat, pulling the water from the pitcher and dropping a sheet of ice in front of Samantha. Watchers! The man's blade bounced off the ice shield and barely missed Samantha's hip.

Samantha screamed and bolted backward, scrambling for the kitchen. The woman leaped out of the booth after her, talons ripping through the tips of her perfectly manicured fingers.

Jacob reached the booth, his broadsword of ice forming in his hand. He thrust at the male. The Watcher dodged left, but not fast enough. Jacob connected with its shoulder, a shallow cut blooming with black blood. The magic of his blade meant the wound would burn like acid.

Leaping straight into the air, Jacob dodged swiping talons,

landing on top of a table with a precarious wobble. He brought his blade around and severed the Watcher's arm. The limb melted into a sizzling puddle of black ooze.

Wounded, the Watcher burst entirely from its illusion. It tackled Jacob in a flurry of leathery wings, talons, and snapping fangs. Jacob slid his blade under the thing's ribs into the cavity where the heart might have been if it had one. In a final burst of energy, the Watcher shredded Jacob's side with the talons of its remaining hand. Luckily, it exploded before it could completely rip Jacob apart. Black chunks of Watcher flesh skimmed across the tabletops and into the walls. Oily blood doused him from head to toe.

Jacob rolled over and forced himself up, gripping his mangled side.

Bursting from the bathroom, Malini gasped. "Oh, Jacob!"

Bonnie's scream cut through the restaurant.

"Go!" Jacob demanded.

Malini bolted for the kitchen door. Jacob hobbled after her. When he reached the kitchen, he saw an ogre holding off the female Watcher with a swinging cleaver, while Grace cowered behind its beefy legs. Both were covered in ripped flesh from the Watcher's talons. Malini tried her best to burn the Watcher with her healing hand, but the creature was too quick. It dodged her advances, closing in on the ogre.

Jacob didn't waste any time. He threw his blade into the Watcher's back. His aim was true. It sliced through the chest and the creature melted into a steaming black puddle that oozed down the kitchen drain.

The ogre separated into Bonnie and Samantha. "Bonnie's really hurt," Samantha said, catching her twin as she collapsed in a bloody heap. Malini rushed to her side and placed her left hand on the wounds. Bonnie healed, but at the same time, the skin on Malini's arm blistered to the elbow.

"I need water."

Thankfully, Grace filled a pot and brought it to her. Jacob was in no condition to use his power. His knees gave out and he landed on his backside on the tile. Pain shot through the torn flesh on his side. "Malini."

She plunged her burnt arm into the pot of water, healing herself, then moved to Jacob. Her touch was a welcome relief. The light flooded through him until he felt his flesh stitch back together and the burn under the skin extinguish.

"This is getting to be a nasty habit, Jacob," she whispered to him.

His mouth pulled to one side. "I think I'm getting better at it."

"Better at getting pummeled?"

He sat up and pushed her hand away. "Hey, I killed both of them. A little respect."

Malini plunged her burnt hand again, turning toward the others. "Is anyone else injured?"

Samantha held out her arm, slashed from elbow to wrist. Malini crossed the room to heal her, then healed herself.

Jacob turned in a circle, taking in the splatters of red human blood mixed with sprays of black from the slaughtered Watchers. The kitchen was trashed. Well, everywhere but the grill, which had been shielded by the vent hood.

"Hey, I think the burgers are still good," Jacob said.

The girls' mouths dropped open at the same time. Grace's eyebrows arced into her curly red bangs.

"I'm just sayin'. They smell really good and, ah, well

there's a little blood but that will come right off." Jacob poked at a burger with a spatula.

The sizzle of the burgers was the only sound as Grace scanned her destroyed kitchen and then her two girls. Her eyes landed on Malini and she sighed deeply. "We'll come. We'll come with you."

Malini pulled the woman into a tight hug.

THIRTEEN

ABIGAIL

Abigail arrived at Pauly's Nightclub just after one and filtered into the back of the crowded dance floor. Malini's note said Ethan would be behind the bar at 1:15 a.m., but Abigail wanted time to scope out the place. With a virgin Soulkeeper, she needed to be prepared. If Lucifer had her followed, there could be trouble.

A throbbing mass of people packed the dance floor, glimpses of the bar flashing between flesh and sweat. Squares of glass lined the walls and the front of the bar, lit from within by blue light. Latin pop delivered an intoxicating rhythm that moved the crowd as one, a living organism rising and falling with the beat. She edged her way around the crowd, near the booths with black leather bench seats and lime green curtains, taking in everyone and everything the way only a creature of the night could.

"Do you want to dance?" The woman who cut Abigail off was stunning, with long brunette hair, blue eyes, and a figure that rivaled Abigail's illusion. She could've been a Watcher, but she smelled human.

"Sorry, I can't," Abigail said.

"Too bad. You're the hottest thing in this place." Smiling, the woman blended back into the mass of bodies.

Abigail perused the faces in front of her, couples pressed against each other in the dark. There were men and women but the men were with men and the women were with women. Yep, this was a gay bar. After so many years of living in Paris, Illinois, she'd almost forgotten they existed. If anyone in Paris was homosexual they were so far in the closet they were halfway to Narnia.

She continued toward the bar, glancing at her cell phone. Two minutes to go. A bartender in a tight black T-shirt fixed drinks and made change as fast as he could. Servers pressed against one corner of the bar and guests leaned on every inch of it. Abigail sifted through the crowd, watching the seconds tick off to 1:15. It had to be the bartender. She waited for a sign, a clue to make sure.

A younger man with a tray of dirty glasses emerged from the crowd and headed for the bar. Blue light reflected off his black hair. He lifted the gate and moved toward the sink. As loud as the music was, the bartender didn't hear him coming. He turned into the young man's tray, sending glasses tumbling. The young man pushed the bartender down to the floor, switched his tray to his other hand, and caught the falling glasses. To the human eye, it looked like they'd never fallen, that the bartender had bumped into the busboy's body, not his tray. The young man had saved the glasses from breaking with his mind. This was Ethan.

"Hey, sorry I knocked you down," Ethan said, offering a hand to the bartender. "I thought I was going to drop these."

"No problem, man. Good thing they didn't fall."

"I've never lost one yet." Ethan bellied up to the sink and started washing the glasses. Abigail moved in.

"Can I speak to you for a moment?" she said across the bar. She had to yell for him to hear over the music.

"What do you need? I'll have Ray get it for you." Ethan continued his washing but tipped his head in the direction of the bartender. A tight-lipped smile stretched across his clean-shaven olive complexion.

"I need to speak to you in private. It's important."

"Sorry, I'm working. Are you sure Ray can't help you?" Now he sounded annoyed. He finished the last glass and dried his hands on a bar towel.

"I'm afraid I must insist that you speak with me, Ethan Walsh, or the consequences could be undesirable."

Ethan's brown eyes twitched at the corners.

"Is this about Vegas?"

"Please, Ethan, someplace more private," she said. If believing she was someone else got him in a quiet room, she'd use it.

"Ray, I'll be right back," Ethan called. He tossed the bar towel on the counter and flipped up the gate. He bolted toward the backroom.

Abigail weaved around the patrons to get to him. "Crap," she said. Why did he have to do this the hard way? Strolling to the darkest corner she could find, Abigail slipped into shadow. An advantage of being a reformed Watcher was that she could do what Watchers did. She folded herself into the darkness, slithering past the dancing couples as a twisting mist. She followed Ethan out the back door, but if he or anyone else saw her it would be only as a ripple of the light, an optical illusion that disappeared in the next blink.

Ethan closed the door behind him and scanned the alley. When he thought he was alone, he placed his hands on his knees and took a deep breath. That's when Abigail materialized from her shadow and leaned forward to whisper into his ear.

"What happened in Vegas?"

"Holy mother of— Where did you come from?" Ethan ran his hands through his hair and shifted sideways.

A force pushed against Abigail's shoulder. If she'd been human, she'd probably be on the pavement.

"Stop, Ethan. I'm not going to hurt you. You're not in trouble. There's something important I need to talk to you about and it has nothing to do with Vegas."

Reluctantly, Ethan pulled over a couple of empty beer crates stacked next to the dumpster and took a seat. "Okay. You've got my attention. Shoot."

"You have certain gifts that were given to you for a purpose. It's time for you to meet that purpose."

"What kind of gifts are we talking about? It doesn't sound like you mean my way with people."

"The telekinesis, Ethan. It's genetic. You are a Soulkeeper, a soldier for God, charged with protecting human souls. It's time for you to train to become what you were meant to be."

"Huh?"

"You're a Soulkeeper, Ethan. Don't act so surprised. Didn't you wonder why you could move things with your mind?"

"Occasionally." Ethan cracked the knuckles on his right hand.

"I need you to come with me. It's not safe here anymore. We need to train you before it's too late." Abigail held out her hand.

Ethan sighed. "Listen, whoever you are, I have a gut feeling that you actually believe what you're saying is true, but there is no way I'm a Soulkeeper. I couldn't be a soldier for God."

"Why not?"

"Well, for starters, I'm gay."

"So?" Abigail said.

"Last time I checked most religious groups would say my lifestyle wasn't exactly godly."

"Huh. I don't know about what other people think, but since you are a Soulkeeper, you're good enough for God, so you're good enough for me."

"I cheated in Vegas. Moved the roulette ball from red to black. Stole a wad of money from a casino."

"Unfortunate for the people who played red, but I have no idea what bearing your deed has on this conversation." Abigail drummed her fingers on her upper arm.

"I can't be a soldier for God. I'm a bad person. I do wrong all the time, big stuff, little stuff. There's no way. You've got the wrong person."

Abigail folded into the darkness and reappeared above him, upside down and clinging to the wall with the tips of her fingers. His head snapped right, then left, until she let out a deep sigh toward the top of his head.

He shouted something unintelligible and leapt to the other side of the alley. Abigail laughed. Gracefully, she pushed off of the wall, flipping her legs over her head and landing on her feet in front of him.

"What are you?" he gasped.

"You may have noticed, Ethan, that I am not like you." She stepped toward him, extending her arm and allowing her illusion to peel back from her true skin. "I am not human and I am not a Soulkeeper." Closer, she forced him to press his back against the brick wall to avoid touching her. She lowered her voice and motioned toward her chest. "In fact, this body is made of evil."

"I don't understand. If you're evil, why are you here? Why are you telling me I'm supposed to work for God?"

Abigail shivered and her illusion snapped into place. "You know, I ask myself that question on a regular basis. Suffice it to say, that despite my past, I've chosen my own path. You, Ethan, need to do the same."

Ethan shook his head. "I don't know. This is crazy."

"As crazy as the first day you moved things with your mind?"

He crossed his arms over his chest defensively, rubbing his shoulders and leaning against the wall.

Normally, when Abigail wanted more information about a new Soulkeeper, she would loosen them up with a cup of her tea, but since it wasn't the time or place, she settled for using sorcery. She didn't know what the magic smelled like. It was different for everyone. But Ethan would smell whatever made him feel most comfortable, whether baking cookies or pumpkin pie. "It must have been shocking the first time. How long have you had your gift?" she said.

He inhaled deeply and all of the tension bled from his torso. "A little over two years. I was seventeen," he said softly.

Abigail leaned against the bricks beside him. "Was there a

conflict, a stressful event that started it all? Someone close to you died or almost died?"

With a groan, Ethan pushed off the wall and returned to his seat on the beer crates. "Yeah, me."

Abigail raised her eyebrows.

"There was this guy, a guy I liked. I thought he was like me, gay, you know? But he wasn't. And worse, he was pissed when he found out I thought he was." He rubbed the back of his neck. "Anyway, I guess he thought it would make him seem less gay if he beat the crap out of me. He did, you know, beat me to a pulp. Until something inside me snapped, and *boom* he was on his ass. I wasn't sure I'd done it at first. The next morning though, I woke up at home, bloody and sore, and thirsty, really thirsty." He swallowed hard. "There was a cup of juice on the counter, probably my sister's. It slid right into my hand."

"And the rest is history," Abigail said, slightly bored. She needed to move this along. He wasn't safe here out in the open.

"Yeah. It took another two years before I could control it."

"Ethan, I think you should come with me now. I can take you where there are people like you that can teach you more about your gift. But we need to hurry. There are Watchers coming for you."

"Watchers?"

"Demons. Fallen angels. Baddies that go bump in the night. If they find you, they'll kill you."

"Kill me? Why"

"To have one less Soulkeeper in the way when they invade our world." She paced the alley in front of him. "Oh, and because they're hungry. They're flesh eaters. If they find you, they'll eat you." She smiled, allowing her teeth to transform into razor-sharp fangs.

He hugged himself. "Do I have time to think about this?"

"Sure. But I don't recommend we go back inside. It's too easy to lose you in the crowd and my gut tells me we're on borrowed time."

"They'll fire me. I'll lose my apartment. There's no way I can just leave."

"We have ways of helping with the practicalities." She waved her hand and a pool of vomit appeared at his feet. "You've become violently ill and need to go to the hospital." She handed him her phone.

He eyed the gadget in her hand and shook his head. "It will be better if I use my own." Pulling his phone from his pocket, he relayed the message, adding something about suspect shrimp dip in the backroom before ending the call.

"Interesting addendum about the shrimp dip."

"The key to telling a great lie is in the details."

She cocked her head to the side. "I have a feeling you and I are going to get along well."

Ethan nodded. "I need to stop at my apartment to pack."

"After you." Abigail motioned toward the end of the alley. She followed Ethan to his apartment, then ushered him into his new life.

FOURTEEN

MARA AND HENRY

Mara prodded Necromancer forward, hoping that Henry would join her soon. She understood he had responsibilities. Even though he could be in more than one place at a time, sometimes he needed to stop to concentrate. He'd go into a trance-like state and that meant Mara needed to keep herself busy. But the In Between was a strange place to be alone.

Henry's castle was a construct of his consciousness. She'd learned it was a replica of an actual castle he'd known of when he grew up in England. As she'd moved beyond the hills surrounding the castle, she'd left Henry's head and that's when things got strange.

She'd shared in Gideon's vision. It was odd to leave a British countryside and end up on an American main street in a matter of steps. Now, she crossed the plush green yard of an Italian villa. This was someone else's construct and by the looks of it, someone powerful. Considering she wasn't supposed to be here, she decided not to stop to say hello. She'd taken enough of a risk visiting Gideon.

Beyond the last rolling green hill, the grass turned to sand and the light from above put off an intense heat to match the desert landscape. Necromancer slowed, her hooves sinking uncomfortably in the sand. Mara tried to change the environment, to form a cloud over them for shade. But this was someone else's handiwork. She couldn't change it.

Necromancer gave a concerned whinny.

"Just a little farther," Mara said. "I want to know what's back here."

Over the next dune, a crystal palace rose out of the sand, shining like a diamond in the desert sun. She pulled Necromancer to a halt and took in the sparkling beauty. The circular structure cast bizarre shadows across the sand, transfixing her.

"Enjoying your ride?" Henry said from behind her.

"I was wondering when you'd catch up with me." Mara leaned sideways and accepted a kiss from Henry, who had sidled up to her on Reaper. "It's so beautiful. Whose place is this?"

Henry grinned. "You of all people should know who this is."

Mara shrugged. "How would I know? I've never even been here before."

"Because your life as a Soulkeeper would have been remarkably different if it wasn't for him."

Concentrating on the architecture, it dawned on Mara that the palace was acting as a giant sundial and she knew immediately whose it was. "This is Time's house."

"Yes. His name is Aldric."

"He controls time the way you control death?"

Henry chuckled. "Control is a strong word. I don't control death; I simply facilitate the soul's journey home. Aldric's job is much the same. Time passes and he facilitates its order in the universe."

Mara frowned. "I don't get it. What does he do?"

"I don't think I would have any more hope of explaining why Aldric exists than I would of explaining why I exist. He is the power that allows me to be in multiple places at one time. And, I am sure, your power came from him, just as Malini's power came from me."

Necromancer tugged the reins and stomped her feet. "I think the horses want to get out of this heat. We should go," Mara said.

"Of course." Henry nudged Reaper around and Necromancer followed, falling into place beside him.

"Do you think Aldric can feel me here? You know, how you can feel when Malini is near you. You said there was a tug, a sort of thrum, that told you she was close by."

"Maybe," Henry said. "We shouldn't get too close." His tone was serious.

"Do you miss Malini? You guys went to prom together and there's the arm..."

The sand melded into the Tuscan countryside and the horses picked up the pace, enjoying the breeze that drifted over them the moment they crossed from one territory into the next.

"No. We have a connection because I gave her my gift and I was excited to experience the human world with her, but I never loved her." Henry glanced meaningfully at Mara.

"Oh." Her heart skipped a beat and she became crucially

interested in the way his shoulder muscles pulled against his jacket as he rode.

"Who lives there?" Mara asked, tipping her head toward the Italian villa.

"Fate. We call her Fatima." His gaze drifted toward the forest in the distance. "I'm sure she knows you are here. Nothing gets by Fatima."

"Do you think she'll turn us in?"

The muscles in Henry's cheek tightened and he turned black eyes in Mara's direction. "She has no reason to, but we can't hide forever."

When they entered the tree line of Henry's forest, Mara's shoulders relaxed. She hadn't realized how being outside Henry's reality had made her tense up. This was coming home, entering into a world that was theirs. It sounded strange. They'd only been together for a short time but it felt both like a lifetime and a fraction of an hour. Time in the In Between wasn't measured like it was on Earth. She couldn't plot their relationship against a calendar or a clock. But whatever it was, it wasn't long enough.

Sighing toward the approaching castle, Mara decided now was not the time to be secretive about her feelings. Who knew how much longer they'd have together?

"I don't want to go, Henry," Mara said. "I know it's only a matter of time before God or Lucifer comes for me. But I don't want to go. I'd stay here, with you, if I had the choice."

They reached the castle. Tom helped her dismount, then led both horses to the barn, the white wig tilting awkwardly on the bones of his skull. She started up the steps, but paused when she noticed that Henry wasn't following. She turned to face him.

"Mara, in six hundred years, I've never met anyone like you." He approached her cautiously, as if she might go up in smoke at any moment. "You fit with my life here. Even surrounded by death, by what I am, you seem as comfortable as if you were made for this place."

"I am comfortable here. I've never had a real home. This place feels like home."

His toes hit the base of the step she was standing on. He ran his hand down the outside of her arm and entangled his fingers in hers. "I'm happy with you here. You don't make me want something more than this existence. Instead, you make this eternity feel like so much more."

She stepped down, her feet falling between his, the front of her jacket pressing into his chest. She slid her hands inside his coat, her palms settling on his hips. An earthy scent of dark spices with a hint of smoke filled her nose. She breathed him in. "What are you saying, Henry?"

He lowered his forehead to hers, his eyelashes brushing softly against her skin. "I'm saying, Mara, that as impossible as it seems, I'm falling in love with you. I want you. I choose you. And nothing would make me happier than if you could stay." His voice cracked.

As much as she knew their situation was hopeless, she couldn't stop herself from pulling him nearer. She tipped her lips up to meet his, her fingers sliding behind his neck. Strong arms wrapped around her and his hands tangled in her hair as his kiss grew deeper, more urgent. He kissed her as if he could breathe her in and hide her away inside himself forever. The way their mouths moved against each other said more than any words possibly could. Desperate, wanting, gripping kisses that tried to master the wind, that begged to hold the river of what was coming back with a shaking hand.

She closed her eyes. At nineteen, Mara had some experience with love, but always from the sidelines, on the fringe of what was real. This was different. This was standing in the center of the ocean and burning brighter than the sun.

When she opened her eyes, they were standing in his bedroom.

"How did we get in here?" Mara asked into his lips.

"Well, I didn't do it."

"Are you saying that I zapped us here just by thinking about it?"

A smile broke out across Henry's face. "Then you admit you were thinking about kissing me in my bedroom."

Heat crawled from her neck to her ears. "Yes."

Placing a hand in the arch of her back, he pulled her against him. "Mara, you've never felt embarrassed before to kiss me. For as long as you've been here, we've spent every spare moment in each other's arms. Why the blush now?"

"Because I think now it means something ... more. I liked you before but the other part was, um, physical. Now, I think it means something. Henry, I think I've fallen in love with you, too."

"My Mara." He kissed her again and the room started to spin. There was no more embarrassment. For Mara the planets aligned. Everything she was, everything she would ever be, was meaningful because of Henry. In some ways, knowing her life was over made everything crystal clear. She didn't have time to take things slow or to analyze her feelings. Every part of her wanted this, wanted him.

She snaked her hands between their bodies and franticly unbuttoned his shirt.

He caught her wrist. "Mara, we've only known each other a short time—"

"I don't care. I don't care. Who knows how long we'll have together? I want you. I want to be with you before I die. I want this to be forever."

"The right thing to do would be to marry you, Mara. That's what I'd do if I were alive. I'd marry you in a church with all of our friends and family watching."

"I have no family and neither do you. Who is there here to marry us? You're immortal and I'm undead."

He took a step back, his eyes never leaving hers, and held out his hand. A ring formed in his palm, platinum with a skull. He slid it onto her ring finger. "Mara, I give this to you as a sign that I am yours, always. No matter what happens, or where you go, if you have this, a part of me is with you."

Mara held out her hand and formed a similar ring, although it took her longer to finish it. It was platinum, too, but instead of a skull, she formed the front into an hourglass, a symbol of her power before she died and the thing she wished she could share with him always, more time. She slid it onto his finger.

"Henry, I give this to you so you will know that no matter what happens or where I have to go, my heart is here with you, forever."

Henry ran his fingers down the side of her face, then brushed his thumb over her lips. "I've never been with anyone before," he whispered.

"Neither have I, but I think we can figure it out."

He nodded, moving in slowly to kiss her again. He swept

her up into his arms and carried her to the bed. The room darkened and candles blazed to life on every surface.

She stretched out underneath him, pushing his riding jacket off his shoulders as his hand found the collar of her blouse. The rest was as easy and magical as falling into each other, as limitless as their imaginations.

FIFTEEN

KATRINA

L ate for class, Katrina rushed across the quad, cursing Mallory for being such a pig. She'd finally found her textbook kicked underneath Mallory's bed, behind a wadded sweater. She carried it in her arms. No time to add it to her backpack. If she was lucky, she'd get to class in time to avoid a front-row seat. Professor Rahkmid liked to give the front row first crack at every question.

Yanking open the glass door to the building, she slipped inside. She almost dropped her book when she saw her professor talking to a boy in front of the lecture room door at the end of the hall. *Crap!* Not wanting to draw attention to her lateness, she ducked to the side of the vending machine in the hallway.

"Saturday," the boy said. "It is imperative that you and your team arrive exactly as I've directed you."

The voice chilled Katrina to the bone. Cord. The Watcher who'd possessed her was only a few steps away. She hugged her book to her chest in an attempt to cover up the bass rhythm of her pounding heart.

"Of course," Professor Rahkmid said. "As you wish."

"Excellent. Go teach your class, Professor. You're late."

The classroom door whooshed open. She wedged her body tight into the wall, wishing she could fit behind the vending machine. Cord raced right by her and out of the building. Tentatively, Katrina stepped toward the glass door and watched Cord disappear into the nearest tree.

A shaky breath escaped her lips. The book tumbled out of her arms onto the floor, her hands shaking and sweaty. Looking left then right, she was relieved no one heard the hardcover slap the linoleum.

She dropped to her knees and fumbled with her backpack, digging for her phone. As she exited the building, she wondered if she'd ever be able to make up what she missed today, but there was no way she could sit in class. Not when she'd just seen Cord influencing her physics professor. She tapped Gideon's number. His greeting was a welcome comfort.

"Meet me in my dorm room," she said.

"Why what's happened?"

"I saw Cord. Gideon, they're here on campus. Something is going down."

"I'll be right there."

Katrina quickened her pace. Her stomach twisted and her heart pounded in her ears. Every student walking across the quad was suspect. Every shadow held the potential for evil. She held her breath until there was a locked door between her and the outside world. Gideon was already there, leaning against her desk. She took a seat on her bed and hugged her knees to her chest. Everything she'd seen and heard tumbled from her lips.

He paced the small patch of carpet between the twin beds. "Why your physics professor, Katrina?"

"I don't know. But this school is one of the best in the country. The brightest minds in the world come here to teach. Whatever Lucifer is planning, it must be complex."

"You are right. If he was simply planning an attack with Watchers and magic, he wouldn't need humans."

Katrina rested her head against the window. The cold glass on her forehead did nothing to squelch the hot prick of tears that welled in the corners of her eyes. She pressed her eyelids together and tipped her chin up, hoping the waterworks would drain away. This was no time to fall apart. Despite her best efforts, hot, wet trails carved their way down her face.

"You are upset," Gideon said. "I have experienced crying once. It is a horrible empty feeling. I can't cry as an angel, although I feel something, here." He rubbed his chest where his heart should have been.

"I thought angels could cry?"

"Some can. I'm not that kind of angel. I'm a messenger and in order to be useful, I can't become emotional over the message."

"But you said you've cried?"

"It's a long story. Tell me, Katrina, what causes you to cry now? Is it fear? I will protect you."

She wiped under her eyes but it was a useless effort. More tears took their place. "I'm afraid but that's not why I'm crying. I have this awful feeling that Lucifer is going to win." She reached for a tissue from her desk and blew her nose. "Ever since I was a little girl, I've always dreamed of having my own family. I thought I would fall in love, get married, have children. The biggest problem I thought I'd ever face was deciding between a career and being a full-time mom. Now, I'm threatened with a lifetime of being some Watcher's flesh slave."

"He will not be successful. Abigail and I, along with the Soulkeepers, will stop him. That's what we're here for. That's what we do."

"I know. I know you guys saved me before. But this time feels different. Like something has shifted. Can't you feel it in the air? It's like, this time, Lucifer is one step ahead of us."

"Don't talk like that," Gideon said. His eyes darted to the shaggy pink area rug between the two beds.

"You feel it, too. I can see it on your face," Katrina said.

Gideon shook his head. "Dane. Dane may be the key."

"Dane Michaels? What about him? I heard he was missing."

"Lucifer has him. He's holding him for ransom. He says he wants the list of Soulkeepers."

Katrina's hands flew to her mouth.

Gideon continued, "Lucifer wants us to believe that Dane is the bait to get what he wants, the Soulkeepers. But what if he's not the bait? What if he's a distraction? Lucifer wants us to concentrate on Dane and protecting the Soulkeepers so that we won't notice what he's doing here with your professor."

Pressing her palms together in front of her lips, Katrina tried to absorb everything Gideon said. "That makes sense. But how do you figure it out? How do you find out what he's planning to do in order to stop him?"

"I need to talk to Malini."

Katrina groaned.

"Katrina, she's our Healer. She'll know what to do."

"She's sixteen."

Gideon placed his hands on her shoulders. "I will figure this out. We'll keep you safe. I promise."

Katrina tossed her arms around Gideon's neck. "Thank you, Gideon. Thank you for being here for me."

SIXTEEN

ABIGAIL

A stagnant ninety-two degrees, the air in Hot Springs, Arkansas, clung to Abigail's skin like a wet blanket. Still, steam rose off the pool at city center. Hot Springs wasn't a misnomer. The water here bubbled from the ground at one hundred forty-seven degrees, dwarfing the June heat. Old women in house dresses and men in worn hats lined up around a spout near the pool with jugs to collect their day's water. Local wisdom claimed it had medicinal properties.

Abigail remembered this place. A few hundred years ago, she knew a Quapaw Indian named Wasa, who taught her about the healing waters and the plants that grew from it. More than a lifetime ago, Wasa's tribe ruled the forest in this area. Now the antique stores and spas reminiscent of the roaring twenties attracted tourists by the busload. She'd heard The Pancake House made the best deep-fried French toast in the south, but she didn't have time to stop for brunch. It was almost 2 p.m. and Abigail promised Malini she'd stick to her instructions. The new Soulkeepers would be expecting her.

Slipping through the door into the brown wood paneling of The Bean Grinder Coffee House, she eyed the only two customers in the place, a man and a girl at a small table. A tired-looking blonde made sandwiches behind the counter. Through a door at the back, a man entered with his arms full of bottled beverages. He rested the haul on a chair and began stocking the fridge to the left of the counter.

"Can I help you?" the blonde said, leaning up against the counter. Dark circles loomed under her eyes.

For the purposes of looking natural, Abigail ordered. "A small vanilla latte, please." She placed a five-dollar bill on the counter. "Keep the change."

"I'll bring it to your table." The woman got busy making her drink.

Abigail turned to the small round table behind her. "Are you August?"

The man stood up and straightened his necktie. He extended a calloused hand. "It's a pleasure to meet you, Miss Abigail."

She accepted his handshake. Despite his crisp white shirt and pressed slacks, August's tanned skin crinkled like leather. He'd spent too much time in the sun. Abigail took the chair next to him across from the girl. "You must be Bridget," she said.

"Yes, ma'am."

The girl's short, brown hair fringed her face unevenly, like she'd cut it herself. Her long, wiry frame made her seem younger than Abigail had expected. If she had to guess, she'd say the girl was thirteen. Freckles danced across her cheeks. Like August, the top of her nose and ears peeled slightly from sun damage but the pale blue dress with tiny yellow flowers she wore showed as much care as August's ensemble.

"I've come to tell you it's not safe for you here anymore," Abigail whispered. "They're coming. They have your names." Abigail lowered her chin.

"We wondered if it wasn't somethin' like this. We've been on the move for weeks. Killed six Watchers between Georgia and here. We've never seen so many." August rubbed his forehead. "I lost count of how many souls we've saved. We thought somethin' big must be comin'."

"Something big is coming. We think Lucifer's trying to make a move to take over our realm."

Bridget frowned at her fingers, tangled on her placemat.

"We'll help any way we can," August said.

Abigail checked over her shoulder for eavesdroppers. The barista didn't seem interested. She prepared the latte behind the counter in slow motion, with her back to their table. "I can't believe they're forcing me to work a double again today. It feels like I haven't slept in a week," she said to the man stocking drinks, who was even less interested.

About to turn back to the new Soulkeepers, pain pounded into Abigail's brain, debilitating pain that made her entire body twitch. A wire whip scraped against the inside of her skull. She yelped and folded forward, her head hitting the table. The pain stopped.

"You shoulda told me you were a Watcher. It hurts Watchers," Bridget whispered, shaking her shoulder. "Humans can't feel it. I'm really sorry. I was just checking to make sure you were who you said you were."

Abigail pushed herself up and swallowed hard. "You saw my thoughts?"

"Yes. I can take them out and I can put them in. I'm sorry, I didn't think it would hurt you."

"That's a formidable gift."

"Thank you." Bridget lowered her eyes again.

August smiled and nodded. "She incapacitates 'em and I decapitate 'em." He chuckled quietly.

A hush fell over the table as the barista approached, latte in hand. "Your coffee, Abigail," she said.

The latte landed in front of her, a curl of steam rising toward the ceiling.

Abigail turned toward the blonde woman and frowned at the knife in her hands. It was the knife she'd been using to cut the sandwiches but it was odd how she twisted it back and forth. It glinted in the light from the window, reflecting a pattern onto Bridget's face. "How did you know my name?"

Abigail reached out, meaning to touch the barista. Something wasn't right. The woman seemed almost in a trance.

Before her hand made contact, darkness shot up around her, swallowing her, transporting her. The coffeehouse dissolved and she materialized inside a pale tube, like an insect trapped under glass.

"Welcome back, Abigail," Lucifer's voice rang out. He swaggered toward her. She was in a different place in Hell this time, a sitting room decorated in gold and red.

"What do you want?" she asked, her breathy voice giving away her trepidation.

"I've told you what I want. I need your help." Lucifer's eyes burned into hers from the other side of the magic wall that surrounded her. "I'm not going to stop until you help me."

"I said, 'no,'" Abigail said, sounding braver than she felt.

She couldn't let him get to her. She turned her back on Lucifer, hoping he'd lose interest.

"Have it your way but know this. You hold the key to what I want, and I won't stop until I get it." He brought his face closer and whispered, "I can peel apart your life person by person until you are begging to be by my side."

She didn't answer his taunt. Closing her eyes, she tried to ignore him. Lucifer wouldn't waste his time keeping her there if she refused to give him the satisfaction of a response. The effort paid off. Smoke filled her tube, buoying her up, up, back into her body, to the coffee shop. She landed in her seat at the table, jerking into the present.

Blood. Everywhere, blood.

Abigail bolted upright, knocking her chair to the floor.

August's body draped across the table. Blood gushed from a stab wound in his neck. It soaked his tie and one short sleeve of his white dress shirt. Bridget had made it as far as the door; well, part of her had. Her arm remained at the table. The rest of her body sprawled dead in front of the glass, the blue dress drenched in her blood.

Abigail turned in a circle. The barista's blood-covered hands poked out from under the seat behind August. Her body lay sprawled on the ground with a gunshot wound to the head. Blood and something more splattered the wall beside her. The stock man stared at the bodies with the same vacant stare she'd noticed in the barista. He was influenced just as she was. Why hadn't she noticed sooner?

The man brought the gun to his head, his hand shaking.

"*No!*" Abigail cried, flinging her power in his direction. He collided with the wall, the gun slipping from his hand.

The door swung open and the sound of a woman's scream

cut through the room. Abigail stared as the stranger ran from the massacre. Blood spattered the window. Blood soaked the floor. Blood oozed across the counter. Blood dripped from the bodies.

Something inside Abigail snapped. Whatever part of her was closest to human shut off and the Watcher inside took over. Numb calm spread across her body. She twisted into shadow, to the sound of approaching sirens.

SEVENTEEN

DANE

D ane repositioned himself on the slab of stone but there was no reprieve from the pain that racked his body. The circle of fire scorched his skin, even when he pulled his knees into his chest. Weakness and pain were constant reminders that his body should have given out by now. Day after day without food or water in the ever-shrinking prison should've meant death. But this was Hell. Lucifer was using him, and death would mean his freedom. Whatever magic kept him alive would end when he was no longer useful. As he pushed himself up to his knees, he welcomed that day, he prayed for that day.

"I heard you were down here."

The voice that filtered through the flames was one he'd never forget. "Auriel." Dane turned to see her figure silhouetted behind the flames.

"The one and only." She laughed and the flames lowered. She hadn't changed. With platinum-blonde hair, icy blue eyes, and a silvery blue gown, she could dice any guy's heart to shreds and have it for breakfast, literally.

"What are you doing here?" Dane rasped.

"I have a meeting with Lucifer." She lowered her voice to a whisper and raised her hand to the side of her mouth. "We're taking over the world. I suppose I can let you in on the secret since you're as good as dead."

Dane buried his face in his hands. "Leave me alone, Auriel. Isn't it enough that you used me and almost ruined my life? Do you have to torment me in my death, too?"

"Oh, but Dane, I have more use for you. Don't you know you're an integral part of the plan?"

He shook his head. "Lucifer can try to use me as bait to entice Malini and Dr. Silva to translate the list of Soulkeepers. But they never will. I'm not that important."

Auriel grinned. "Hmmm. If that was what Lucifer was really after, it would be a total loss. I'm pretty sure your friends are gonna let you burn."

Dane jerked. Every muscle in his body ached in response. "Then how am I an integral part of the plan?" His voice broke as he said it.

"We need an innocent living sacrifice, and you, pathetic as you are, qualify." Her lips peeled back from her whiter than white teeth.

He might have asked her more about his fate but at that precise moment Lucifer appeared in front of her in a shower of sparks. Applause broke out from the shadows. Auriel clapped the loudest and gave a little bow at the waist.

"An elegant entrance, my lord," she said.

"Thank you, my dear. And what are you doing? Playing

with the tool?" Lucifer wrapped his arm around Auriel's shoulders.

"Just keeping myself occupied while I waited for you to grace me with your presence."

Dane snickered.

Lucifer shot him a look that made his skin burn. Dane squeezed his knees to his chest, determined not to scream. The burning stopped when the devil turned his attention back toward Auriel.

"Has our guest arrived?" he asked her.

"Yes. She's in your chambers, my lord." Auriel motioned toward a door in the stone a few yards from his prison. Dane had seen Lucifer come and go through the door, but hadn't known what lay beyond it.

"Well, let's not keep our guest waiting."

Lucifer guided Auriel toward the door and pulled it open, wide enough for both of them to fit through. Dane had a moment to absorb the opulence of the red-and-gold entryway before his eyes fell on the guest that waited there.

"Dr. Silva?" he called.

Her icy blue eyes flashed to his in recognition.

"Dr. Silva! Please, please help me!" he begged. He crawled to the side of the fire.

Lucifer patted Dr. Silva's shoulder. *Pat-pat-pat,* like a father pats a daughter.

Her expression became as emotionless as a reptile. The door closed slowly behind them, severing her heartless stare. She'd abandoned him with nothing but the flames and the pain.

For a moment, Dane was confused. Why was Dr. Silva in Hell and why was she talking to Lucifer? Then he realized it didn't matter. Auriel had given him all the information he needed. If he was the key to Lucifer's plan, he needed to take himself out of the equation.

What was it his parents used to say? Suicide is a mortal sin. If he killed himself, he'd lose his soul. But some things were more important than one soul. Like stopping Lucifer. Like saving the Soulkeepers.

With everything he had, he pushed himself to his feet. Before he could chicken out or think too hard about the consequences, he sprinted toward the flames. He landed squarely on the ring of fire. Intense pain swallowed him whole. His hair burnt off in an instant. His skin bubbled black. The rancid smell of burning flesh filled his nostrils and the sound of his screams ricocheted off the stone around him. Eventually, there was nothing left to feel pain and he welcomed death with open arms.

But his sacrifice was for naught. When he came to, he was right back at the center of the circle. Death wasn't an option, it seemed, at least not until Lucifer wanted him dead. Dane buried his face in his hands, hopelessness blanketing him like a shroud.

EIGHTEEN

MARA AND HENRY

Mara woke with fireworks in her heart. She'd never expected her first time to be so perfect or that she'd love someone the way she loved Henry, with every part of herself. Memories of their night together came back to her in luscious flashes, a bare shoulder, the sight of his hip, the weight of his body above her.

Henry's arm was draped over her waist but she could tell he was sleeping because he wasn't breathing. It was weird to think she could stop breathing, too. She'd tried it a few times but could never keep it up. After a few minutes, she'd get distracted and start again out of habit. How long, how many centuries, had it taken for Henry to lose the urge to breathe? Now, the only time he did was when he thought it would make her more comfortable.

The ring Henry had given her fit snugly on her finger, the platinum skull spanning the space between the knuckles on her left hand. She thought of the one she'd given him, the hourglass. Her heart ached. Time was how she'd defined herself since she was twelve, but now her power was gone. Who was she? Would she ever have a chance to find out?

"Sorry to disturb you, but there is something we must discuss," a small voice said from the end of the bed.

Henry startled awake. He sat up so fast, Mara struggled to keep the sheet in place. Pulling it tighter around her body, she propped herself up on the headboard. The woman on the end of the bed looked identical to Mara. Well, a better version of Mara, with no piercings and an inner glow that filled the room with homey warmth.

"Who are you?" Mara asked. Henry elbowed her hard in the side.

"I am," the woman said.

"Oh, you're God!" Mara sounded dense even to herself. "Sorry, I thought ... why do you look like me? I always thought you were a man."

The look Henry shot her could've soldered iron.

"I am neither. I am. You see me as I exist in you." God's voice held a soft echo that gave it the hollow quality of wind chimes. "It is easier for you this way."

Henry shifted uncomfortably but Mara didn't know why. She felt completely at peace in God's presence. "Are you here for me?" Mara asked.

"Yes. Your soul is clearly mine," she said. "You have a good heart, Mara Kane. It's time for your soul to move on to Heaven."

Mara beamed with pride. Something about the way God said it made her feel good to be her, to have lived the life that she lived. She leaned forward, drawn to God by some invisible force, but stopped when she realized Henry was statuesque on the other side of the bed, his face conspicuously blank.

She twisted the ring on her finger. "I'd like to stay here," Mara said. "For my heaven, I'd like to stay with Henry."

God rose from the end of the bed and glided toward the window. Birds flew to rest on the sill, looking toward her presence and singing their happiest song.

"I'm afraid that's impossible. The In Between isn't any place for a soul. You should have never been brought here."

Mara intertwined her fingers with Henry's. "Will you force me to go?" She was surprised how raw her voice sounded.

God's eyes lingered on their connected hands. "You have free will, Mara. I will leave a door for Death to usher you through. When you are ready, come to me. Whenever you are ready."

Mara's heart leaped as she considered God's words. She had to go, someday, but not today. She could stay with Henry longer, maybe until the end of forever.

Henry's face looked like he just won the lottery. He pulled her into his chest.

"Oh, thank you. Thank you," Mara said. She bowed her head, overwhelmed by the gift God had given her.

But her relief was premature.

A dark hiss came from the corner of the room. Inky shadows crawled across the walls, knitting the air into a dense tar. Lucifer stepped from the darkness, shaking his blond head and wagging a finger. "Not so fast. I demand a consequence."

God glowed brighter, sparks of electricity dancing on her skin. "A consequence? Her soul is mine. There shall be no consequence," God said, her voice rising.

Lucifer lifted a corner of his mouth and focused unnaturally blue eyes in Mara's direction. "Death broke the rules. I am entitled to a consequence for his indiscretion."

God narrowed her eyes and twisted her mouth as if the room stunk from Lucifer's presence. She sighed. "Fine. What consequence shall you enact on Death?"

He held out a hand and an obsidian hourglass the size of a gallon of milk formed in his palm. He turned it over and sand began trickling into the lower chamber.

"Mara must go through the door before the last grain of sand falls, or her soul is mine."

God's presence thundered against the walls. She levitated two feet off the floor, charging the air with electricity. "This is unacceptable," she boomed. "The consequence is his not hers to pay."

With his hands on his hips, Lucifer gave a cocky laugh. "Since Death doesn't have a soul to take, losing her is the only suitable punishment. Besides, as you said, she shouldn't be here."

"Leave my sight, beast!" God bellowed, and this time Lucifer flinched.

"Do you agree to my consequence?" he hissed.

The room quaked. Mara thought the walls might come down.

"*Yes,*" God said, but the word was filled with anger and resentment. She took a deep breath and blew it out at Lucifer. He came apart like dust, his pieces dissolving into the ether. God returned to the floor, her power folding within her, until she looked peaceful and almost human.

"I must go now," she said to Mara. "Do not miss the door. I cannot save you from where he will take you."

Mara nodded.

God turned to Henry. "Perhaps it is time for you to share with Mara how you came to your station."

Henry's head snapped up and his lips parted in a silent gasp.

"She seems up to the challenge." God strode to the window, broke apart into the light, and was gone.

Watching the sand rush through the hourglass, Mara burst into tears, rolling her face into Henry's chest. He hugged her to him and rubbed her back in slow circles.

"Mara. Mara, don't cry. It's going to be okay. I need to tell you something. God gave me a way for us to be together."

Mara tipped her head back so she could see his face. "What? How?"

"I need to tell you how I became Death."

NINETEEN

MARA AND HENRY

O ut of surprise and confusion, Mara pushed back from Henry's chest and wiped the tears from under her eyes. "I thought you said you couldn't tell anyone? I thought there were cosmic handcuffs on your vocal cords or something?"

"There were. But God just gave me permission to tell you. You might say the handcuffs have been unlocked."

Mara slid out of bed and wrapped herself in a fluffy red robe that appeared on the chaise lounge by the window. She took a seat at the table and conjured a cup of coffee from the ether. The steaming mug she lifted to her lips read *Instant Undead, Just Add Coffee.*

"Would you like one?" she asked Henry, bobbing the cup.

"No. I'm fine."

"I'm ready. Spill this super-secret story about how you became Death. Then tell me how it's going to keep us together."

Henry got up and walked to the window. He rested his

hands on the stone sill and stared out across the rolling English hillside. "Where should I begin?"

Mara brushed her hair back from her face. "At the beginning. I want to know everything about you."

Henry nodded but kept his eyes fixed on the horizon. With the far-off nostalgia of long-distant memories, he began his story. "I was born in 1332, in a village called Wickshire in England. People say that you come into this world alone and you leave alone but that wasn't the case for me. I was a twin. I came into the world with William.

"Our parents, Richard and Mary Gravel, owned an inn called the Golden Goose. There were only about two hundred people living in Wickshire at the time, but because our inn was on a well-traveled road, my parents earned a fine living and due to that, William and I grew up with more comforts than most people in our town.

"Things were different then. There were no computers or telephones. Often we were the first to hear news because messengers would rest at the Golden Goose on the way to more important places.

"Once we were old enough, William and I spent our time in the tavern talking with the guests about any number of things. Our conversations and interests varied widely. Although we were twins, William was always a strapping boy. From the time we were twelve, he already looked like a man and worked like an ox. I, on the other hand, was sickly as a baby. I was smaller and thinner. Often my gaunt cheeks would provoke some concerned traveler to ask if my parents were feeding me. I was eating, better than most at that time, but I couldn't gain weight.

"William talked with patrons about hunting and sword-play. He once met a knight who thought he'd make an excellent squire. That's what William wanted to be, a knight. I'm not sure why he didn't take the man up on his offer. I can't remember now. I hope it wasn't because he didn't want to leave me, but it probably was. We were like that, as different as we were, wholly together."

"What did you want to be?" Mara asked.

"Unlike William, I spent my time talking to messengers and religious men. My dream was to become a priest."

"A priest?" Mara's eyes widened.

Henry grinned. "It might have been different had I known a girl like you, Mara. Priests were the scholars of my time. I eventually learned to read and even owned a Bible."

Mara interrupted. "Learned to read? Didn't everyone know how to read? Didn't children go to school?"

"Not necessarily. If you were a boy and your parents had money, you might go to the monastery for an education, but most people only learned what they needed to for their occupation. By the time we were thirteen, William and I helped run the inn. I knew how to make all different kinds of ale by then. We never went to school. I learned from our guests. It was rare to be able to read as well as I could. And owning an actual book was almost unheard of in our town."

Henry planted both palms on the windowsill, as if he needed the stone to keep upright. "Our father died in his sleep when we were sixteen," he said.

Leaning forward, Mara placed her hand on Henry's, rubbing her thumb across the back. "I'm so sorry."

"It was a long time ago." Henry's eyes met hers. "The night he died, the sound of footsteps outside my room woke me, and I watched a man with flaming red eyes enter my father's bedchamber. I crept to the doorway in time to see the man pull my father's soul from his body. Of course, I thought I was dreaming but in the morning he was dead."

"How awful," Mara said.

"Our father's death was extremely difficult for William and me, but we learned to carry on. By that time, we were running the inn anyway. Our mother handled the cooking and the cleaning. We brewed the ale and managed the tavern. Then one night a messenger came with a story that would change everything. The Black Death had come to England."

"Wait, the Black Death, like the plague?" Mara's face twisted in horror.

Henry nodded gravely. "At first it seemed like a faraway thing. The messengers brought word of an illness. Boils on the armpits and groin were the harbingers of certain death. We heard of entire towns dying out and the places discussed by our patrons grew closer and closer. People abandoned their homes and livelihood and ran from the disease, often staying with us on their journey. Then the unthinkable happened. A man staying with us grew ill and was found to have the Black Death."

Mara swallowed hard. Her hands were sweating and she wiped them on her robe. "We had to learn about the plague in school. They say it was spread by rats and fleas."

"We didn't know. Life was different then. Faced with their impending death, people became animals. They abandoned their families, took part in drinking and debauchery. Others became hermits, isolating themselves from everyone. Eventually, we feared for our lives and closed the inn. Still death came for us. My mother fell first, then my brother. I cared for them both, knowing I'd be next."

"Weren't you scared? It must have been terrifying. How did you make yourself stay?"

He turned toward her, leaning his hip against the windowsill. "I'd spent enough time studying with the priests to believe that only the body dies. I knew I couldn't leave and still keep my soul. I was prepared to die if it meant doing the right thing."

Mara always felt Henry was a good person, despite having the position of Death. As she looked into his dark eyes, she was sure of that now. She could see the soul inside the man shining like a star.

"William died in my arms a few days after my mother. That's when things became bizarre. I saw the man with the flaming red eyes again. He came to my brother and pulled his soul from his body. I hadn't eaten in days and I thought I might be hallucinating but when I saw the door open and the light shine on my brother, I rushed forward and dove into the light before William.

"Death stopped me. 'This door is not for you,' he said. I struggled against his grip, all the time watching William move into the light behind me. 'Let me go!' I said, but Death looked me in the eye and asked, 'Do you challenge me?'"

"He asked you if you challenged him?" Mara shook her head. What did it mean?

"Yes. I wasn't sure what he meant. I just wanted to be with my brother, to know that he'd be well wherever he was going. But he asked me again, 'Do you challenge me?' I said, 'Yes.'"

Mara grimaced. "You challenged the existing Death? While you were still alive?"

"Yes, Mara, I did. I had no idea what I was doing, only that I desperately wanted to join William in the light. But words are weapons when it comes to old magic. I had challenged Death and there was no going back.

"The next thing I knew I was in the woods with Death. God was on our right and the devil on our left. God issued the challenge. Somewhere in the woods was a scroll. Whoever found the scroll and read it would become immortal. Would become Death. The other would die and must move on to Heaven or Hell.

"I ran through the trees as fast as my legs would carry me. I searched until I thought I might collapse from exhaustion. Deep within the forest, I came upon a meadow. The scroll was tethered to a tree in clear sight and Death waited there for me. He could have easily read the scroll himself first but instead he watched me pluck it from its hiding place. As I read the words from the parchment, I knew without a doubt that Death had wanted me to challenge him. He had invited me to win. When I was done reading, I became this, and he moved on to his eternity. The Black Death had left him worn and tired. He was relieved to walk into the light."

Henry rubbed his eyes with the heels of his palms.

"You never got to see William or the rest of your family?" Mara lamented.

"No."

She grabbed his wrists and pulled them down from his face, wiping his tears away with her thumbs. "What about your servants here, Tom and Andrew with the horses. They are dead and they are here. What makes them different?"

"They were destined for Hell and chose to be servants here instead of serving that eternity. I am allowed a few but their existence is shallow and owned, nothing I would want for my brother. I am happy he joined my parents in the light. I do miss him though."

Mara pressed her lips against his forehead, then lowered her face to meet his and closed her eyes. "Thank you, Henry. It couldn't have been easy to relive that story."

"No."

"Why do you think God wanted you to tell me?"

"I think she wanted me to know that if you moved on, there was a way I could go with you. I could offer someone else the challenge."

Mara frowned. "Oh. I don't like the thought of you sacrificing yourself for me."

"Maybe it's time, Mara. You, William, my parents, it might be nice to be together. It would be nice to rest."

Pressing her cheek against Henry's, she watched the hourglass out of the corner of her eye and wondered why going to Heaven, with or without Henry, didn't feel like a happy ending at all.

TWENTY

JACOB AND MALINI

Inside the secret cavern under Laudner's Flowers and Gifts, Jacob led the new Soulkeeper, Ethan, to the boat wedged in the white sand. After helping Malini over the side, he motioned for Ethan to take a seat at the bow. Jacob positioned himself next to Malini near the mast.

"Are we being mean, Jacob?" Malini whispered into his ear.

"Absolutely not. If we have to take him, we might as well enjoy it." Jacob grinned.

Since Dr. Silva and Gideon weren't human, they couldn't get past the cherubim at the gate into Eden. Lillian was already in Eden, as were the Guillians, Jesse, and Master Lee. That left Jacob and Malini to chaperone the newest Soulkeeper.

At the front of the boat, Ethan was roughly the color of glow-in-the-dark slime. "I didn't ask about the creepy passageway under the flower shop, or why there's a boat in a cavern without any water. But I'd really like to know how we plan to get where we are going." He eyed the solid wall behind him. "Is this going to hurt?"

Malini unhooked her sunglasses from her T-shirt and slid them on. Jacob did the same. "Nope. Won't hurt, but you might want to hang on." Jacob yanked on the rope to raise the sail.

A roar like a freight train rumbled through the cavern, starting far off and low but growing to an eardrum-crushing decibel. The ball of fire that exploded toward them surrounded the boat with heat and light before ricocheting off the back wall and catching the sail.

"HOLY SHIIIIII—" Ethan white knuckled the wooden hull.

Jacob and Malini exchanged grins and stretched their arms above their heads roller coaster style. A few seconds later, the boat drifted down an aquamarine river surrounded by white sand.

Ethan turned toward them in his seat. From under a mop of disheveled black hair, his brown eyes gawked at Jacob, rimmed with dark half-circles and sunken into an unshaven face. He looked like someone found him on the side of the road, and maybe Dr. Silva had. Jacob hadn't had the chance to ask.

"That was ... that was..." Ethan stuttered.

Malini reached for Ethan, as if she were going to apologize. Her eyebrows knit together in empathy.

"That was *awesome!*" Ethan said. "If this is the ride there, I can't wait to see what Eden's like."

Malini laughed and returned to her seat.

"You *are* a Soulkeeper." Jacob reached his fist forward to bump Ethan's. "What can you do, anyway?"

Ethan leaned against the side of the boat and gave a half grin. Jacob's sunglasses flipped off his face and landed on Ethan's, who then tilted his chin toward the sun.

"Thanks. It's bright out here."

Malini arched an eyebrow. "Impressive."

The boat coasted under the perpetually flaming swords of the cherubim. Jacob's body slid through the invisible membrane like gelatin through a strainer. Even though he'd been through it before, he never got used to the way the gate to Eden sifted his cells, making sure he was worthy and human. Ethan must have felt it, too, because he brushed his hands over his face like he was clearing away spiderwebs.

"It takes a few times to know what to expect," Jacob said.

"Do you get the slice and dice on the way out, too?" Ethan asked.

"No. It's a one-way security system," Malini answered.

A purple and red Macaw flew overhead, disappearing into the exotic foliage as the boat docked itself. Jacob climbed out first, offering Malini his hand. Ethan tossed his bag over his shoulder and got out on his own.

"This way." Jacob headed up the path toward Eden.

"Where are you from, Ethan?" Malini asked.

"Los Angeles. I'm supposed to be a freshman at UCLA, but I guess that's on hold now."

"How much has Dr. Silva told you about what's going on?" Malini asked.

"Not much. Aside from convincing me I'm a Soulkeeper, she wasn't exactly forthcoming with the info."

Jacob grunted. "Sounds like Dr. Silva."

"So, she's always a distant, self-serving crab?" Ethan laughed.

"Not always, but frequently, yes."

Malini nodded in agreement.

"I would have asked more questions but she said I needed to get some rest to be ready for today."

"Well, that was probably good advice," Malini said.

"Might have been if I actually got any. The fighting was too loud. Dr. Silva and Gideon were at it for hours."

Malini stopped mid-stride. Jacob did, too, turning toward Ethan on the path. "Gideon and Dr. Silva were fighting?"

"Like cats and dogs, no pun intended."

"What were they fighting about?" Malini asked.

Ethan crossed his arms over his chest. "I didn't hear the whole thing but there was something about loyalties. Gideon didn't want her to do something because he was afraid they couldn't be together if she did. She wanted him to realize they might never be together anyway. He offered to fix the problem. Someone broke something. I've gotta tell ya, it was scary. More than once I thought about sneaking out and going home. But then it was over. I guess Dr. Silva left because Gideon brought me to the shop this morning."

Jacob narrowed his eyes toward Malini. "What's going on, Healer?"

"I don't know. She's bringing in two more Soulkeepers this afternoon. Maybe she wanted to get an early start. When we're done here, I'll talk to Gideon and find out." She placed a hand on Ethan's shoulder. "Don't worry. I know this is overwhelming. Dr. Silva isn't usually that bad. I don't know what's going on but we'll figure it out. We're going to take good care of you here, I promise."

Ethan bobbed his head. "Thanks."

They continued around the corner and up the hill, until

the jungle ended and a manicured lawn reached toward a stucco mansion. The freshly painted sign in the yard read Eden School for Soulkeepers, Est. 10,000 B.C.

"Mom has spruced up the place." Jacob opened the door and led the way into the jewel-encrusted foyer. "She's even dusted."

"How did she get this done so fast? This place is huge." Malini eyed the cobweb-free chandelier inquisitively.

Jacob advanced down the main hallway to the lecture hall in the west wing. His mom's voice filtered through the door. He slipped inside and took a seat in the back. Malini and Ethan followed.

Lillian lectured to the five Soulkeepers at the front of the room. "We know that becoming a Soulkeeper requires a specific gene, hereditary and recessive. Those with the gene may or may not become Soulkeepers in their lifetime. The gene activates when the person is put through an extreme circumstance, usually a threat to their life or the loss of a loved one, sometimes both."

She used a pointer to circle the adrenal gland on a medical diagram. "We think that the flood of cortisol in the system triggers the gene to activate. Once activated, the gene produces proteins that enable our special abilities. Much of this is speculation as we have limited capabilities to perform medical testing here. What we know for sure is that practicing the use of your skills decreases the side effects associated with the flood of proteins in the body.

"For example, my gift is the ability to wield any weapon. In the beginning, using the gift would result in severe muscle fatigue. But with practice, Master Lee and I were able to exponentially increase my endurance. In addition, practice helps us fully expose the extent of our power. So, continuing with my personal experience, practice brought out complimentary qualities of super-human speed and superior kinesthetic intelligence."

"Kinesthetic intelligence?" Ethan asked Malini.

"It means she's a whiz at acrobatics. I've seen her hit a bull's-eye with an arrow she shot while executing a full layout."

"Oh."

Lillian pointed to a list on the whiteboard. "Besides fatigue, here are other side effects we've logged within our Soulkeeper population: burning heat, freezing cold, nose bleeds, dehydration, migraine headaches. Have any of you experienced any of these or other symptoms?"

Jesse raised his hand. "If I try to disperse for more than five minutes, my molecules snap back together on their own, and it feels like I have the flu."

Lillian nodded.

Samantha piped up. "When Bonnie and I join, if we stay together too long, we can't always separate equally. Once it took us an entire day to get back to our normal size."

"Interesting," Lillian said. "As we practice, be aware of your body and know when you need to stop. I'll be teaching you basic defensive skills so that even if your power wanes, you can get yourself out of a dangerous situation. Any questions?"

All five heads shook.

"Excellent. First training session will be in two hours in Room 115. Right now, it looks like we have a new student." Lillian looked toward Ethan, as did the rest of the class. "I'll get him settled in and we can make his acquaintance before we start."

Everyone stood and waved their hellos on their way out the door.

"You must be Ethan," Lillian said. "I'm Ms. Lau."

He accepted her hand. "Nice to meet you."

Lillian stepped to the side and embraced Jacob. "Good to see you. Are you enjoying your summer?" She winked.

"Right, Mom. I love traveling all over the country fighting demons," he said sarcastically. But then his face softened. "Actually, you know what? I do. I'm having a great summer."

Lillian smiled. "I thought so." She gave Malini a quick hug. "I need to talk with both of you once we get Ethan settled in. It's important."

"Of course," Malini said.

She led all of them into the hall. "Ethan, come with us and we'll show you to your dorm room. It's in the east wing."

"Mom, the place looks great. How did you get everything cleaned up so quickly? The grounds alone must have taken days." Jacob eyed the polished brass room numbers to the right of each door.

"You know, it's the damnedest thing. The school had its own..." She cleared her throat.

"Its own what?" Jacob asked.

"Maintenance system," Lillian drawled. "The system stopped working when everyone left, but has revived with our presence here."

Malini giggled. "What type of system mows the grass and clears away branches? You'd need a team of landscapers for that."

Lillian smiled and shook her head. "You won't believe it, Malini, but Eden is a garden and the Lord provides."

Just then, a small man with a face like a monkey's

appeared in the foyer wearing green lederhosen and a tall pointy hat. He didn't walk in the front door; he literally appeared out of thin air. Ethan leaped backward into Jacob.

The man removed his hat and held it in his green-stained hands. "Ms. Lau, the room has been prepared for the new student. Is there anything else I can do for you today?"

"Yes, please, Archibald, I would love it if you and the other gnomes took a long break before dinner to do as you please."

Archibald flashed a set of ragged yellow teeth. "As you wish, Ms. Lau." He disappeared as quickly as he'd come.

"Mom, what was that?" Jacob asked.

"Shhh. Jacob, be respectful. Who, not what. That was Archibald. He's the head of the pod of garden gnomes that takes care of the school. They've been here from the very beginning. Besides getting the place cleaned up, he's shared a wealth of knowledge about the school's history."

Malini nudged Ethan, who was still staring at the place Archibald had been. "Lillian, what were the gnomes doing this whole time? When Jacob found this place it was completely overgrown and left to rot."

"Before Warwick left, he ordered the gnomes to take care of themselves until his return." She lowered her voice. "The gnomes do exactly as you tell them. Exactly and nothing more." She crossed the foyer leading the others into the east wing and up a spiral staircase.

Cave-like drawings covered the walls of the stairwell. One, a stick-figure boy riding a horse, caught Jacob's attention. White dots of paint shot out of the boy's palm toward black shadows gathered behind a tree. "Look, Malini. Neanderthal Soulkeepers."

Malini stopped and perused the painting. "Not Neanderthal, Jacob, Native American. Look at the handprints on the horse. It's domesticated. And over here, behind the rider, those look like stone dwellings."

"This place really has been here a long time."

Lillian cleared her throat. "This passageway is a progressive mural. Look in the upper right corner at the top of the stairs."

Jacob followed her line of sight as they climbed. A peace symbol and a flower were spray painted in neon colors. Overwhelmed by the legacy of Soulkeepers that had come before, Jacob reached out for Malini's hand. She squeezed it three times, a silent 'I love you,' their own personal sign language.

"So, how did you find the gnomes?" Malini asked.

"I didn't. They found me. When I moved into Warwick's office, Archibald came and asked if he'd returned. After my heart started beating again, I realized he wasn't a threat. I explained Warwick was dead and that I had taken his place. The rest was just a matter of me asking the right questions."

They reached the second floor landing, and Lillian opened the door for them.

"Everyone stays up here?" Ethan asked.

"No. Just the boys. The girls are on the third floor. For now, while Jacob is on the outside, it's just you, Jesse, and Master Lee." Lillian walked to the third door on the left and turned the knob. "Here we are. Room 206."

The room was about the size of a college dorm with walls in the same stucco as the rest of the building. One window brightened the room from the far wall. A dresser, a nightstand, and a twin bed were the only furniture.

"I'll warn you, the bed takes getting used to. Everything in Eden was designed to be at one with nature. The mattress is stuffed with leaves. We can get you a hammock if you have allergies."

"No. It's perfect." Ethan walked into the center of the room and tossed his duffle on the bed. He turned a slow circle. "Is there a bathroom?"

"Down the hall. It's all geothermal and solar. Don't waste water or energy, unless you want a garden gnome to speak harshly to you. And trust me, you don't."

Ethan nodded, staring into the room. "Yeah, a shower would be good," he said absently.

"We'll leave you to settle in." Lillian ushered the others into the hall. "Class in two hours, Room 115." She closed the door behind them, leaving Ethan staring out the window. "Don't worry, he'll be fine," she said to Jacob and Malini.

Jacob wasn't so sure. The guy looked shell-shocked.

"What did you have to talk to me about anyway?" Malini asked.

"Not here. I have to check with Archibald. I just remembered I never specifically said to prepare food for Ethan and you two for dinner. They do *exactly* as you tell them." She shook her head. "Meet me in my office in five minutes?"

Jacob and Malini nodded in unison.

TWENTY-ONE

THE VISITOR

On the other end of Eden, Malini led Jacob into Lillian's office. The shelf of geodes and gemstones from when Warwick Laudner walked the halls still cast colorful light across the desk, but Lillian had added her own personal touches. A framed print of Van Gogh's Starry Night hung on the wall and a floral-patterned rug covered the floor. A picture of Jacob was taped to the side of a new computer, solar powered, Malini presumed.

"What do you think my great-great-grandfather did with these stones?" Jacob ran a finger over the shelf in front of the window.

Malini hugged him from behind. "It probably had something to do with his gift. I don't know for sure but my red stone enhances my abilities." Releasing Jacob, she lifted a large amethyst geode. "I think these stones were tools, but we may never know for sure how he used them."

Lillian walked through the open door, her long, quick

strides guiding her to the leather chair behind the desk. "Archibald says Warwick used them to communicate with Soulkeepers outside of Eden. I haven't been able to figure out how they work. We might need them. No cell service here."

Malini took the seat across the desk from her, next to Jacob. The metal frame and hard pad reminded Malini of the chairs in the Paris High School office and judging by their split pea color, were probably made in the same year.

"So, what did you need to talk to me about?" Malini asked.

Lillian folded her hands. "You've made a mistake. I know you assigned me to run this school for a good reason, but I can't do it anymore. You need to find a replacement."

"What? But everything looks perfect. You're doing so well!"

"And Laudner's Flowers and Gifts has been closed two days this week. I still don't know how I'm going to explain it when the Laudners come home from their cruise. I'll have to say I was sick or something. I know this is more important, but we're spreading ourselves too thin. I can't pretend to help John run a business, while simultaneously running a school, and preparing my skills to fight off Lucifer."

"I'm sorry, Lillian. I know I've asked too much. Maybe one of the new Helpers can become more involved. Let me think about it and get back to you."

"Please do, and quickly. I needed help, yesterday. And to be perfectly honest, I never wanted this job. I'm a Horseman, not a Helper. I don't mind teaching the Soulkeepers about weapons, but running a school just isn't my thing."

"I know. I know, Lillian. Let me meditate on it. I'll find someone else. But promise me you'll hang in there until I do," Malini pleaded.

Lillian sighed. "Okay. But not forever. I'm fine with going back to the way things were before we found Eden. I'm serious about this. I don't want to do it another day. For you I will, but you better get to work on finding a replacement because I'm not sure how much longer I can force myself to do this."

Malini nodded. "We should probably go," she said. "I need to speak to Gideon and we still have three more Soulkeepers to round up. Abigail should have August and Bridget ready by now."

"Of course. I'll walk you out to the boat." Lillian stood and led the way into the hall. "By the way, I heard from your Uncle John last time I was in the shop. He and Carolyn are enjoying their cruise. They send their love."

Jacob grinned. "I'm glad it's working out for both of us, but what are we going to do about them when they get home? I can't make excuses forever."

"Me neither, but we'll cross that bridge when we come to it," Malini said.

A few minutes later, the three reached the edge of the jungle and stepped onto the dock. "Hey! Where's the boat?" Malini asked.

Her eyes darted around the harbor. The boat's dark hull appeared at the gate on the horizon. It passed under the flaming swords and drifted toward them.

"Who else knows about this place?" Jacob asked.

Malini blew air through her nose. "No one."

Lillian reached for her calf and pulled a dagger from a sheath there. She assumed a defensive pose as the boat docked and the sail lowered.

The bench seats were empty but there was a body in the bottom of the boat. A corpse? Pale but smudged in ash, the skin hung off the skeletal remains in a way that hardly seemed human. Malini jumped in and turned the head to face the light.

Dane.

TWENTY-TWO

JACOB AND MALINI

Jacob watched Malini's fingers feel for Dane's pulse with a heavy heart. Dane's pale skin hung on his skeleton, his body covered in cuts and bruises. He looked like a corpse.

"Quick! Help me get him up to the school. His pulse is weak and he's dehydrated. I can heal him but only if we get some nourishment into his body," Malini commanded.

Jumping into the boat, Jacob peeled off his T-shirt and tossed it over Dane's naked hips before gathering his friend into his arms. He was much too light.

Lillian reached forward to help Jacob out of the boat but he didn't need it. The adrenalin coursing through his veins was help enough. He leapt to the dock and jogged up the path, unable to comprehend that the sleight weight in his arms was Dane Michaels. The first time he'd met Dane, he'd been intimidate by his size. Now, the stocky bully turned friend was utterly wasted. It blew Jacob's mind.

When he reached the school, his mom was already there,

holding the door. "West wing, fourth floor. There's an infirmary."

Jacob bounded up the spiral staircase to the clean white room. Gently, he positioned Dane on one of the six hospital beds.

Malini rushed to his side. "He needs water."

Lillian disappeared behind a divider and returned with a glass and pitcher. "I added some sugar. He needs the calories."

"Good thinking." Malini lifted the glass from Lilly's hand and brought it to Dane's lips, cradling his head in her left hand. "I'm going to give him enough healing energy to drink but I won't be able to heal his body until he has enough calories inside of him to rebuild his cells."

Dane swallowed a few gulps of water without opening his eyes.

"It's going to take some time. We'll have to take shifts. I'll go first, until he's strong enough to drink on his own. Jacob, you can go next." She tipped the glass to Dane's lips again.

Jacob nodded. "Maybe we can get Dr. Silva to mix an elixir to heal him faster."

The room plunged into silence, Malini and Lillian exchanging glances.

"What?" Jacob asked.

Malini groaned. "If Dane is here, Lucifer must have gotten what he wanted." Panic crept into her voice. "Dr. Silva must've—"

"No. She wouldn't." Jacob shook his head.

Lillian rubbed her forehead with her fingertips. "Yes, yes she would, Jacob. She's always been a loose cannon."

"And Ethan told us she was fighting with Gideon. We have to face the possibility that she gave up." Malini's eyes darted around the room, like she was searching for answers in the corners.

Jacob paced like a caged animal. "No. How could she do that? We can't do this without her. We need Dr. Silva."

Lillian placed her hands on Jacob's shoulders. "We may have to. We may not have a choice."

Malini took a deep, cleansing breath and let it out slowly, seeming to beat back her earlier panic by force of will. "Jacob's right. We shouldn't jump to conclusions. There might be some answers in the In Between. I'll go over as soon as I can. And we need to talk to Gideon."

Jacob looked at Dane's emaciated body in Malini's arms. "I don't think we can leave him yet."

"We won't, Jacob." Malini's eyes welled with tears. "One thing at a time. Saving Dane comes first."

❦

THE GARDEN WAS DARK BY THE TIME JACOB FINISHED with his shift caring for Dane. He found Malini sitting cross-legged at the end of the dock, face tilted toward the tranquil waters. The moon was low, appearing larger than life on the horizon. Her dark silhouette was a humble contrast.

"My mom asked Ethan to help with Dane. She's going to teach that defense class to the Soulkeepers, just in case. Plus, she needed to run the school. Did you know that the gnomes won't eat unless she tells them to take care of themselves?" Jacob lowered himself to the wood beams behind Malini. At her level, he could make out the glint of wetness on her cheeks. She'd been crying. He placed a hand on her shoulder. "What is it, Malini?"

She swept her fingers under her eyes and cleared her throat. "I went to the In Between for guidance and to center myself."

"Why are you crying? What did you see?"

Turning her body toward him, she slipped her fingers into his. "I can't tell you."

Jacob whispered into her ear, "I know you can't always share the specifics, and you have to be careful not to upset the balance of nature or change the course of history, but, look at you. Your head is going to explode if you don't talk about it. Can't you tell me anything?"

Malini rested her head on his shoulder. "Before I became a Healer, do you remember when I went to the Abraham Lincoln Presidential Museum with my parents?"

"Vaguely."

"Well, did you know that his decision, the Civil War, resulted in the deaths of over six hundred thousand people?"

Jacob squeezed her hand. "No, I didn't. I knew there was a Civil War, though."

Malini snorted derisively. "You really should pay more attention in school."

"I'll start as soon as I think anything they teach us will save our lives." He chuckled.

Her mouth tugged downward. "Even though so many people were killed, it was the right thing to do. Did you know a Healer was helping him? Panctu. I used to wonder what it was like for her to know her guidance would mean the deaths of so many. But it was the right thing to do. A Healer's job is to guide people toward the greater good, no matter what." A tear traced a sparkling trail down her cheek.

Jacob swallowed hard. "You've seen what we have to do and it means death, maybe for a lot of people."

"Sometimes one person seems as valuable as a whole army of them." She sobbed in earnest and Jacob pulled her into his arms.

Was it him? She might have seen his death or his mom's and of course she couldn't say. Doing so might change what was meant to be. The thought stuck in his throat, a swollen egg that made it hard to breathe. He tipped his face until his forehead met hers. "This is why God made you a Healer. Another person wouldn't be as brave. We have to do what we have to do. I've died before, you know, twice. It's practically a habit."

She straightened. "It's not you! Do you think I'd be able to have this conversation if it was? I'd be a sniveling idiot, completely useless. No, it's not you, but it's bad enough." Her hand lifted to his cheek and her lips found his in a kiss that was as comfortable as breathing.

Eventually he pulled back, remembering that neither of them had eaten dinner yet, and he was supposed to have her home in a couple of hours so that she could check in with her parents. "Where does your father think we are right now?"

"Movie."

Jacob chuckled. "Are they enjoying the cruise?"

"I think so." Malini picked at the side of her nail.

"What's our next move? Do you think Abigail ever met with the two Soulkeepers this afternoon? And there's a third out there somewhere. If Lucifer has the list, we should have rounded them up yesterday."

"The two Abigail met with are dead."

Jacob swallowed. "Did Abigail do it?"

"No."

"What about the last Soulkeeper? Do we try to find the last one on the list?"

"That's what Lucifer will expect us to do. It's the logical thing. But Lucifer's game was never about the list."

"What?"

Malini rolled her eyes and groaned. "We've been playing into his hands the entire time, Jacob. It's all so clear to me, now. It's true that someone needs to gather the last Soulkeeper, but not us and not now. We need to use the element of surprise and go after what Lucifer really wants."

Jacob pushed himself up to his feet. "I don't suppose you know what that is? Aside from rounding up a bunch of humans to farm for flesh after he takes over the world."

"That is what he wants to do, but if we are going to stop him, we need to know how he plans to do it. I can't see that part. But I know who can."

"Who?"

"Gideon."

"Gideon?"

"Yes. He's our link to what's really going on." Malini used Jacob's hand to pull herself to her feet.

Jacob shook his head. "You mean what's going on with Dr. Silva?"

"No, I mean with Lucifer. Gideon may not know it yet, but he's the key to undoing Lucifer's plan. You and I need to find him and make sure he stays on our side."

"Why wouldn't Gideon be on our side?" Jacob asked. He intertwined his fingers in hers and led the way up the path.

"I'm not sure yet."

"I don't suppose you could be more specific," Jacob pleaded.

Malini shook her head.

"Okay." He sighed. "Gideon it is." They'd reached the school and Jacob held the door open for her.

"I wonder what's for dinner?" Malini asked.

Jacob smiled. "A hot, gnome-cooked meal."

Malini groaned.

"Hey, Malini, guess which dessert you should skip?"

"What?"

"The forbidden-apple pie."

Malini giggled, wiping the remnants of tears from her face. "Thank God you're good looking, Jacob, because you are not getting anywhere on your sense of humor."

Jacob followed her toward the dining room, wondering how long they had to laugh about anything at all.

TWENTY-THREE

MARA AND HENRY

As hard as she tried, Mara couldn't keep her eyes off of the hourglass. Henry, on the other hand, couldn't look at it. He avoided it by staring out the window, his fingers rubbing the bricks of the sill impulsively.

"Don't worry, Mara. Once I've helped you through the door, I'll find someone to challenge me and I'll meet you on the other side. Of course, it might take me some time. I have to find the right person."

Mara's face turned from the hourglass. "How do you find the right person to challenge Death?"

"They have to be a champion, someone who doesn't give up easily. The first days are difficult, even painful. Lucifer will try to sway the new Death to his side by promising to take the pain away. I have to find someone who won't be swayed."

"What? I thought everyone here was neutral?"

"We are neutral. But sometimes remaining neutral means doing things to counteract Lucifer's cheating ways. When he doesn't follow the rules, we don't either."

Mara walked up behind Henry and slid her hands up his chest. "If Lucifer doesn't follow the rules, isn't there some kind of punishment? What about God?"

Henry turned in the circle of her arms and placed his hands on her shoulders. "God never breaks His promises. He never breaks the rules. When Lucifer cheats, He can't match cheating with cheating. But we can. Those of us in the In Between have been keeping the balance for good for a very long time."

Brow furrowed, Mara pulled back a little. Henry described God as a He, which seemed odd to Mara, who had seen God as female. But then she remembered that everyone saw God as the best part of themselves. For Henry, God was a He.

"The immortals keep the balance. How?" she asked.

Henry fixed her with an intense stare. "I mean, when a murderous dictator meets an untimely death, often it is exactly that, untimely. Much can be accomplished when Death, Fate, and Time work together. Have you ever wondered why time in Nod and Hell is different from here and on Earth? Aldric keeps it that way to give us the advantage. Everything there takes longer, giving us more time to respond. Fate sees when her loom becomes tangled by Lucifer's trickery. She shares those incidents with us and we conspire to set things right. But imagine, Mara, if someone were to win my role who had a proclivity toward evil."

"The balance would sway in Lucifer's favor."

Henry nodded.

Mara pressed a finger to her lips and lowered her eyes, twisting from his embrace. She couldn't believe what she was about to say. "I don't think you should find a challenger. I don't think you should come with me to the other side. Not right away."

Henry's face snapped up. "Why?"

"Yesterday, I saw Gideon. He used the stone to seek guidance from Malini's power."

"Gideon? Who's Gideon?"

"He's the angel who's in love with Dr. Silva." Henry looked confused and Mara realized he hadn't met either of them. "Dr. Silva is a fallen angel who helps the Soulkeepers. Gideon is the angel who's in love with her."

"I think I remember seeing them before you kissed me at the prom. They were huddled around Malini's body. I can't hone in on their souls like I can with humans."

"Anyway, Gideon was here and I had a chance to talk with him. He said that Lucifer is up to something. He's kidnapped a friend of ours named Dane Michaels and has been holding him for ransom, to obtain the list of all Soulkeepers who have come to power."

Henry paused, shaking his head and frowning. "Dane Michaels is in Eden. His soul I can see."

"What? What does that mean? Does Lucifer have the list?"

"I don't know the circumstances, only the soul. I remember him."

Mara sighed. "Even more reason that you have to stay in your position. I think it was a little too convenient that Lucifer showed up with the hourglass just when all this crap started going down with the Soulkeepers. I have a feeling that he created this consequence to try to force you out of service. He's up to something. He wants you to offer someone the challenge so that the In Between will be weak when he makes his move." She pointed at the hourglass, now half empty. "That is to ensure you are at your most vulnerable precisely when he wants you to be."

While Mara had always understood that Henry was Death, the air he assumed taught her exactly what that title meant. The bones of his face became more prominent and his eyes darkened into black holes of anger. The skin peeled back from his hands. He formed a bony fist and the temperature in the room plunged.

"You are right, Mara," he said. "We've been played for fools. He has used my love for you to attempt to further his wicked scheme." Henry's skeletal fist came down on the table, splintering the wood into a million pieces. Her coffee mug rolled across the floor.

In this form, his presence was overwhelming. Mara backed toward the door instinctively, her hand pressing into her collarbone. "Please, Henry. Don't give him the satisfaction of wasting one more minute of our time together."

Henry bowed his head and Mara felt the cold retreat into him. His face fleshed out and his hands returned to normal. When he looked at her again, it was with soft brown eyes, filled with love and longing. He opened his arms and she ran into them.

"It won't be forever, Mara. Where you are going, you will hardly notice my absence. Someday, when this is all over, I'll come to you. My predecessor did it and I will do it. We'll be together."

Mara pressed her face into his chest, trying to absorb every detail about him, from the sound of his voice to the way she fit into his embrace. She believed him when he said he would come for her. But someday was a long way off and Mara knew, as good as heaven was, it wouldn't be paradise without him.

TWENTY-FOUR

MALINI AND JACOB

Malini sighed impatiently from the passenger seat of Jacob's truck. He'd circled the block three times and still couldn't find a place to park near Katrina's dorm. Students rushed in all directions, trying to make their afternoon classes and cutting off Jacob in the process.

"Just park, Jacob. I'd like to do this before my first gray hair."

"The parking lot is all meters and I don't have any quarters. I'll get a ticket."

"What's more important: a parking ticket or saving the world from tyrannical rule by the ultimate evil?"

Jacob turned into a restricted parking lot mumbling, "Tyrannical evil," resentfully under his breath. Hopefully, saving the world would not mean getting towed. They exited the truck and crossed the street to the boxy brown dormitory. Katrina was waiting in the atrium.

"Geez, I thought you guys would never get here. Could

your text be any more vague?" She backed inside and pressed the button for the elevator.

Jacob waved his hand. "Hello, Katrina. How are you? I miss you, too. I can't believe it's been as long as it has. Time flies."

The look she gave him could strip paint off the wall.

"Not now," Malini said to both of them as she stepped onto the elevator. She waited until the doors closed to continue. "Let's get upstairs. We need to talk."

Katrina led the way to her room, unlocking the door and holding it open for all of them. "My roommate is studying at the library. We have at least an hour."

Jacob strode into the room and took a seat on one of the two twin beds he assumed was Mallory's because the rumpled bedspread didn't reflect Katrina's neat freak compulsion. Malini plopped down next to him.

"Where's Gideon?" she asked

Katrina glanced toward the window. "He hasn't come back yet. He left this morning to snoop on my physics professor."

"Why is he watching your physics professor?" Malini asked.

"Because I saw him with a Watcher—Cord."

Jacob shifted toward her. "Cord? What's Cord doing here?"

"That's what Gideon is trying to find out. I heard Cord talking to Dr. Rahkmid yesterday. He gave him specific instructions to bring his team to a rendezvous point on Saturday."

"That's tomorrow!" Jacob said.

"Do you think your professor knows what Cord is?" Malini asked.

"I don't know. I think he was influenced. The way he hung on Cord's every word and was agreeable to everything he said..."

Malini narrowed her eyes. "Tell me about Rahkmid. What do you think Lucifer wants with him?"

"Gideon and I have been over this again and again. We can't figure it out. He's from the Middle East and it's not like he's a rocket scientist." Katrina laughed but Jacob and Malini looked at each other in confusion. "I mean that his job is all textbooks and equations. He doesn't actually help make anything. If Lucifer is trying to create some master weapon, he chose the wrong guy."

Scratching his ear, Jacob stood and approached the window. "So Lucifer is using a man who teaches classes and stares at equations all day to somehow be a part of his plan to take over the world. It's like a bad instructional video: World Domination Through the Magic of Science."

Malini frowned. "Katrina, can you take us by his office? I'm guessing a physicist has seriously detailed notes. Maybe we can find something about what he's planning to do. Plus, hopefully we'll run into Gideon. You did tell him I was coming, right?"

"I did and he told me he got your text, Malini." Katrina joined Jacob at the window. "It isn't like him not to be here."

Tugging on Jacob's arm, Malini led him toward the door. "I don't like this. Let's go see if we can find him."

Katrina stayed where she was, staring out the window. A shiver slithered down her spine, and her arms wrapped around herself like she was holding her chest together.

"Katrina, do you have a map of how to get to Dr. Rahkmid's office? I think it would be better if Jacob and I went alone. You should stay here. The enchantment on this room will keep you safe."

With a sigh of relief, Katrina gave Malini a telling hug. A folder on the meticulously organized desk contained the map. Katrina starred a building a few blocks away and wrote a room number next to it. "His office is number 375. According to my syllabus his office hours are over for the day, which usually means he's teaching another class."

"Excellent. Thank you." Malini reached for the doorknob.

"Good luck," Katrina said, her voice breathy.

Malini opened the door and followed Jacob into the hall.

Across campus from Katrina's dormitory, Malini glanced at the map in her hands and then up at the building in front of her.

"This place looks like a castle," Jacob said.

"Altgeld Hall. John Altgeld was a governor of Illinois in the late 1800s. He had a certain taste in architecture and a bunch of the public universities in Illinois erected these castles in his honor," Malini explained.

"This isn't the only one?"

"Nope. There's a castle on the Illinois State University quad, Eastern, Northern, and Southern universities too."

"Weird."

"I know, right? They're beautiful but eccentric. What is it about Illinois governors?"

Jacob shrugged and held the door open for her.

They climbed the stairs to the third floor and down the deserted corridor to 375. Malini jiggled the doorknob.

"It's locked," she said.

Jacob bent over. He kept a flask of water strapped to his ankle and had become very good at springing locks. Before he could reach it, the mechanism engaged and the door opened on its own. Malini stepped backward, hoping whatever excuse her muddled brain developed would be believable. But there was no one on the other side of the door.

"Dr. Rahkmid?" Malini called.

Gideon's hushed voice responded. "Come in, Malini. It's me."

She entered the crowded office, amazed that someone so intelligent could be just as untidy. Closing the door behind her and Jacob, she eyed the stacks of papers and books piled precariously on every conceivable surface. Gideon sat in the chair behind the desk, fingers buried in his hair.

"Gideon, what's going on? Have you found something?" she asked.

He lifted a document from the desk and turned it toward Malini and Jacob. It was covered in mathematical and scientific equations. "Do either of you know what this means?" he asked.

Jacob moved closer, squinting at the numbers and symbols scribbled across the page. "It means this guy is smarter than me. Who could understand this? It's like a different language."

Eyeing the equations, Malini sighed and shook her head.

"I don't understand it either but I do understand this." Gideon flipped the document over.

Hand sketched in black charcoal, a human sacrifice was depicted strapped to a stone altar. No hair or facial features defined the sacrifice except for the mouth, agape in a silent scream. A figure with outstretched wings drove a jagged blade into the victim's heart. Blood dripped from the wound, pooling at the base. Watchers crawled from the blood, as if the sacrifice had ripped a hole in the paper large enough for them to fit through.

Malini took the drawing from Gideon. "What does this mean?"

Gideon folded his hands on the desk. "Do you remember how Oswald became Abigail's portal?"

"It's not something you forget. She buried her dead husband and a tree grew out of his body and blood. Somehow his soul was bound to the tree, which gave it the power to transport."

Nodding, Gideon sighed heavily. "To bring a portal into existence, you need something from Heaven, Abigail, something of Earth, the dirt Oswald was buried in, and blood. You need blood, human blood. Look at the picture. The angel, the stone, the blood, and a million demons shadowed in it. Lucifer never cared about killing the Soulkeepers; that was just a ploy to distract us from his real plan. He's trying to open a portal."

The diagram slipped from Malini's fingers and her head shook emphatically. "They already have a portal, the tree in Nod. Why would they need another one?"

Gideon snatched the sketch from the desk and pointed at the blood. "Look at the number of faces in this blood, Malini. Watchers can only come through the tree one or two at a time, but if Lucifer wants to take control, he needs to bring forth an army, a legion of dark angels that will sweep the state, then the country, then the continent. One at a time, Watchers can be killed. The Soulkeepers have time to react. The Watchers have time to collapse under their own self-serving ways. But a legion of Watchers..." Gideon shook his head. "Lucifer is planning to create a portal big enough for a legion to step through."

"Um, not to shoot down the best theory we have so far, but it won't work." Jacob spread his hands. "Lucifer doesn't have something from Heaven. He doesn't have an angel to make the sacrifice."

As if the air around him turned to lead, Gideon's shoulders slumped forward, his wings falling limp from his back. He scrubbed his face with his hands and his voice came out in a whisper. "Abigail gave herself to him in exchange for Dane. As long as she doesn't eat flesh, she doesn't share the Watcher's curse and will work in the ceremony. Lucifer never wanted the list. He wanted her."

Malini's fingers pressed over her lips. Jacob fell forward, catching himself on the desk and knocking a pile of books to the floor.

"Why? Why would Abigail give herself over?" he asked Gideon.

"She wanted me to believe it was to save Dane. That's what she told me before she left. But I've been thinking about things she said to me over the last month we were together. She thought Lucifer might win, and she wasn't sure she wanted redemption. She wasn't sure she trusted God to do what he promised us."

Tears streamed down Malini's cheeks and she noticed Jacob had turned to face the wall of the windowless office, an obvious ploy to hide his face. Gideon's body crumpled across the desk, sending papers flying and books toppling to the floor.

"Can I speak to Gideon alone please?" Malini asked Jacob.

Jacob nodded and exited the office, closing the door behind him.

Gideon raised his head.

Bending at the waist, Malini rested her fingers on the desk and met Gideon's eyes. "What I say to you now, I say not as your friend but as your Healer. I've had a vision, Gideon. You will have the opportunity to either save Abigail or to join her. You must not do either. You must let her go, even if that means losing her forever."

"But—"

"No, Gideon. I am certain of this. What I share I don't share lightly. This message is for you and you alone. You must let her go. If you don't, we are all doomed."

Gideon shook his head.

"She's made her choice. You have to make yours. If you are with us, if you will help me save this world, you will believe me and trust what I say. Do not try to save her. Do not try to join her. Do you understand?"

Rising to his full height, Gideon ruffled his wings. He frowned at Malini and stepped around the desk, nudging past her. He paused at the door, his hand hovering over the knob, and his back to her.

"You are very young, Malini. Very young for a Healer."

"Yes, but my power is old. I'm sure about this, Gideon. You have to trust me. Are you with us?"

Silence stretched out between them. Malini's breath came and went in long, even draws. She had no idea what she would do if Gideon refused to follow her instructions. The Soul-keepers needed him, now more than ever.

"Yes. I'm with you," he said toward the door. Then he opened it and dissolved into the light of the hallway.

TWENTY-FIVE

DANE

D ane opened his eyes with no idea where he was. A glass appeared in front of his lips and a strong arm tipped his body forward. Sweet liquid poured down his throat.

"Good job. Hey, you're awake," a deep voice said.

He turned his head toward the voice but the glow from the window left him blinking at a dark silhouette.

"I'm Ethan. I'm going to take care of you for a while." The silhouette shifted. A guy with Latino coloring and a physique like he lived at the gym leaned against the bed. The room looked like a hospital, but the guy was too young to be a doctor.

Dane tried to speak but his throat cracked. He licked his lips, fighting to sit up against the weakness that seemed to permeate every part of his body.

Ethan placed one strong hand on Dane's shoulder and the other on his hand. He leaned forward, giving Dane a closer view of his face. Stubble peppered his chin and dark circles hung under his eyes, but Ethan's was the kindest face Dane had seen in what seemed like a lifetime.

"Just relax, Dane. You're safe. Nobody is going to hurt you here." Ethan straightened slightly. "Geez, you're cold, let me get you another blanket."

Tightening his hand around Ethan's fingers, Dane tried harder to speak. "Malini?" he rasped.

"She's gone, dude. Jacob and Malini left to go talk to Gideon. And Lillian and the other Soulkeepers took off for Dr. Silva's in case they needed back up. It's just you and me for a while." Ethan walked away and returned with a warm blanket.

Dane pushed against the mattress, trying to sit up, but he wasn't strong enough. Ethan's arms hooked behind his shoulders and under his knees and lifted him up in the bed, plumping the pillow behind his head. The warmth of the new blanket encircled him as Ethan spread it across his body.

"There. That's better," Ethan said.

What happened next didn't involve any thinking on Dane's part. It was instinctual, like drinking the water that was brought to his lips. He used what little energy he had left to throw his arms around Ethan's neck.

At first, Ethan's arms tensed, but then he returned the hug, rubbing Dane's back and cradling his head as tears Dane didn't know he was holding, rushed down his face. "Man, you've been to Hell and back ... literally."

Dane fell back onto the pillow with Ethan's help.

"Whole time," Dane croaked, "no one touched me."

Ethan frowned. "You don't have to explain. I get it and it's okay with me." He held out his arms. "Hugs are free."

The smile that Dane cracked hurt his cheeks, but he didn't care. "Why are you here?" he asked.

RETURN TO EDEN   181

"You mean, why was I left behind?" A scraping sound echoed through the room as Ethan pulled over one of the chairs from the patio to Dane's bedside. He took a seat. "Someone needed to stay to look after you and I've had the least amount of training as a Soulkeeper. I guess they thought I'd be safer here anyway. Besides, no one knows me yet, so..."

"You're a Soulkeeper?" Dane asked.

In response, Ethan reached out his hand and made the glass of lemonade float into it from the bedside table. "Yeah, I guess I am. No one was more surprised than me. Are you?"

"No," Dane said. "Friend."

"I see. And you ended up in Hell for it?"

Dane nodded.

"Sounds like you're a friend worth having."

The muscles in Dane's face twitched. His vision blurred and he closed his eyes against a floaty, spinning sensation.

"You're tired. You should rest. I've asked one of the gnomes to bring you dinner. You'll want to have enough energy to eat it once it's here," Ethan said.

"Gnomes?" Dane's eyelids flipped open.

Ethan grinned. "Yeah. The Garden of Eden has garden gnomes. Like real useful garden gnomes that know how to do, like, everything."

Dane's eyebrows lifted.

"The food is great. Save your strength. Like I said, Jacob and Malini are on it. They said they're going to talk to Gideon about Lucifer and Abigail. They're afraid she traded the list for you."

The sound of her name made Dane stutter. He needed to tell Ethan. Someone needed to know.

"What's wrong, Dane?"

"Traded herself for me," Dane spat out. "Saved me."

"You mean she traded herself, not the list?"

Dane nodded.

"She saved you? Was that who put you on the boat?"

"Yes. Tell them."

Ethan nodded and smoothed the covers. He pulled his cell phone from his back pocket and held it toward the window. "No service here. No cell towers in Eden."

Guilt weighed on Dane's heart. Had Abigail lost her soul forever to save him? He didn't know for sure, only that Abigail had met with Lucifer, then carried him out of Hell and to the boat. Lucifer never gave something for nothing. She'd traded something valuable. He shook his head, the tears starting anew.

"Listen, Dane," Ethan said in a soothing voice. "I've been part of the Soulkeepers for a matter of days and I'm already certain Malini and Jacob know what they're doing. When Abigail came to get me, she was creepy for sure but she was trustworthy. I've got to think that all of the Soulkeepers know that. They're going to do the right thing. They'll figure out what's happened and they'll make it right."

Ethan's eyes seemed so sure and Dane was too weak to do anything but cling to the hope he offered. He relaxed against his pillow and closed his eyes again.

"That's it," Ethan said. "Rest up. I'll wake you when your food gets here."

This time Dane allowed himself to slip into darkness, feeling oddly safe in Ethan's presence.

TWENTY-SIX

MARA AND HENRY

Wrapped in Henry's arms, Mara watched her last minutes fall through the hourglass. She squeezed him tighter, wishing that her bell still worked and she could stop time, preserving this moment forever. It was so unfair. All of it, all of the rules, all of the consequences, seemed arbitrary and purposeless.

"It's time, Mara. Let's not give Lucifer the chance to argue the particulars."

She nodded, sobbing, and climbed from the bed. She'd dressed in the gray dress from the day they met. If she had to spend eternity in one outfit, she wanted it to be the one she was wearing on the happiest day of her life, the day she met Henry.

He kissed her softly on the lips. They had said everything there was to say. To draw it out any longer would be torture for both of them. With a wave of his hand, her door glowed to life.

"I'll come to you," he said. "Eventually, when I find the

right person to replace me and Lucifer is less of a threat, I'll pass on and we can be together forever."

She twisted his ring on her finger and nodded, although she found his words less than comforting.

He pulled the door open. Light and warmth welcomed her, coaxing her forward. She stepped into a world of joy. Children played in the distance. Figures danced in the beyond to the drifting notes of a far-off melody. Even the air smelled sweet, a combination of freshly cut grass and blooming roses. Cherry blossom petals showered down from above like confetti welcoming her home. She took another step into the light and sensed the door behind her close but didn't turn around to check.

In the blink of an eye, a dark figure blocked her path. Her first thought was disappointment. She desperately tried to step around the dark silhouette. But curiosity got the best of her and she looked up, way up, into the figure's face. A blood-red toga wrapped around his body, in stunning contrast to his espresso-colored skin.

"Do you challenge me?" he said.

"Who are you?"

The man tipped his bald head, giving her a better view of his face and his large gauge ear piercings. "I am Time. Do you challenge me?"

"Aldric?"

"That is the name some call me." He met her eyes.

Mara squared her shoulders and silently weighed the choice before her. Heaven was clearly paradise and she had no idea what becoming Time meant, not really. A moment ago, she'd been ready to move on.

She played with Henry's ring on her finger. Heavy.

Squeezing. What was God's purpose, having Henry tell her the story of how he became Death? Could it be for her benefit instead of his? She thought of the ring she'd made for Henry, an hourglass. There was more she wanted to do, more she wanted to be.

The loving light behind Aldric tempted her, warming every particle of her being with joy. She closed her eyes to keep it out. Heaven could wait. It would still be there when she was the one being challenged. This chance would never come again. The chance to be with Henry might never come again. When she'd said she wanted Henry as her Heaven, she hadn't been exaggerating. Every part of her wanted to spend eternity with him. This might be her only hope.

"Have I chosen unwisely or do you challenge me?" Aldric whispered.

"I challenge you," she said.

At once, God appeared on her right, again in Mara's likeness. Lucifer's platinum-blond illusion appeared on her left.

The devil's red face spewed an obscenity she could hardly comprehend. "I have things to do. Let's get this over with," he hissed.

God smiled. "Is the timing not convenient for you? It was your hourglass that marked the minute of her crossing over."

"Yes, a process that shouldn't have involved me. Surprising there should be a challenge now." He rolled his eyes.

"Why? She is clearly worthy."

"On with it then. Aldric, the coin."

Aldric produced a large golden disc and tossed it into the air. Mara watched it spin, noticing one side was engraved with an all-seeing eye, the other with a horned beast. Aldric caught it and flipped it onto the back of his hand.

"God," he said, exposing the all-seeing eye.

Lucifer groaned. "Trial or consequence?"

For a moment, God seemed to be weighing Mara with her eyes, taking her in from head to toe, looking into her soul. "Consequence," she said. "If Mara does not succeed or dies during the trial, her soul is mine."

Mara breathed a sigh of relief.

"Humpf." Lucifer scanned Mara with equal interest. Each part of her body burned where his gaze touched her, a red-hot poker testing her soul. He waved his hand and the warm glow of heaven disappeared, replaced by a rural landscape. A vast field of corn stretched as far as she could see.

Aldric shifted, glancing from Lucifer to the field. "What is this game?"

"If I get to choose the trial, there sure as hell will be some entertainment value, Aldric." Lucifer shrugged. "Don't be concerned. Should either of you die, you are guaranteed a spot in heaven, after all." He sighed deeply. "Although there may be some suffering." The corner of his mouth curled.

"What do we have to do?" Aldric's hands tightened the knot on his toga.

With a grin that seemed to hold too many teeth, Lucifer pointed his hand toward the cornfield. "Simple. Find the scroll within this cornfield. Read it and you become or remain Time."

"What's the catch?" Mara asked. "Is the field so large that I'll die of old age before I reach it? Is the scroll hidden inside an ear of corn?"

God shook her head. "The trial has to be possible to navigate. This field is five miles square and the scroll is on the ground within it."

"No more helping!" Lucifer snapped. "Or I will demand a retrial."

He kept talking but Mara couldn't hear it. A whisper echoed through her brain, God's whisper. *Beware. The field is filled with hellhounds. Kill them to survive.*

Aldric held out his hand. "I am allowed a weapon." A sickle formed in his palm, out of the ether.

Mara didn't give Lucifer a chance to argue. She held out her hand and knitted a short sword. "Me, too," she said.

"Fair," God said firmly.

Lucifer narrowed his eyes. "On my count. Three, two, one, go!"

By the tone of his voice, it was obvious that Lucifer wanted her to race into the corn, but Mara noticed that Aldric stepped cautiously into the stalks. She did the same. It didn't take long for her to figure out why Aldric hesitated. The leaves of the corn had thin, sharp edges. By moving slowly, the leaves bent against her weight. Even so, she already had several paper-cut like red marks on her bare shoulders.

The gray dress and sandals that had seemed symbolic when she'd stepped through Henry's door now seemed like a ridiculously poor choice of dress. But how in the world could she have foreseen this? She attempted to conjure jeans and a flannel shirt but the magic didn't work. Apparently, the knife was the only tool she was allowed.

Mara stopped short. Why did Aldric offer her the challenge? Henry was with her the entire time. He couldn't have had anything to do with it. Was it God? Someone else? No immortal offered a challenge without expecting they would lose. She needed to know why Aldric was willing to sacrifice himself for her.

Veering left, Mara hoped to intersect Aldric's path. If he truly intended to give her immortality anyway, then why not work together to find the scroll?

As she chopped at the stalks, she envied Aldric's sickle. Her straight blade required her wrist to turn awkwardly and made for slow progress. She walked at a diagonal, toward where she thought Aldric's path would lead. The point where she'd entered the field was a distant memory. The corn loomed above her head against a purple and red sky. Twilight. How long before she'd be lost in the dark?

Breathe. Just breathe. Mara tried to slow her racing pulse. There was a reason that Lucifer had chosen a cornfield. Having grown up in trailer park near the city, Mara had no experience with rural life. Cornfields had always held an exotic creepiness. The farther she journeyed into the stalks, the more the corn seemed to crowd her shoulders and steal the air around her.

She couldn't help it. Fear gripped her by the lungs. Whacking at the stalks with her sword, she cleared a circle around herself. She needed air. She needed the corn to stop touching her. *Whack-whack-thwack.* She chopped at the field. It wasn't enough. She couldn't breathe. She was going to die!

At a full-out run, she raced through the corn, letting out smothered yelps as the stalks sliced at her face and shoulders. Bright red blood oozed down her arm. She swung the sword haphazardly in front of her, somehow knowing she shouldn't scream but finding it impossible not to. A loud rustle to her right stopped her in her tracks. She lifted her sword toward the noise, trembling.

"Aldric?" she whispered.

A stalk whipped forward, forcing her to dodge left to avoid

it. No one. Silence. Another loud rustle, closer now, behind her.

"Aldric?" she asked again.

Shadows lurked at the base of the corn. Mara stared at the dark patch of dirt to her left. A bit of her blood dripped from one of the leaves onto the earth. That small drip grew wider, like oil bubbling up from a hole. She watched in horror as the oil grew into a wolf-sized black beast with more teeth and claws than body. It blinked glowing green eyes and licked a drop of her blood from its jowls.

All rational thought abandoned her. Mara's scream pierced the twilight. The thing pounced. Wielding her blade, she lost her balance, falling between the rows of corn. Her back slammed against the rock-hard dirt. Somehow, she managed to slap her blade against the creature's side. It rolled, flattening the stalks next to her.

Mara leapt to her feet, pointing her sword at the creature's throat. It paced in front of her, driving her back into the corn. *Crack!* Another hellhound appeared behind the stalks. The first hound closed in. She dodged diagonally but the second hound was already there. Together, they herded her. Hunted her.

As good as dead, Mara reached deep inside, to that place she'd called on the day she'd picked up the bell that had changed her life. With a warrior's howl, she swooped down on the first hound, a whirlwind of slashing sword and dodging feet. Her blade landed in the creature's throat. A spout of oily blood poured from the wound. She yanked the blade free, somersaulting over the first hound to avoid the claws of the second. From flat on her back, she stabbed upward, skewering the second hound through the chest. The beast exploded above her, its black contents raining down.

From out of nowhere, a third hound leaped at her from the side. She scrambled to get to her feet and wedge her blade between herself and the creature. Claws thrashed at her face. Her body fell to the ground once more.

A hooked blade whistled from the right, throwing the hound from the air and simultaneously slicing off its head. Aldric stood above her, turning in a circle, scanning the corn.

"Get up!" he ordered. "With all the blood, there will be more."

Mara scurried to her feet. "I'm a bloody mess, Aldric. What do I do?"

He tore a strip from the bottom of his toga and tied it around the deepest gash on her arm. "Don't let the blood touch the earth." He motioned toward the crimson trails on the corn.

She didn't waste any time. Ripping the bottom of her dress, she wiped the remaining blood from her skin as best she could, and then tucked the gray cloth behind a corncob so that it wouldn't touch the ground. "Let's go."

Slowly, carefully, Mara followed Aldric into the stalks. The one bonus of the attack was it had moved her beyond panic into survival mode. Heaven or no Heaven, Mara would not be a victim of Lucifer's trial. She owed it to Aldric, to Henry, and to herself to survive.

TWENTY-SEVEN

JACOB AND MALINI

J acob dreamt he was in an earthquake. He held Malini's hand while buildings crumbled around them. Everything inside him told him to run, but Malini wouldn't budge.

She was saying something over and over. "It's time. It's time."

He woke with a jolt, Malini shaking his shoulder. "It's time, Jacob. Dr. Rahkmid is pulling out of his driveway. We need to follow him."

He shook his head and reached for the keys.

"No. Wait. Don't start the car until he's a few blocks up. I don't want him to suspect anything."

Forcing his lips to form words, Jacob mumbled, "What if I lose him?"

"You won't." Malini dug in her purse and handed him what looked like a piece of candy. He unwrapped it and popped it into his mouth.

"EWW! This is horrible. What did you feed me?"

"It's a Swedish cough drop. The horehound root will help wake you up."

Jacob manipulated the hard lump to the side of his mouth. "How about a Red Bull instead?" He rolled down his window and spat the lozenge onto the road.

Malini laughed. "No time to stop."

Jacob turned the key and pulled onto the road as Rahkmid's car hooked left up ahead. "There are a few behind your seat, along with some snacks."

Checking the six-inch area behind the bench of Jacob's truck, Malini gave an appreciative squeal. "Jacob Lau, you prepared for this. You planned for something in advance."

"I did."

"When did you become so responsible?"

"Oh, I don't know. Sometime between being expected to save the world and wanting to spend the rest of my life with a Healer."

Silence.

Jacob glanced toward Malini who was gaping at him. "What?" he asked.

"Did you just say you wanted to spend the rest of your life with me?"

"Well ... yeah. Obviously that wasn't a proposal or anything." He laughed. "That would be the lamest proposal ever."

He heard her shift in her seat. "But you think about it?"

"Sure. I mean, after all we've been through, it's kind of ridonkulous to think we'd end up with anyone else. Could you imagine bringing someone new into this life?"

Silence.

Jacob groaned. "That came out wrong. That's not why I

RETURN TO EDEN   193

think about growing old with you, Malini. I love you. We've
tried the apart thing and it does not work for me."

The force of the kiss she planted on his cheek almost made
him swerve off the road.

"You are the best boyfriend ever," she said.

"Yeah, I know."

The crumpled wrapper from the cough drop hit him in the
temple. "Jacob, look, he's turning onto the highway."

Jacob followed the professor up the ramp and merged into
early morning traffic. "This is good," he said. "He won't notice
we're following him with the other traffic."

Hours ticked by with nothing but the hum of the engine.
Jacob forced himself to concentrate on the road, guzzling Red
Bull to stay awake, while Malini dozed against the passenger
side window. It wasn't helping that Rahkmid's car drove at a
steady two miles under the speed limit. No unnecessary or
sudden moves to wake Jacob up. It was early, much too early.

As the sun broke the horizon and stretched its golden rays
across the countryside bordering the highway, Jacob couldn't
stand the silence a moment longer. He reached over and shook
Malini's shoulder.

"Look, Malini, the sunrise."

She opened her eyes and stretched. "It's beautiful."

"Yeah. That's why I woke you up and not just because I
was bored out of my mind following this guy."

"Do you want to know something weird about the
sunrise?"

"What?"

"The name Lucifer means literally light-bringer, or
morning star."

Jacob grimaced. "That's the misnomer of the year."

"Some people think that it was his name before the fall, when he lived with God, but the truth is he invented that name after he came to Earth. It's part of his illusion."

"Sneaky."

Rahkmid turned his blinker on and exited toward the Chicago suburbs. "It's about time," Jacob said. He dropped back, following the blue Honda Accord as the suburbs melted into a more rural landscape. In the distance, a herd of large animals grazed in a field.

"Those look like—"

"Bison. Pull over, Jacob. I know where he's going."

Malini reached for her cell phone and his mom's face filled the screen before she hit the call button.

"What? Where are we?" Jacob asked.

"Lillian," Malini said. "Fermilab ... Can you bring the others? ... Yes. Send Grace and Master Lee ... Perfect." She tapped end call.

"Malini! What is this place?" Jacob placed a hand on her shoulder.

"Fermilab. It's a government laboratory that studies subatomic particles. They accelerate and smash pieces of atoms together to see what will happen. They discovered the top quark here."

"Uhuh. Maybe you should skip to the part that explains why Lucifer is here with a team of physicists."

Malini brought up an image of Rahkmid's diagram on her phone. "Look at the picture, Jacob. Lucifer is trying to create a way to bring an army of Watchers into this reality. To do that, he has to rip a tunnel between Earth and Nod. Fermilab is the home of the largest particle accelerator in the world next to CERN in Switzerland. It's called the Tevatron. For years scientists have tried to use particle accelerators to replicate the conditions of the Big Bang, you know, the force that started it all. But it's never worked because scientists don't have God to produce the magic that made the collision happen in just the right way." Malini pointed at the sketch of human sacrifice on her screen. "I think Lucifer has figured out a way to tap into that magic. Only, if we've learned anything about Lucifer, this Big Bang won't create, it'll destroy."

A lump formed in Jacob's throat. "How do we stop him?"

"The same way we always do. Kill anything or anyone that bleeds black."

Most of the time the finer points of Malini's plans escaped Jacob. It wasn't that he was unintelligent but that he knew his strengths. He trusted Malini with the details and brought the muscle when she needed it. But this time, a tone in her voice tugged at a sore spot deep within his chest. He turned away from her and rested his forehead on the steering wheel.

"I can't kill her, Malini. Dr. Silva bleeds black and we both know she's fallen off the grid since we got Dane back. You haven't said anything to me about her, but I can put two and two together. I won't kill her. I can't. I just can't."

Malini placed a hand on his shoulder. He turned his head, surprised that Malini was weeping in the passenger seat. It seemed like she was always crying lately. Not a good sign.

"It's not you who has to," she said, her voice trembling. "But you won't be able to save her."

At the words that sealed Dr. Silva's fate, an involuntary sob escaped his throat. He accepted Malini's hug, their tears mingling where his cheek touched hers. "I hate knowing the future," he said.

"Me, too."

Jacob nodded and wiped under his eyes. By the time they'd pulled themselves together the sound of a firecracker signaled Lillian's arrival, her enchanted staff in hand.

DEEP BENEATH THE EARTH, WITHIN A FOUR-MILE-LONG tunnel, Abigail watched a group of influenced humans build the altar necessary for the sacrifice. She had no idea if their work was accurate or why Lucifer was oddly missing from the construction. Whatever distraction pulled him away must be of ubiquitous importance, and she knew it would probably never happen again.

The muffled sobs of Stephanie Westcott were audible, despite the girl's gag. Her hazel eyes, so like her mother Fran's and brother Phillip's, begged for release. Abigail had known Stephanie since she was a toddler racing through the aisles of her parents' grocery store.

With a wave of her hand, Dr. Silva veiled the girl from the workers, even though she was sure in their influenced state they would never notice what she was about to do anyway. Placing her finger over her lips, Dr. Silva signaled for the girl to remain silent. She smoothed the dark-brown hair from Stephanie's face and pulled the gag from her mouth.

"I can't stop what's going to happen today, Stephanie, but I *can* stop your suffering." A thermos appeared in her hand. She screwed off the lid and poured a steaming cup in front of the girl's reddened eyes. "This is a tea I've made. If you drink it, everything will become much easier for you. You won't feel any pain."

Stephanie gave a short nod, although tears continued their

silent journey down her cheeks. "Will you tell my mother that I love her?" the girl choked out.

Abigail didn't respond, but raised the cup to Stephanie's lips. The girl drank every last drop. Immediately, Stephanie's eyes glossed over, her tears dried, and her breathing calmed. Abigail made the thermos disappear and replaced the gag. She lowered the veil.

With the sobs abated, the only sounds were of the torches and saws that constructed the altar.

TWENTY-EIGHT

MARA

"Thank you for saving me," Mara said, following closely behind Aldric. The words sounded pathetically trite to her ears.

He looked over his shoulder and raised an eyebrow. "If I hadn't, this whole experience would've been a waste of time. I'm not here for my health." His deep voice rumbled with frustration. "This field is made to feel menacing, to terrify you, but if you run, you will bleed, and if you bleed the hounds will come."

"Got it. I'm sorry I fell for that."

"Lucifer is ruthless. Be on guard, always." He glanced in her direction as if he could tack the advice to her mind with his stare.

"Why did you open yourself up to the challenge?" Mara asked.

Aldric chopped a path through the stalks with his sickle. Stalk after stalk whooshed to the ground but he didn't answer her question. Mara cleared her throat. Maybe he hadn't heard her? Would it be rude to ask again?

"Your question has more than one answer." His voice startled her. Finally. "I have been Time for over two thousand years. You might say a change was in order." He chuckled. "But that would not explain why I chose you. It's true I'd heard of your love affair with Death and if I were a sentimental old fool that might be reason enough. I am not. Love is fleeting. Immortality is not." He stopped swinging his blade and met Mara's eyes. "You cannot quit being Time because you break up with your boyfriend."

Mara nodded. "Of course not." She hadn't given the challenge enough thought. Had she pondered immortality for more than five minutes before she agreed to this? Probably not. Did she make the decision based on her feelings for Henry? Probably. She mentally slapped her forehead.

"I chose you because I thought you were uniquely qualified for the job."

"Do you mean because my gift was to stop time?"

"Yes, but also because you used your gift responsibly. Even when your life became difficult and lonely, you didn't abuse the power. Did you know that your power came from me?"

"Not until recently. Henry told me."

"Each immortal is allowed to give one Soulkeeper a gift. All Soulkeepers have power; it's in their genetics. But not every Soulkeeper has a gift from an immortal. Without my gift, your power would have been different, weaker. When you were born, I was having lunch with Fate and she pointed you out to me in her weaving. Your parents were a waste of skin and bones, even then. She mentioned that a little girl like you, raised in a home like yours, would be unspoiled, the perfect canvas for a gift from an immortal. I'd waited a long time to give my gift. You seemed like a worthy candidate.

"I came to Earth while you were still in the hospital. I held you, next to your crib. And I gave you my gift. I've watched you these many years. You've used it well." His smile gleamed beautifully white against his dark skin.

Mara lifted an eyebrow. "That's what Henry meant about it not being the right time for him to move on. He's given his gift to Malini—her hand—which makes her his natural successor. But Malini won't die until another Healer comes to power. That's why he couldn't know when. It would be difficult for him to find another."

Aldric tipped his head. "And choosing another is a great risk to all of us. If the wrong person becomes an immortal, think of how it would affect the balance? Time, Death, and Fate are forever linked to each other, and have been friends of God from the beginning. If any one of us should be replaced by someone sympathetic to Lucifer..." He shook his head. "You must survive this challenge, Mara." He returned to hacking the stalks in their path.

They walked for hours, their eyes sweeping the dirt around the stems for any sign of the scroll. Rubbing her sore neck, Mara tipped her head backward to stretch her aching muscles. The sight of the darkening sky made her stomach twist.

"Hey, Aldric," she said.

"Yes?"

"Do the silks on these corn stalks seem lighter to you?"

He stopped chopping and looked up. Most of the silks they'd passed had been dark brown. These were bright white.

"Yes. They are different."

"I have an idea. Lift me up."

Aldric grimaced. Certainly, he was just as tired and sore as she was.

"Just for a minute. I think it's a clue."

He lowered himself to one knee and she climbed onto his shoulders. With a grunt and enough effort to make him tremble, he rose to his full height. Once her head emerged above the tassels, she saw exactly what she was looking for. Excited, she pushed off his shoulders and landed on the ground behind him.

"It's a bull's-eye!" she squealed. "The tassels are colored deliberately. We are in the second light ring from the center. If we start moving northwest we'll hit it. The scroll's got to be there!"

Aldric's mouth dropped open. "You brilliant, brilliant girl."

"This way." Mara pointed toward the center, then moved out of the way so that Aldric could swing his sickle. Soon, they exited the light-colored ring and entered the dark.

"One more light section, one more dark, and then we'll be in the middle," Mara said. It was obvious but it made her feel better saying it out loud. They were close. So very close.

It was a good thing, too, because her sandals bit into her blistered feet. Every step was excruciating. Mara noticed that Aldric's hands were similarly raw and blistered. Each swing of the sickle filled his face with pain.

"I could go in front for a while," she said. "My sword won't be as effective but we could switch weapons. My arms are in much better shape than my feet."

A mixture of reluctance and relief played across Aldric's

features. He sighed but nodded in acceptance of the idea. He traded his sickle for her sword. With renewed zeal, she attacked the stalks in front of her.

Aldric's voice came over her shoulder. "I know you chose this because of Henry but you need to know that, at first, becoming what I am may be completely engrossing. It may take practice before you can see Henry and not disrupt your responsibilities."

Mara swung harder at the stalks in front of her. "Like what? I get that there are places like Nod and Hell where you slow time in order to give everyone else an advantage. But doesn't the rest of it just happen? What's so hard about what you do?"

Behind her, Aldric's feet shuffled to a halt and his deep laugh rumbled. "How big is the universe, Mara?"

Annoyed, she shrugged. "Infinite, I guess."

"As Time, you control the rotation of every planet in the universe. Picture eternity as a giant grandfather clock. You will be the center cog, the piece that makes the others move."

"How is that possible? No one could control all of that."

"It is only possible when you become Time itself," Aldric said.

"Phhhft." Mara narrowed her eyes and focused her frustration on the stalks in front of her.

"Don't 'phhhft' me. This is what you signed up for."

"It sounds made up. I'm still wondering if I'm going to wake up in my bedroom."

"Very soon, you will know for sure. Look." Aldric pointed at the tassels. "We've entered the last dark ring."

A hellhound ripped through the corn. Mara swiped with

the sickle, slicing its shoulder. One of its claws ripped across her chest before it rolled to the floor. Aldric decapitated it with the short sword. Mara's blood dripped to the packed dirt. The corn around them came alive, rustling ominously from all directions.

Aldric eyed the blood that oozed from her wound, discoloring what remained of her gray dress. "Run, Mara! Run! Kill anything in your path!"

"But—"

"I'm right behind you. *Run!*"

With a burst of speed that came from some panicked recess of her soul, Mara launched forward, weaving between the stalks. Every step sent pain rippling through her destroyed feet, and the open wound at her chest. The leaves sliced her skin into ribbons. The rustle of her body knocking into the stalks made an eerie din.

A hound leapt at her from the left. She swung the sickle, slicing through its neck. Ducking, she avoided another from straight ahead. She could see the bull's-eye. Almost there.

Aldric's scream brought her up short of her goal. She turned back, a soul-shattering wail crossing her lips. A hellhound had ripped open Aldric's abdomen. His sword was stuck in a second and a third was approaching his bloodied face.

Run, he mouthed before the hound's teeth came down around his throat.

Tears burned in her eyes, but she pushed on. As she broke through into the bull's-eye, she told herself that she must survive. With Aldric gone, who knew what would happen if she didn't? His soul was in God's hands. Now Mara had to make sure he hadn't died in vain.

Frantically, her eyes swept the ground for the scroll. There, among the browning stems, she saw its ancient parchment. She dove for it, ignoring the pain of the stalks she barreled through to get there. On her hands and knees, she dropped the sickle and unrolled the scroll.

Corn rustled behind her. She rolled to her back. A hound leapt from the shadows. She kicked at it, its claws digging into her legs.

"I claim the prize of eternity," she yelled. "I am the beginning and the end, the drifting sand and the source of wind. I am the stars and the turn of the moon. The bringer of dawn, power mine, I am sworn!"

The ground shook, an earthquake that originated from within her. The hound backed away, whimpering. A ray of light poured from the sky into her heart, filling her with a liquid fire that closed off her throat and crushed her from the inside out. Just when she thought she would die a second death, her insides adapted, growing, growing, growing, big enough to contain the energy from above.

She stood, balancing on shaking legs, moving in time to the rumbling earth. The corn around her flattened to the ground. She faced God and Lucifer, still waiting at the edge of the field.

"I win," she said to Lucifer, but her voice was a deep, hollow echo.

Her face lifted to the heavens. A star fell toward her, then right through her. As it passed, she noted the direction it spun, the speed, how planets revolved around it. Each of the planets had its own rotation, its own speed, its own time. She learned them one by one. The entire solar system, like music connected in perfect harmony, flowed through her new immortal body. More. More. More. The galaxy, then the universe poured into her. She was the clockwork. She was the machine that powered it all. *Tick, turn, tick.* It all worked together.

Spreading her arms, she opened herself up, and invited it all in.

TWENTY-NINE

THE SOULKEEPERS

Malini paced along the road in front of the bison exhibit. Lillian, Jesse, the twins, and Jacob lined up, eyes fixed on her, waiting for instructions. Gideon, in his cat form, paced at their feet. Helpers Master Lee and Grace had continued their search for the last Soulkeeper and Ethan remained in Eden caring for Dane. They had strict orders of what to do if Malini and the others failed. They were to return to Eden and keep the Soulkeeper line alive until a new Healer rose to power. Malini prayed they'd never have to use that particular backup plan.

With a deep breath, Malini addressed the group gathered on the side of the road. "Today, we face the greatest challenge of our lifetimes. The devil himself plans to rip a hole in this dimension and flood our world with his minions. Months ago, a Watcher described Lucifer's plan as bringing on the next great flood, only this time humans would perish while Watchers survived. We think he plans to bring forth a Watcher army with the intention of destroying life as we know it. We cannot allow any Watchers to escape this property."

Samantha reached for Bonnie's hand for comfort. Jesse adjusted his glasses, a fidgety ball of energy. Lillian stood statuesque at his side.

"There is a team of physicists here under Watcher influence. If possible, restrain or incapacitate the humans. They are not acting in their own will. We have reason to believe that Dr. Silva has joined Lucifer's ranks. Do not exercise restraint when dealing with Dr. Silva. Kill anything with black blood. Do not hesitate."

Lillian squirmed, gripping the handle of her knife in the sheath on her leg. She flashed a forlorn look at Gideon, whose green cat's eyes bore into Malini's.

"You both heard me correctly." Malini waited while her words sunk in. The Soulkeepers glanced at each other, some with greater understanding than others.

"I've been studying the satellite view of the area and I see three potential entry points to the Tevatron. The loop is four miles long, but the CDF Control Room is here." Malini pointed with a stick at the drawing she'd made in the dirt based on the images from her phone.

"Gideon, Jacob, and I will go there. It's the most likely place for Lucifer to plan the sacrifice. We'll launch an offensive and attempt to take the crew out before the ceremony takes place. If we fail and the tear occurs, there are two subterranean access points, here and here." She drew X's over boxes on her drawing. "Those access points are the most likely places Watchers will attempt to exit if they get through. The twins will take the east, Lillian and Jesse, the west. Kill anything that gets through."

Bonnie and Sam huddled together nervously. Bonnie gripped a medieval-looking spiked club in her hands, a weapon they'd brought from Eden. It was blessed and would cause damage beyond the force the twins could wield. Just like Lillian's knives and the spiked chain Jesse brought, the material would burn a Watcher on contact. Malini hoped it would be enough to hold back the flood if she and Jacob weren't able to turn the water off at the tap. "Any questions?" she asked, eyeing them one last time.

Gideon leaped toward her, transforming into an angel in a grotesque twist of flesh. When he was done, he stood toe to toe with Malini, his eyes challenging her. "I have a question," he said into her face.

"Spill it," Malini said, fists going to her hips.

"How do you know? How do you know that Abigail has turned herself over to Lucifer? How do you know this isn't all the devil's elaborate trap?" He snapped the words at Malini, his voice rising with the tide of anger that reddened his face.

Malini shook her head. "I know because it's my job to know. When I became Healer I was given the ability to determine the greater good."

"The greater good for humanity, not the greater good for us."

Malini nodded and lowered her voice. "You know that's how it works, Gideon. You taught me that."

He brought one fist down into the other with such force it made Malini take a step back. "You are a sixteen-year-old girl who has been a Healer for less than a year. Maybe this time you are wrong. Maybe this time there has been a mistake." His eyes cast downward.

Malini shook her head. "There's no mistake, Gideon."

His upper body collapsed and he caught himself on his knees.

Stepping forward, Malini placed her healing hand on his shoulder. "I can't force you to trust me. I know this is hard for you but I also know that this time I'm right. The future is always changing based on our choices. I can't see every possible scenario. But I do know that in this case, this plan will lead to the best outcome." She turned her face toward the others. "You have to trust in my abilities as a Healer. If you don't, we're as good as doomed. We might as well go in fighting blind."

Gideon shrugged her hand off his shoulder.

"I need to know if you are with us or against us," she said to him.

The angel ruffled his wings. The air around him sparked and crackled. "I told you before, I'm with you," he said reluctantly. He spat the words and refused to meet Malini's eyes.

She steeled her resolve and rose to her full height, facing the Soulkeepers, who watched Gideon nervously. "This is my guidance to you as your Healer, not my personal will. If we are to have any hope of defeating evil, we have to work together. That means you are in one hundred percent or not at all. You can't do this halfway. Are you in?"

One by one they nodded their heads.

"It's time. We go on foot. Spread out and don't get caught." Malini turned and used the car to launch herself over the fence into the buffalo exhibit. Jacob followed. Gideon lagged behind but eventually moved in their direction.

"Wow, Malini, great speech. 'You're either with me or against me.' Damn. I didn't know you had it in you." Jacob smiled in her direction.

"It's not funny, Jacob. We're going into battle. People could die. Did you see how they looked at me? They think I came up with this plan on a whim. They don't respect me. They don't trust me."

Jacob shook his head. "That's not true. It's not about you, Malini. Everyone knows you're brilliant. They're scared. Gideon's heart is broken and the twins and Jesse have almost no experience with this type of thing. I know it's hard but you can't take it personally."

"That's easy to say but I have a hard enough time trusting in my abilities. They're right, Jacob. I'm only sixteen and I'm not sure that everything's going to be okay. People might get hurt. People might die, and it might be my fault. But this is the only way I know how to lead. My gifts tell me this is the right thing to do."

Jacob scanned the horizon, watching the bison eye them cautiously from their watering hole. "Don't step in it," he said.

"I don't have a choice. I have to do what I have to do."

He yanked her arm toward him, pulling her against his chest. She narrowly missed a steaming pile of dung. "I meant literally," he said.

"Oh, thanks." Silently, she worked her hand down into his. As they crossed the miles toward the small building that marked the entrance to the control center, Malini glanced back occasionally to check that Gideon was still there. He was, but he made no effort to catch up. If he'd wanted to, he could travel through the light the way that Dr. Silva could travel through shadow, but he didn't.

"He's there, Malini," Jacob said, tugging her forward. "He told you he would be. Don't expect him to be happy about it."

When they reached the entry point, Jacob made short

work of the lock with the water from his flask. Gideon showed up just as they approached the elevator.

"How is this going to work, Malini? There's nowhere to hide. As soon as we step on that elevator, they're going to know we're here."

Malini lowered her eyes. "Yes. We won't get in undetected. Lucifer's been tracking me for weeks." She placed one finger over her lips and turned toward Gideon. *Disappear*, she mouthed.

He did, dissolving into the light that poured through the windows. The elevator doors opened and Malini stepped inside, pulling Jacob in behind her. She pressed a button on the panel. With a jerk, they descended below the Earth's surface.

Nervous energy poured off of Jacob, who positioned himself slightly in front of Malini, his fingers never leaving the top of the flask he'd tucked in his waistband.

After a ridiculously slow ride, the thick metal doors opened.

Dr. Silva stood on the other side, her face an icy sculpture of fury. Her eyes narrowed at Malini, the illusion fading to the slit pupils of a Watcher. "You have to leave, *now*."

THIRTY

JACOB AND ABIGAIL

J acob leaped forward, the water from his flask freezing into the blade that was perfectly weighted for his hand. "Back off, Abigail. I don't want to kill you, but I will if you come near her, I swear." He crouched defensively.

"Kill me?" She laughed. "Do you think you could?" Her body twisted into shadow and reappeared behind him, inside the elevator. "I'm very hard to kill, Jacob."

Lifting Malini by the waist with one arm, Jacob sprung from the compartment. "Shouldn't you be somewhere doing Lucifer's bidding?" he said through his teeth.

"As it so happens, Lucifer was called away," Abigail said.

Malini stepped around Jacob's body. "That is his weakness, isn't it? Only one place at a time. While he's gone, why don't you tell us how to stop this from happening?"

Abigail strode from the elevator, lighter than air. When she floated like that it was easy to tell she wasn't human. It reminded Jacob of the first night he'd seen her, outside his bedroom window.

"This can't be stopped," Abigail said. "You are fools to try. A team of humans has been altering this facility to prepare for this sacrifice for weeks. The place is swarming with the influenced and the Watchers who manage them."

"We're not leaving, Abigail," Malini said.

Pivoting on her heel, Abigail's black cloak flowed organically with her, the cloth arcing as if it had a life of its own before settling around her ankles. Her platinum-blonde hair floated to rest at the center of her back. "Then follow me," she said over her shoulder. "If you refuse to leave, you might as well have a front-row seat for the show." She walked away from them, toward a railing at the end of the hallway.

Jacob pleaded with Malini in hushed tones, "Why do I have a feeling this isn't going to end well? Maybe we should leave. We're no good to anyone dead."

Malini shook her head but offered no explanation. Jacob walked to the railing, following in Abigail's footsteps. His breath caught in his throat when he saw the scene beyond. In a pit three stories deep, a monstrous black machine loomed against the concrete. A stone altar had been welded to a steel platform at the center. A room the size of a school gymnasium held a row of computers, and panels of toggle switches, buttons, and blinking lights. A dozen humans buzzed between the electronic equipment, while other humans worked to perfect the platform and altar.

As promised, there were Watchers, too. Jacob looked down upon Auriel and his mouth filled with the taste of maggots. A second later, he recognized Cord on the other end of the room. He pointed them out to Malini. Others came and went with the humans, only discernible from this distance by their other-worldly beauty.

With a grave purse of his lips, Jacob watched Abigail descend the stairwell and join the chaos below. "She isn't telling them we're here."

"She's still hoping we'll leave," Malini said.

"Why? I don't get it. She either wants us dead or she doesn't."

Malini brought her lips to Jacob's ear. "No matter what Abigail says or does, don't think for a minute that she wants you to see her like this, Jacob. Her illusion covers loads of imperfections, but her feelings for you are not one of them. She doesn't want us to see her do this and she doesn't want to be the cause of our deaths."

"Ironic considering she's the focal point of a plan to bring about the end of the world," Jacob whispered.

Malini nodded.

An explosion of sound and light turned their attention toward the pit. A pillar of red, sparkling smoke dissipated into a chorus of coughs from the surrounding humans. Lucifer's blond curls and white smile beamed from the center. The tailored suit he wore made the corncob he nonchalantly juggled in his left hand seem out of place.

"What's with the corncob?" Jacob whispered. Malini placed a finger over his lips.

"Don't fight until I tell you to," Malini cautioned under her breath. "Go along."

Lucifer's voice boomed from below. "The inconvenience of my absence has been rectified." He pointed the cob at Abigail. "Tell me good news. I need a pick-me-up after what I've just been through."

216 G. P. CHING

Abigail glided to his side and whispered something in his ear. Her eyes flicked up toward Jacob and her finger pointed at Malini. Lucifer grinned.

"This *is* good news." He pointed a hand at Jacob and Malini. "Look who's joined the fun. Come on down, kids. You won't want to miss this."

Jacob glanced back toward the elevator only to find a thorn bush had erupted from the concrete and filled the hallway.

"You won't be going back that way." He shook his head and coaxed them forward with his hand. "Cord, Auriel, would you mind escorting our guests to the viewing area."

"What was that you were saying, Malini, about Abigail not wanting us to die?" Jacob said.

Shhhh.

The Watchers materialized to their left and right, grabbing Jacob and Malini's elbows and pushing both forward. Down the industrial metal stairs, Jacob faltered, catching himself every third step, trying to keep up with the Watcher's rough handling. If Malini was afraid, Jacob couldn't tell. Her face was completely blank. He tried to trust in her bravery, that she'd know what to do, but his heart betrayed him, pounding in his chest. Every drop of water within twenty yards called to him. It was all he could do not to use it. When they reached Lucifer, Auriel and Cord pushed him forward and he crashed to the concrete floor at the devil's feet.

Malini tilted her face up. "What is this, Lucifer? What are you doing?"

He glanced around the room laughing, his narrowed eyes landing back on Malini. "The Healer wants to know what I'm doing." He lifted her by the back of her T-shirt. "Don't mess with me, Malini. You know exactly what's going on here, and you have just become a part of it."

Lucifer jerked Malini into a chair that manifested itself in front of the platform. The black wood splintered, erupting grotesque gray arms that wrapped around her chest and held her in place. Dead arms of the damned that stunk of decay and sulfur. She turned her head to avoid the stench.

Jacob reached out to the water, but Malini shook her head.

"Don't try it, Horseman," Lucifer said. He grabbed Jacob by the neck and forced him into a chair next to Malini. Struggling to stand, Jacob fought against the corpse arms that forced him painfully into the chair.

He turned his face toward Malini, noticing the fear that had taken up residence in the corners of her eyes, and he wondered if any of this was part of the plan. She looked away quickly. Was she afraid of what he might see? Did she have doubts about her own plan?

Lucifer clapped his hands together. "Places, people. These Soulkeepers are like bugs, once you see one, the place will be lousy with them before you know it. Let's make them fallen heroes." He jogged up to the platform. "Abigail, it's time."

Gideon watched from his place on the stair landing. He'd blended into the light as Malini had asked but it was becoming harder and harder not to act. Malini and Jacob, captured and constrained, would be useless if the portal was opened. The Soulkeepers couldn't afford to lose their Healer now, not with their numbers so low.

It all came down to trust. If he trusted that a sixteen-year-old Healer could lead, then he should wait for her signal. Her role made her privy to information she couldn't always share. She must know what he didn't and he had to support her role.

But the truth was he didn't fully trust her abilities. It wasn't simply because she was young. It was because she treated Abigail as if she were a hopeless case. When you loved someone, it was impossible to believe they were hopeless. He knew if he could talk to her, he could save her.

As an angel, it should have been easy for him to have faith. Maybe his distance from heaven had changed him. The idea of spending eternity with Abigail, with or without heaven, wasn't without merit. He'd thought about falling, too. They could live in Paris as she had, walking their own path between Heaven and Hell. It might work.

The main level suddenly teemed with influenced humans and Watchers. They'd passed around black hooded cloaks that they donned over their clothing. The floor became a sea of black robes, ceremoniously facing Lucifer on the platform. The devil folded his hands like a groom waiting for his bride.

Gideon's heart ached. Abigail was the bride.

Descending the steps, Gideon carefully navigated the crowd. He remained transparent but knew that his scent might give him away. If he passed too close to an astute Watcher, he was doomed. Still he made his way to the front, stepping up beside Malini and placing his hand on hers. She didn't look down at the pressure, but when her fingers curled, he knew she felt his touch.

Yes, Gideon? he heard in his head. He hadn't known Malini could communicate telepathically, but he was sure it was her.

I think it's because you used the stone. This is new for me, too.

We have to fight. We have to get you out of here, Gideon thought.

No. It's not time yet. Plus, you know as well as I do that you won't leave her. Whatever Abigail does today, you need to see it.

Then, I should stop her?

No.

Abigail entered the room, escorting a young girl who Gideon recognized from Paris. He'd never met her personally but he was sure it was Stephanie Westcott. He'd seen her picture in the paper when she'd gone missing. The girl walked willingly to the platform. Abigail trailed behind, her eyes empty and soulless.

I've got to stop her.

You can't. Even if you try, you won't succeed.

I can't watch this.

You have to. I'll need you when it's over.

Gideon's fingers clutched Malini's hand.

I know you've thought about falling, Gideon. Don't. After today, Abigail won't be the same. You'll give up your salvation and she will slip through your fingers.

Stephanie climbed onto the platform. Her face was brave, sad but resolved, as if she had accepted her fate. With an eerie calm, she lay down on the stone slab and turned her head to face Malini and Jacob. Abigail stepped behind the altar, in front of the machine that was now emitting a loud roar.

Gideon tried to force his thoughts into Abigail's head. *Run! Fight! Don't do this!* She'd never been able to read his mind and the blank look on her face was a clear indication that any connection they'd had was completely gone.

Lucifer raised his hands. Fire swirled from his palms, forming a sphere of red and gold that encompassed Abigail, Stephanie, and the machine behind them. The smell of sulfur filled the room. A chorus of moans joined the mechanical roar. As the sound grew louder, Gideon realized it was the screams of the Damned, their tormented souls calling out from the pits of hell. Lucifer fueled his magic with their suffering.

The hooded forms behind him began to chant. Out of the corner of his eye, he watched them rock back and forth, a hideous congregation cheering on the ceremony. Gripping Malini's hand for strength, he looked back up toward Abigail, the ache in his chest threatening to consume him completely.

The lights blinked into darkness, as if all of the power was drained into Abigail, into what she was about to do. She lifted a knife from the altar, an obsidian blade glinting in the light of Lucifer's circling magic. Of course it was obsidian. They weren't just sacrificing Stephanie's body; they were sacrificing her soul. She would pass to neither Heaven nor Hell. It would be the saddest of conclusions, doomed to oblivion.

Abigail's hands came together on the hilt of the blade. She raised it over her head.

No! NO! Gideon reached his free hand toward her, silently begging for her to stop. Malini's grip kept him rooted to the spot. She was right; there was nothing he could do. Abigail was a shell, completely given over to Lucifer's will. Her eyes were vacant.

Stephanie, that poor girl, stared right at him, as if she could see him crouched next to Malini's chair. Her ice-blue eyes held a deep understanding, soulfulness he never expected to see in one so young.

Stephanie's lips moved, but it was Abigail's voice that

reached Gideon's ears. "Some things are more important than love. Some things are more important than any of us. I'm sorry, Gideon."

The knife plunged into Stephanie's chest. Black blood sprayed from the wound, showering Abigail, whose body shrunk. Her hair darkened and her mouth opened to a scream. But the scream was a human scream and, as Gideon watched in horror, Abigail became Stephanie and Stephanie became Abigail. The illusion faded away as the black blood ran from the sacrifice's body.

Forgetting where he was, Gideon dropped Malini's hand and let out a battle cry.

THIRTY-ONE

AFTERMATH

Gideon's howl went unnoticed in the chaos that ensued. Stephanie, released from Abigail's influence, eyed the knife in her hand and the body in front of her. Her mouth fell open and her chest pumped out a scream that Gideon could see but couldn't hear over the shaking walls, the roar of the machine, and the cacophony of voices.

One voice did rise above the rest. "*No!*" Lucifer boomed. He tried to run forward but his magic, the revolving flames, kept him from the sacrifice. Pounding his fists against the sphere of tortured souls, he narrowed his eyes at Abigail's blood dripping to the floor. Black hoods scattered, trying to avoid Lucifer's wrath.

Gideon, now! Free Jacob and me, now.

Manifesting, Gideon's light sent the crowd into a panic. He shattered the chairs, tossing the corpse arms away from them. Jacob leaped into action, a sword of ice forming in his hands as soon as his feet hit the floor.

"Can I kill something now?" he yelled to Malini.

She nodded her head. "Anything with black blood. Gideon, come with me. We have to get to Abigail."

Gideon's eyes widened. He clapped his hands together and a sword of blue fire erupted between his palms. With a surge of his powerful wings he jumped to the platform, swinging the blade at Lucifer's waist. It passed through the devil's abdomen and harmlessly out the other side, leaving a trail of black smoke.

"You have got to be kidding me!" Lucifer yelled, turning on his attacker. He backhanded Gideon, sending him flying off the platform. He landed next to Jacob, who was frantically slicing the shoulders of anything in a black robe. He kicked someone who bled red in the gut, sending them flying backward while simultaneously plunging his blade into a Watcher behind him.

"Gideon, what are you doing? Get up there and help Malini!" Jacob yelled. He twirled and sliced across the chest of another black robe. Red. "Damn!" he said, kicking toward the man's gut.

Still seeing stars, Gideon shook his head and pulled himself up. Of course he couldn't fight fire with fire. Taking to the air, he rolled energy in his palms. Not the fire of destruction all angels could rain down, but the power that came from deep within, a combination of faith, hope, and love. To humans, it was a healing power, but Gideon hoped it would have the opposite effect on Lucifer. He hurled it at the center of Lucifer's back. Jackpot! The devil writhed in pain and turned away from Abigail and Stephanie.

"That's right," Gideon said. "Let's play." He dodged a fireball flung from Lucifer's hand. The devil's eyes turned yellow, his illusion faltering with his anger. Gideon let forth a barrage of blue energy, rolling through the air above the crowded pit.

The other Soulkeepers swooped in from their stations to help. Below him, Lillian diced up Watchers with Jesse, who popped in and out of existence, pulling off hoods and incapacitating the humans in the group. The twins arrived on the other side of the crowd, melded together in the form of a giant. Swinging their club, they launched a Watcher into the air. Gideon dodged the flying body, just as Lucifer regrouped and opened fire.

A ball of flame singed Gideon's wing, sending him tumbling to the platform. He landed in a heap of feathers and muscle behind Malini. She was halfway into the sphere Lucifer had created around the altar, her skeletal hand holding open a window that she carefully stepped through.

Gideon flipped to his feet, pounding Lucifer with another purple sphere. The devil broke from his illusion entirely, becoming a towering mass of horns, claws, and cloven hooves. He returned fire, sending Gideon somersaulting off the platform. The fire tore through the bones of his left wing, sending searing pain through him. Broken, the wing dangled uselessly.

Lucifer's lips peeled back from a grotesque fang-filled grin. He jumped down from the platform and straddled Gideon's body. "I'll enjoy crushing you." He licked his lips with his forked tongue.

There was no escape. Gideon crab-walked backward, his white blood leaving a glittering trail across the floor. Faced with oblivion, Gideon had only one thought: *Abigail*. On the platform, Malini's healing hand lowered toward her chest. He prayed with everything he had left that somehow it would work. Even if he should die, he prayed Abigail would live. Her surviving would make it all worth it. He collapsed to the floor and looked up into the face of the devil, his heart peaceful and ready for what may come.

Everything went white. Lucifer turned his face toward the small sun that glowed from above, shielding his eyes with his hand. All around him, the fighting stopped. Soulkeepers and fallen alike stood dumbstruck at the power, light, and warmth that shone down. Gideon stared into the light, equally awestruck, although he knew exactly who it was above him.

A soft voice cut through the sound of the machine, barely a whisper yet louder than anything in the room. "Your debt has been repaid."

A beam of light hit Gideon's body, a lightning bolt of energy that came with a clap of thunder. The room washed away. Blinded, he let himself go. The warmth and heat washed through him, stripping away the pain of his broken wing, the sight of the death around him, and the hum from the platform. Everything dissolved but peace and light.

Then it all came back to him.

WITHIN THE SPHERE, MALINI LOWERED HER HEALING hand toward Abigail's chest. She couldn't heal Watcher flesh, but her gut told her it was the right thing to do. Before her palm touched, a white light blinded her, causing her to pull her hand up short. She forgot herself in the awesome power that filled the pit. God hovered above them all. Her commanding presence burned like the sun. A bolt of lightning flowed from her into Gideon and Abigail. The power cut right through the rotating red sphere, and blew Lucifer off of Gideon like a flake of dust.

Thrown back from the force of it, Malini watched in wonder as Abigail's body seized with the power flowing through her. Abigail's black scaly skin smoothed to a peachy flesh tone. Her leathery wings dissolved under her back. Straight, platinum hair darkened into honey curls. The hard features of her face softened, and her body changed. Shorter, rounder, softer. The lightning changed Abigail into something almost...

"Human," Malini whispered.

When the light stopped and chaos erupted on the floor once again, Malini lowered her healing hand onto Abigail's chest. The new body trembled under her touch. A charge of electricity flowed from her hand into Abigail's new human heart. Once and again her body flailed on the altar, until her mouth opened and Abigail took her first breath of air as a mortal.

Beneath Malini's hand, Abigail's lungs expanded and contracted. Her heart beat strong and true against her palm. And although the wound from the obsidian blade was difficult to heal, Malini focused until the hole closed. The black blood turned red between her burnt fingers.

Abigail's eyes flipped open, soft blue eyes that were beautiful but ordinary. They locked on Malini as the red blood seeped from under her hand and dripped to the platform below.

"No!" Abigail screamed, clutching the blood to her chest. She sat up, her face terrified by the trail of crimson that trickled from the altar toward the machine. Malini realized what was happening and reached for the rolling drop of blood, trying to stop its progress with her palm. Abigail did, too, but she dropped from the altar awkwardly, her new human body learning to move all over again. Both hands fell short of their goal.

Only a dribble got through. It worked its way under Malini's palm and channeled into the machine, still pulsating with the magic of the sphere. For a moment, nothing changed. Then the sphere opened, melting into the platform. A hurricane-force wind blew out from behind the altar. Malini tripped backward, grabbing Stephanie and Abigail by the arms and tumbling into the pit.

The room shook. The earth split, cracking the altar and the platform down the middle. The machine peeled back, a black hole tearing through the center to reveal an army of Watchers in formation. Nod. The wall unraveled behind the platform and Lucifer's battle cry rose from the place where he recovered against the wall of the pit.

Then all Hell broke loose.

THIRTY-TWO

INVASION

G ideon tried to react to the army of Watchers marching into the pit, but his body and mind fumbled on the floor. Jacob's hand appeared in front of his face.

"Let me help you," Jacob said.

Pulled to his feet, Gideon couldn't keep his balance and fell forward, barely catching himself with his hands in a kind of weak push-up before his face slapped the floor.

"You don't have wings anymore," Jacob yelled, yanking him back up to his feet. He thrust a bow and quiver into his hands. "No time to celebrate. Take these. A human tried to kill me with them earlier. Lucky for us, he didn't succeed."

Slinging the quiver over his shoulder, he allowed Jacob to drag him back against the staircase. Jacob propped him up in the corner and helped him string an arrow.

A Watcher came too close and Jacob spun around and sliced it in half. "Give it a try, Gideon. That one there." Jacob pointed at a Watcher who'd slipped past Lillian and was advancing toward them.

The string pulled to his cheek, Gideon did his best to aim at the Watcher and released. The arrow fell short of its target, skimming harmlessly across the floor. The Watcher stepped over it.

"Whoa! You really are human." Jacob dodged the Watcher's talons and thrust his blade through its chest. He kicked the body away and returned to Gideon to help him string another arrow. "I'll tell you what. Shoot if you have to, but if anything gets too close, reach behind you and poke it in the eye with an arrow."

Gideon nodded. His throat was too tight and dry to respond.

Jacob winked then launched himself into the advancing army, wielding his blade. Black limbs flew from the trail Jacob forged and a head rolled toward Gideon's feet. He flattened against the wall when it melted into a pool of black ooze near his toes.

His bow rattled in his shaking hands. His arm ached from pulling back the string. And for the first time in his existence, Gideon was afraid the way a human might be afraid, knowing that he had only one fragile and mortal life. His new heart pounded against his ribcage, and his skin felt strange. A drip of sweat hit his fingers drawn to his cheek. He wiped under his eye and focused in on the brutal battle.

The Soulkeepers didn't lack for skill. Jacob plowed through a dozen Watchers with superhuman precision. But the Watchers poured from the portal tear and overran the pit like ants. Malini picked up the obsidian blade and was trying her best to protect Stephanie and another human woman

Gideon didn't recognize. They'd escaped the onslaught by hiding under the platform.

The twins, melded together in the form of a giant, held their own but the fatigue was evident in the hesitation before each swing of their club. Lillian guarded the base of the steps, knives flashing and body covered in black blood. The close combat made it more difficult for the Watchers to use magic, but not impossible. Jesse strategically materialized anywhere a Watcher rolled a fireball, making use of the chain in his hands. The method worked. So far none of the Soulkeepers were burned, even though several Watchers had burned each other.

Gideon had to help. He drew the bow, aiming at the crowd of Watchers again, and released the string. The arrow hit his target but only succeeded in sinking an inch or so into the Watcher's shoulder. The beast yanked the arrow from its black flesh, growling like an animal. Claws and teeth flashed toward Gideon's face. With his human eyes, everything happened so fast, he didn't have time to react. He thought he was doomed until the Watcher's head snapped back, pulling its talons up short.

"A little help, Gideon!" Jesse yelled from behind the Watcher, his chain burning into the dark flesh.

Gideon reached into the quiver and grabbed an arrow. Throwing his weight forward, he stabbed the Watcher in the eye, his hand driving through until his palm hit scaly skin. The body dropped to the floor.

"Sweet!" Jesse broke apart and disappeared.

Gideon strung another arrow. His muscles ached and he couldn't believe how heavy he felt, as if gravity had become three hundred times stronger with his humanity. Not to mention that the stomach of his new body twisted uncomfortably, sending heaves of air up his throat. His skin prickled like it was too tight. How did humans survive like this every day? All he wanted to do was to find someplace to hide.

Another Watcher broke from the crowd and headed for him. Drawing the bow, Gideon aimed for the eye and pulled as hard as he could on the string. His muscles burned but he waited until the beast was closer to let go. The arrow cut through the Watcher's head, dropping it where it stood. Gideon blew out a breath. A mixture of pride and bravery flooded him. Surprise, surprise, his human body was capable of other feelings and this one was huge. Gideon could do this. He could help.

Turning toward the stairs, he slung his bow over his shoulder and jumped. The first time he wasn't able to grab the railing but the second time he hooked his toe on the middle stair and wrapped his fingers around the steel. He hoisted himself up and over onto the mesh stairway behind Lillian. From above, he had the advantage. He aimed into the crowd, scanning the faces of the Soulkeepers to see who needed the most help.

True to form, Lucifer stood on the platform shouting commands to his army but avoiding the fray. Below him, Malini's healing hand was burnt up to the shoulder, the glove on her right hand shredded, as she fought from her position under the platform. Stephanie Westcott cowered behind her. The other human had taken over with the obsidian blade.

Who was she? For a moment, Gideon paused, one eye focused down the length of the arrow. The human captivated him. Her honey-blonde waves bounced over her shoulder as she thrust the blade into one Watcher then the next. She was soft but strong, vulnerable but brave. The way she dove at the Watchers, it was like she was a Soulkeeper.

He aimed at the Watcher closest to her and fired. His arrow pierced its head and the woman lifted her face toward him, following the arrows flight. Gideon's human heart skipped. For a moment there was nothing in the world but blue eyes and pale skin. Abigail. She was alive and she was human! She turned back toward the fight, taking out another Watcher. Lucifer's army closed in all around her.

Gideon reached for another arrow but his hand came up empty. He'd used them all.

"Looks like you could use some help."

On the platform beside him, Mara grinned as if she had a pocket full of hand grenades. Well, it looked like Mara, except for the eyes. Her eyes sparkled with a thousand spinning stars, supernovas exploding in distant galaxies. Gideon took a large step back.

She shook her head. "How things have changed." Her voice held a hollow depth it hadn't before. "Don't worry, Gideon. Once a Soulkeeper, always a Soulkeeper."

Raising her hands, she focused on the chaos below, those glowing eyes calculating the hole between Earth and Nod, Lucifer's place on the platform, and the Watchers in the pit. Lucifer pointed at her and opened his mouth to say something but he never got the chance. A blast emanated from Mara, a wave of thick air that washed over the fight below, all the way back to the Watchers that poured from the portal.

The power ricocheted back into Mara. Every Watcher her magic touched slowed down. Lucifer's lips moved to utter a curse that came out too slow to be understood.

Mara flipped him the finger. "Suck it, Satan. Times have changed. Things are 'bout to get real tedious for you."

The battle waged on, but with the Watchers fighting in slow motion, the Soulkeepers had no trouble slaying them all. Watcher cowardice kicked in and those who were able to retreat, including Lucifer himself, slipped back into Nod.

Jacob attacked. "Kill them, kill them all," he yelled, running toward the opening.

With a wave of his hand, Lucifer collapsed the portal, saving what remained of his forces from annihilation.

The earth shook. Piece by piece the machine came apart, sending huge chunks of metal toppling into the pit.

"Run," Mara said with a grin. "Amazingly, you'll have just enough time to make it out alive. Take the elevator."

Lillian barreled up the stairs, grabbing Gideon's arm and rushing him toward the elevator. While she hacked through the thorn bush in the hall, Gideon watched Malini usher Abigail and Stephanie toward the west exit with Jacob and the twins. Jesse appeared beside him and followed Lillian into the opening doors.

They shot toward the surface as the earth crumbled around them.

THIRTY-THREE

CHANGES

Bursting from the small building, Gideon ran toward the road behind Lillian and Jesse, dodging shingles that shook from the roof. Glass exploded from the window and cinder blocks pounded the dirt behind his feet. Gideon searched over his shoulder for Abigail, but the subterranean access point she'd exited from was far away and the shaking made it impossible to see clearly.

Lillian grabbed his shoulder. "Don't look back. The whole thing is going under. We've got to move!"

Out of the corner of his eye, Gideon saw the building they'd just exited implode. Metal and concrete folded in on itself and the widening crater swallowed it whole. With her Soulkeeper speed, Lillian could have easily outrun him but she stayed close. He did as she said, pumping his arms and focusing on the landscape ahead. They'd almost reached the fence to the bison exhibit when he realized he couldn't return the way they'd come. Behind the fence, the bison stampeded across the prairie, frightened by the earthquake. His fragile human body would be crushed.

"I can't go through there. I need to go around!" Gideon yelled.

"This way." Lillian hung left, following the fence.

At a full run, they sped toward the cars. An explosive boom threw Gideon forward, sending him skidding across the grass. With his cheek plastered in the dirt, trees toppled beside him and the ground rumbled below his flesh. The shaking threatened to tear him apart, then dissipated into a gentle vibration before stopping all together.

Slowly, he pushed himself up onto his hands and knees, and scanned the landscape for Lillian. Something was wrong with his face. An intense discomfort he'd never experienced before bloomed in his head and warm liquid dripped into his eye. Wiping his hand across his face, it came away red and gritty. Blood. Real human blood. He sat back on his heels, staring at the stuff he'd waited so long for. Pain. His cheekbone and forehead throbbed. He tapped his face lightly with the pads of his fingers, testing the edges of the place where he'd scraped himself.

A shadow crept over him. "Crap, Gideon, you're hurt," Lillian said. He heard a shuffle, then a cloth pressed against his forehead. "I wish I had something better than my sock but we have to slow the bleeding. I think you need stitches."

He pressed his hand over the compress and stumbled to his feet.

"Easy. Take your time."

"Are we safe?" Gideon slurred.

Lillian turned him around by the shoulders. The place where they'd come from, the land over the Tevatron, was a smoking crater. The ground just ended, the buildings, the machinery, gone, completely gone.

"We have to find Abigail." Gideon scanned the wreckage, cursing his inept human eyes. "Where's Jesse?"

"He took to the wind five minutes ago. We'll meet him at the car." She hooked her arm around the middle of Gideon's back, guiding him away from the wreckage. "I'm sure the rest of them will be there."

With Gideon's bloody knee and sore body, it took them more than fifteen minutes to hobble to the road. He spotted Jesse first, leaning up against the truck, comforting a trembling Stephanie Westcott. Jacob kneeled next to Malini, using his power to help heal her burnt skin. The twins stood up from the place they were resting near the front of the car. Separate, but not quite equal yet, they waved their hands in unison.

And then, there she was. Abigail wore the same thing as before, all black from her throat to her toes, but that's where the similarities ended. She was slightly shorter now, and her skirt pooled around her feet. The front of her dress was ripped from the knife that had killed her, but her change in size left the hole lower on her torso than it should have been. Her once straight, platinum hair had become a wavy mass of honey-colored softness. The hard edges of her face, shoulders, and hips had dulled into rounded curves.

Despite all of the changes, Gideon knew exactly who she was. The way she held herself, the shape of her eyes, the hesitant turn of her lip. It was Abigail. He wondered how he looked to her. Would she recognize him, face bloody and utterly wrecked? Would she still want him this way?

He stopped a good ten feet from her. Lillian left his side and crossed the road to hug Jacob.

"Why didn't you tell me?" he asked. The words hurled harshly from his mouth, reminding him of the hurt. He'd thought he'd lost her forever.

She took a tentative step forward. "I couldn't. I didn't know I'd be coming out of this alive. I knew you would stop me."

"Of course I would stop you. We were supposed to be in this together. After all the years we've spent waiting, how could you do this to me? How could you give up your life without knowing the consequences? What if you had died? Where would that leave me?" He pointed at his chest.

"It would leave you and the others alive. It would leave Lucifer foiled another day. It would leave hope for a better future for everyone."

"But you would be gone," Gideon said through his teeth.

"Yes." She nodded and looked at the ground.

Her face twisted as if she were in pain and before he could think about what he was doing he stepped toward her. Tears flowed from her cornflower blue eyes. An ache he'd never known before filled his chest and he reached out to her but stopped short of her shoulder. He returned his hand to his side.

"I'm sorry, Gideon," she said. "I'm sorry for everything. I did it for you but I realize now I should have told you. You should have been prepared for my death, even if it was necessary." She stepped closer. "But I'm not dead. I'm here and I'm human. If you can forgive me..."

She raised her hand and brought it toward his face. He jerked away. Her hand hung awkwardly in the air between them before coming to rest on her stomach.

Gideon swallowed hard. "Old habits die hard," he said. He reached for her fingers. The back of his hand grazed her abdomen as he pulled her hand toward him. "You feel cool." He smiled at her, his eye darting from their hooked fingers to her face. "They feel cool, Abigail. They don't burn."

Licking her lips, Abigail lifted her other hand to his face. This time he didn't jerk away. He felt the press of her palm next to his good eye. With his free hand, he reached for her hair, feeling his fingers thread into the silky warm softness at the base of her neck. She closed her eyes and sighed. A parade of tears dribbled down her cheek.

He used his thumb to wipe the tears from her jaw. "I will forgive you, Abigail, on one condition."

"What?"

"You never do anything like this again. We move forward together or not at all."

Her eyes opened and her full lips parted. She buried her hand in his hair. "Deal," she whispered.

Trembling, he pulled her to him, closing the remaining space between their bodies and lowering his lips onto hers. Whatever happened inside Gideon's human body could not be explained with mere words. His head filled with visions of Heaven. A tumble of electric sparks started in his chest and traveled south, setting off a chain reaction of sheer bliss. He pressed into her, believing he could never get enough of the feeling, or of her.

"Whoa!" Malini's voice called out. "Don't make me get Jacob to hose you down."

Reluctantly, Gideon pulled back.

"Yeah. Now that you guys are human, you need to learn when it's time to get a room," Jacob said.

Malini approached Gideon and peeled the sock from his forehead, now adhered to his skin with dried blood.

"Ow!"

"I need to touch it," she explained. She placed her left hand over his wound. At first the touch of her hand stung, but by the time she removed it, he could arch his brow without pain. He shifted and Malini reached for his knee, healing that too.

"Thank you, Malini." Gideon stepped back into Abigail, running his fingers through her hair. He turned his head toward Lillian. "I don't suppose you would lend Abigail and me your staff?"

Lillian giggled. "I would but you're human and not a Soul-keeper. It won't work for you anymore."

Abigail giggled and placed a hand over her mouth.

"What are you laughing at?" He scowled at her.

"Gideon, your face. It's priceless." She reached for his hand and led him to the truck.

"We'll take turns with the staffs and meet you back at the house," Malini said.

As he wedged himself onto the seat next to Abigail and Stephanie, Gideon sighed. Jacob turned from his spot behind the wheel and chuckled. "Don't worry, Gideon. It's only a three-hour drive."

Gideon rolled his head back against the seat. Abigail rested her head on his shoulder and they began their long journey home.

THIRTY-FOUR

NEW LIFE

B y the time Abigail arrived in Paris, she'd succeeded in persuading Stephanie Westcott not to share her experiences. The honest truth was she didn't remember anything between drinking Abigail's elixir and finding herself on the platform with the knife in her hand. The part she did remember, being held in a warehouse like an animal by a group of scaly skinned monsters with leathery wings, was a story no one would ever believe anyway. She promised to conceal the Soulkeepers' identities.

Jacob dropped her off a quarter mile from her house, then circled the block and watched as Stephanie climbed the Westcotts' porch stairs and rang the doorbell. Fran Westcott squealed with joy and hugged her daughter in the doorframe. Her father, brothers, and sisters rushed out and joined in welcoming Stephanie home. There would be questions and stories to be told, but for now all that mattered was that Stephanie was home.

"We have to free the rest of them," Abigail said to Jacob, wiping tears from her eyes. After thousands of years of not being able to cry, the waterworks were quickly becoming a habit. "I know where they are. Lucifer planned to farm them for food."

Gideon squeezed her hand.

"Let's get you two home and talk to Malini. She'll know what to do," Jacob said. A few minutes later, he pulled into the driveway of Abigail's sprawling Victorian home. She exited the truck, stretching her cramped legs.

"I never realized how creepy this place looks to human eyes," Abigail said.

Gideon lifted the corner of his mouth. "I was thinking it had a cheery glow now that my vision is three hundred times less accurate."

She laughed. "It must've looked like a morgue to you."

He nodded. "You were worth it."

"Come on, you two. This is the part where we debrief, remember?" Jacob jogged up the stairs to the door and let himself in without knocking.

Abigail knew she was expected to follow. She had to use the bathroom, a human sensation that was turning out to be downright inconvenient. Instead, she grabbed Gideon's hand.

"Everything has changed," she said.

His face sagged. "It has. But this is what we wanted. It's worth it, Abigail. To touch you, to hold you."

Gideon looked the same to her. Sure, his once fiery auburn hair was now more of a dark brown. And his emerald green eyes, still stunning, didn't glow from within like before. He was still taller than she was, and the muscles of his chest and arms stretched the black T-shirt he wore. To her, even with the differences, he looked the same.

She touched her face. "This body is weak. I don't think I can be a Helper anymore. I'm not a Soulkeeper. And I'm not..."

"You're just as beautiful as ever. More so because I know what you went through to earn that body."

She tried to look away but he gently tipped her face up to his.

"You're perfect to me. I want us to live out our lives together. I never want to be apart from you again."

Warmth flooded her heart, and for the first time in thousands of years, Abigail remembered what it was like to be in the presence of God. Love, pure and unconditional, poured into her, overflowing the cup of her heart.

"You're glowing," Gideon said. "In a human way." His smile was as perfect as when he was an angel. Maybe not as white, maybe not as straight, but perfect.

She placed her hand on his cheek.

His lips curled upward. "I'd like to buy you a diamond as big as your head and take you to some exotic locale where seagulls spelled out your name in a series of acrobatic dives. I'd like to get down on one knee and ask you to marry me. But, as it so happens, I don't have a human job and I can't conjure things out of the air anymore. All I have to offer you is me. A much-too-human and fragile me. Is it enough for you?"

Abigail tossed her arms around his neck and fell into him, as ungracefully as she'd ever moved. "Yes. Oh yes, it's enough. I know this won't be easy, but we wouldn't know what to do with our lives if it was, would we?"

He planted a kiss on her lips that left her feeling dizzy and more than interested in exploring the electric tingle in her belly. But the group of Soulkeepers who had gathered on the porch had other ideas.

Malini clapped her hands and whistled. "Hey, time to wrap up this mission, you two."

Her face strangely hot, Abigail nodded and followed her into the house, hand in hand with her soul mate.

❦

ABIGAIL STOOD IN THE CIRCLE OF SOULKEEPERS FEELING oddly out of place. She couldn't pass through the wall to get to the tower anymore, so the group gathered in the parlor. Lillian, Jacob, and Jesse stood near the fireplace but there was no fire. Without sorcery, it would take too long to light it. The twins sat on the sofa, hand in hand.

"I want all of you to know that the humans at Fermilab got out safely," Malini began. "Mara made sure that the timing of the collapse allowed them to escape to the main parking lot. None of them remembers anything. After being influenced for so long, it will be days before they're truly back to normal."

"What about the hole? Do we need to find a way to cover it up?"

"No need. They're calling it a sinkhole, a natural geological occurrence. The government shut down the Tevatron last September. No one was supposed to be in there anyway, so they're not looking too closely at the damage."

Awkwardly, Abigail stepped forward and gestured to get Malini's attention. She had nothing to offer but her human wits and the bit of information she'd gathered from her time in Lucifer's inner circle.

"What is it, Abigail? Just speak out, like we always do."

She lowered her head. "Right. There are more, like Stephanie. The Watchers have been collecting people all year. There are six warehouses of humans as far as Colorado." The passion in her voice increased with every word. "We have to free them before Lucifer has a chance to recover and take them to Nod."

"You know where these warehouses are?"

"Yes."

"Excellent. We'll split," Malini said. "Abigail, I want you to create a map of each location and assign a small team of Soulkeepers of your choosing to each. Tomorrow, we act on your plan. For now, everyone break. Get some rest." Malini looked at Abigail expectantly.

After a few moments, she got the hint. "You are all welcome to help yourself to a room upstairs." She spread her hands and glanced at the faces around the parlor.

There was a clatter of movement and appreciative gestures. The room emptied, aside from Gideon and Malini, who frantically texted on her phone.

"Grace and Master Lee are still in Arizona," Malini said. "They haven't answered my last text. We need someone to return to Eden to tell Dane and Ethan what's going on. We'll need Ethan for the mission, and if Dane's strong enough, it's time for him to go home to his family. The Michaels have been destroyed since he went missing."

"What about the last Soulkeeper?" Gideon asked.

Malini frowned. "The person is from Sedona, Arizona. I only had a first name, Cheveyo. I couldn't get an exact location and I'm not even sure if they are male or female. I didn't get the details of their search before we lost service but they confirmed they're giving up and coming home."

"Do you want me to pop down there and make sure they're okay?" Gideon asked, and then seemed to realize his mistake. "Oh, I can't anymore. Sorry, Malini."

"Don't worry, Gideon. Grace's last text indicated she was on a trail in the mountains. Terrible cell service there. I'm sure if we give her and Lee some time, they'll find their way back to us."

Nodding, Gideon rubbed Abigail's shoulder. "I'm going to go upstairs and take a long, hot, human shower."

Malini smiled. "I highly recommend it."

He walked down the hall and rounded the banister.

"What's on your mind, Abigail?" Malini asked, once he was out of sight.

Flopping down on the sofa, she let out a deep sigh. "I don't think you should use me for this. It's not like before. I have no power."

Malini leaned forward, meeting Abigail's stare. "Is that what's bothering you? You feel weak and powerless?"

"That and I'm not a Soulkeeper. I don't belong here anymore. Even my own house feels foreign. I'm not the same person. I'm vulnerable and clumsy. You shouldn't trust me with something as important as this."

Malini placed her small, brown hand on top of Abigail's. "If anything, I trust you more." Malini shook her head and walked to the window. "When you were a Watcher, I always wondered if you were truly loyal to the cause. You helped us, but I always had this feeling that you were only in it for you. I didn't know for sure what you would do today on the platform.

I saw three possible futures, and let's just say this was the happiest of outcomes."

"If you didn't know what I would do, why did you turn yourself over? If I'd performed the sacrifice, you might be dead."

"You could say I was increasing the odds of a favorable outcome. I had a gut feeling about you. I don't think you could perform an act that evil in front of Jacob. I wanted you to know he was there, that he was watching. I knew it would break your heart for him to see the evil in you."

Abigail rested her head in her hands. "You were right, of course, but I'd made my decision long before that. When I saw Dane in Hell, I couldn't bear it. After he'd helped us the way he did and I knew how much his death would weigh on your hearts, I had to take action, even if it meant losing myself."

Turning back toward the parlor, the last rays of twilight framed Malini's torso. "And that's why I trust you. That type of selflessness is hard to find."

"But—"

"I don't need your sorcery. I need your true strength."

"But—"

"Your true strength, Abigail, is your heart, your mind, and your brand-new soul. Someone like you who has come so far, who has journeyed through Hell and chosen a life of faith, is the most useful of all. It's easy to choose what's right when right is your only choice. You've seen the evil that could be and rejected it. I need you. I need your experiences."

Abigail leaned back against the sofa, hugging herself. Malini's words rang true. After staring into the face of evil, Abigail was sure she would never go back there. Lucifer wouldn't waste his time trying to tempt her again. He knew what she was capable of now.

"Okay. I'll do it. I'll make the maps and build the teams."

Malini approached and sat down next to her. "There's more." She placed her hands around Abigail's. "I want you to teach the Soulkeepers. No one understands Watchers like you. Nobody understands evil like you. Lillian is a Horseman and belongs in the field. She's never been comfortable running Eden and we are going to need her here when Lucifer regroups. I want you, and Gideon if he'll agree, to run the school and help us teach the new Soulkeepers."

Abigail's mouth fell open. "Can I ... go there?"

"You can. Dane made it through and so can you. I've seen it."

"Then, yes, Malini. Yes. I will gladly share what I know with the Soulkeepers. I'll talk to Gideon. I'm sure he'll help, too."

"Welcome to the team, Dr. Abigail Silva, human and honorary Soulkeeper." Malini shook her hand formally and then pulled her into an embrace.

For the second time that day, Abigail's heart swelled with gratitude for the new life she'd chosen.

A SINGLE RED CANDLE BURNED ON HER DRESSER, BARELY illuminating the room that was now too dark for her tastes. Behind the bathroom door, the groan of the pipes shutting off preceded the clank of the shower door. Drawers opened and closed and bottles clanked together. Gideon.

Fumbling in the darkness, she found a long silk nightgown

she'd had since the 1920s. She pulled it over her head. It fit differently than before. In the dim light she turned back and forth in front of the mirror, trying to get used to the new curves that pulled against the silk.

"You look beautiful." Gideon's voice was all gravel, low and rough.

She spun around. Framed by the bathroom light, he adjusted the towel wrapped around his waist. Stray drops of water lingered on his broad chest. With his hair slicked back, his left eyebrow was slightly lower than the right, a human imperfection she hadn't noticed before. Somehow it made her heart beat faster and her fingers ache to touch him. Human feelings didn't make sense, but she liked them.

"I didn't know you were watching."

"I wasn't. Good timing I guess." The corner of his mouth twitched.

Her insides fluttered. A hot tingle rose up her chest to her cheeks. She smiled. "It used to be if I didn't like something about my body, I could snap my fingers and change it. I guess this is me now. This is the only body I have."

"It's a good body. You're perfect, just as you are."

She stepped closer, suddenly nervous. She forgot to breathe. When she remembered, her breath was too loud and shaky. Padding on bare feet, she traversed the space between them and placed her palms on his bare chest.

He closed his eyes. Warm hands found her face. Thumbs traced her mouth.

She met him halfway. Full lips. Warm breath. The kiss was soft at first, searching. Every sensation was sharp enough to cut to her soul. He pulled her closer, until her nightgown pressed into his chest.

Gideon's touch used to cause a painful, blistering burn. The fire he ignited now didn't hurt. It was a different burn, the dull, hot ache a woman feels for a man. As his fingers threaded into her hair, she rose up on her toes, her hands gripping his shoulders. She *wanted* to be consumed by this fire. She couldn't get enough of it.

THIRTY-FIVE

MARA AND HENRY

For Mara, time had no meaning anymore. Inside her glass house in the In Between, she played the universe like a musical instrument. The planets and stars spun at her fingertips. Galaxies expanded or contracted at her will. She didn't know why Aldric thought this would be difficult. For her, it was as easy as breathing. For her, it was what she was born to do.

Of course, she had a faint memory of difficulty. An eternity ago she'd had to learn to keep the planets spinning at different speeds. She'd practiced splitting herself and visiting Earth during specific periods of time. But for her, the past, present, and future were as one. She was beginner, novice, and expert, all in the same immortal body. And with a hand in everything, it was easy for her to help the Soulkeepers.

A crystal tube spanned floor to ceiling in the center of her palace, the result of lightning striking the sands of time. The shiny black crystal glinted in the sunlight. Mara concentrated, and soon images played out across the glass.

Jacob and his mom broke into a warehouse in Ohio. The faces of skeletal-thin prisoners beamed as the Horsemen killed the Watchers and wrestled the human guards to the ground. Mara clapped her hands. The human captives were freed by the authorities who swept in, anonymously tipped off by the team who had done the real work, the Soulkeepers.

The scenario played out again and again: Ethan and Jesse in Colorado and then Indiana. The twins in New Orleans and then Mississippi. By the time Jacob and Lillian reached the sixth warehouse, the remaining Watchers had fled. Mara giggled. Left without instructions by the Watchers, the influenced human captors gave up without a fight. The Soulkeepers had won this round.

Smiling at her work, she walked to the wall of her glass estate, thinking about all the people returning to their human homes. Proud of the part she'd played in it, she looked out across the blowing sand. There was something she was forgetting. Something important.

Where the sand collected into a dune, a pale gray horse with a straight-backed rider stood watching over her realm. Henry. Splitting herself, she arrived on the dune behind Reaper, dressed in a silver gown and heels.

"Hello, Henry."

The horse startled, and then pranced in a circle at the rider's coaxing. Henry slid down from the saddle in front of her.

"Mara, do you remember me?"

The corner of her mouth twisted skyward. "Just because I became Time and have a universe to control, doesn't mean I would forget the love of my life—er, death."

His eyes wrinkled at the corners. "I thought I'd have to move on to see you again."

"I changed the rules."

"I see that." Henry slid his gloved fingers over the ends of the leather reins. "Excellent work saving the world."

"It was the least I could do. I'll always be a Soulkeeper at heart, after all."

He stepped forward, until the front of his riding coat skimmed her dress. "Mara, I know you have your own place here, and your own immortality, but I was wondering if you might like to share mine again. Or we could meet in the middle. Maybe a picnic, or a hunt. I miss you, Mara. I want to pick up where we left off."

She placed her hands on his chest and leaned into him, brushing her cheek against his. Her lips found his ear and her eyelids fluttered closed. "Mmmm. I want to pick up exactly where we left off."

When she pulled back, they were in his darkened room. Henry raised his eyebrows and the candles flamed to life. She wrestled the riding jacket from his shoulders and kissed him hard, her lips frantic and needing. In one smooth motion, he scooped his hands under her, wrapping her legs around his hips, and slammed her back against the stone wall. What might have bruised her human body merely ignited her immortal one. She pulled him closer.

"I love you, Mara." Henry's hot breath caressed her ear.

"I love you, too, Henry. Today, tomorrow, and always."

EPILOGUE

Behind the doors of their cheery yellow home, Carolyn sipped her coffee across from John, who flipped through the Paris Daily newspaper. Only a day ago, they'd returned from their cruise, but Carolyn had worked hard to catch up on the town gossip.

"It's a miracle, John. The Westcotts got their daughter back!"

"Uhuh." John sipped his coffee and turned the page.

"Martha said that Stephanie Westcott doesn't remember a single thing that happened to her. Well, of course, they took her to the doctor. She's lost a bunch of weight but she's gonna be fine. Strange though about the not remembering."

"Uhuh."

"Dane Michaels came home, too. Just showed up on Luke and Mary's doorstep. Well, the boy was half starved to death but he's going to be okay, too. Guess what, John? Guess what?"

"What, Carolyn?"

"He doesn't remember a thing either. Not a thing. Neither one of them can remember anything that happened while they were gone."

"Uhuh."

"It sure is a blessing they are home." She took a long sip from her coffee mug and allowed her eyes to wander across the street. That man was there again with Abigail. What was his name? Gideon. He didn't ever seem to leave. Her eyes narrowed suspiciously at the place where the couple sat on the dark blue porch.

"Lillian couldn't remember either," John said from behind his paper, bringing Carolyn back to their conversation.

She lowered her voice. "You are right about that, John, and she was missing for over a year." Leaning her chubby face against her palm, she drummed her fingers on the table. She sat up straighter in her chair. "I think I know what's going on here."

John lowered his paper and met her eager stare. "Are you going to tell me?"

"Aliens."

With a snort, John returned to his paper.

"Alien abduction, John. It's just like that movie *Fire in The Sky*. They probably did all sorts of tests on Stephanie, Dane, and Lillian that we'll never know about. Tests to see if the aliens could survive on our planet. *Anal* probing. Then they wiped their memories clean."

John chuckled.

Carolyn banged her fist on the table. "What other explanation could there possibly be?" she squealed.

Flattening the paper on the table, John flipped back to the

front page. In bold font across the top, it read, FBI THWARTS HUMAN TRAFFICKING. John read the story aloud. "The largest human trafficking ring ever found in the United States was toppled yesterday when government officials freed hundreds of people from six warehouse prisons. Working on an anonymous tip, authorities reportedly stormed the warehouses and apprehended twelve suspects. Adding to the mystery surrounding the tip, the suspects were found incapacitated upon arrival and a few of the captives had already been freed. Hundreds of others have been reconnected with family members. Authorities speculate that the captives had been drugged, as none of them have any memory of their time missing."

Carolyn stared at John blankly. "I guess that would explain things." She laughed. "Martha is going to be so disappointed it wasn't aliens."

It was John's turn to laugh. "That hat she wore to church last month looked like it was alien enough, I'll tell you that much."

"Oh, John." Carolyn slapped his arm playfully.

He flipped back to the sports section until Carolyn's hand grabbed his arm and shook. "John, look. Abigail's crossing the street. She has a letter in her hand. Do you think the postman brought us another cruise?"

John shrugged and pushed his chair back from the table. By the time Abigail reached the porch, they were standing in the open door.

"Good morning, Abigail. How are you today?" John asked.

"I'm well." Abigail held out a beige monogrammed envelope. "I have something for you two."

"Is it another cruise?" Carolyn quipped.

"Not this time, but I hope you can make it."

Carolyn ripped open the envelope and pulled out the thick card stock inside.

You are cordially invited to attend the wedding of
Dr. Abigail Silva
and
Gideon Newman
On Saturday, July first at twelve o'clock in the afternoon at
Sunrise Park.

"Ooooh, I knew it." Carolyn stomped her foot. "I knew that man was special!" She handed the invitation to John and pulled Abigail into a hug.

"You're getting married!" John exclaimed, running his finger over the raised letters. "Congratulations."

"The flowers will be our gift," Carolyn said, patting her chest. "We wouldn't miss it for the world!"

"That's very generous of you, Carolyn. We'd appreciate it." Abigail pointed her thumb at her house. "Well, Gideon is waiting for me. I better head back."

"Okay. Congratulations, dear!" Carolyn waved excitedly as Abigail crossed the street for home.

John's eyes narrowed. "Did she look different to you?"

Carolyn hmmphed in his direction. "That's what love does to a woman, John. Now that she's landed her man she can stop starving herself and put some meat on those bones."

"She looks shorter."

"No more heels. Poor woman has earned her right to spend a few years in flats."

"I guess."

"Don't you remember how I changed once we were married?" Carolyn asked.

John blinked twice in her direction. "How could I forget?"

ON THE FIRST OF JULY, WHEN THE SUN WAS AT ITS highest point in the sky, Abigail readied herself inside a small white tent in Sunrise Park. Breathless, she checked her dress in the mirror for the three-hundredth time. The gathered silk of her strapless gown crisscrossed her bodice, then draped to the grass in a graceful swag.

Swept up on top of her head, Abigail's new curls were as novel as the curves that held up her dress. She was still getting used to the new her. She'd applied makeup for the first time that morning in neutral tones that gave her the glow she used to get by illusion.

"You look beautiful," Malini said from the flap that acted like a door.

"Do you think so? I wonder if it was too much for me to choose white, being a widow and a former demon. Do you think people will talk?" Abigail joked.

"People in this town have been talking about you for years. What's one more thing?"

They laughed together toward the mirror. Malini's dark hair and violet dress offset Abigail's pale silhouette.

"I have something for you," Malini said, holding out a small box. "It's from Jacob and me. Since you are technically old but your soul is new, and the setup outside is borrowed, we thought we'd get you something blue."

Abigail cracked the box. A platinum cross pendent reflected back at her, inlaid with sapphires. "Will you help me put it on, Malini?"

"Of course."

Small brown hands scooped up the pendant and hooked it around her neck. It rested between her collarbones.

"I love it," Abigail said. "Tell Jacob it's perfect."

She touched it lightly with her fingers, enjoying the cool feel against her skin.

"It's time, if you're ready."

"Oh, I'm ready. I've been ready for more than a lifetime."

Malini smiled and held the flap to the tent open. Abigail lifted her bouquet from the small white table near the mirror. Three orchids formed the focal point. Carolyn said she could only picture Abigail with exotic flowers. There wasn't a rose or carnation in the entire wedding.

Outside, she took her place behind Malini at the back of the aisle between two blocks of white folding chairs filled with friends and neighbors. The Laudners, the Westcotts, and the Guptas rotated in their seats for a better view, along with a slew of other townspeople Abigail barely knew. The other Soulkeepers were there, too. Dane, who'd gained some weight, sat next to Ethan as if his mere presence warded off evil spirits. Dane's parents sat separately in the back row.

Flower sprays arched over the aisle and a string quartet played a classical piece. Abigail couldn't enjoy it. She focused on a man who stood in the shadows of a tree behind the six-inch platform that would serve as the altar. His blond curls didn't move even though a distinct summer breeze blew from the west. His suit was black and his face was grave.

Lucifer.

Malini started down the aisle, blocking the devil from her view, step-together, step-together, until Jacob, in his black tuxedo met her at the front. Frowning, Abigail's eyes drifted back to the shadowy place where she had seen Lucifer. He was still there but so were two others. Henry and Mara stood between her and the devil, arm in arm in the full light of the sun.

The music changed. The crowd rose to their feet. Lucifer wanted her attention again. She wouldn't give it to him. Not today. Abigail smiled broadly and stepped one foot in front of the other. She walked down the aisle alone. There was no one to give her away. But maybe that was how it should be. She'd earned her own soul.

Gideon waited at the altar. For a moment, she couldn't move. All she wanted to do was to chisel the sight of him into her memory. His dark hair was combed back and curled against the collar of his black tuxedo. Human as he was, to her he would always be an angel, and today he glowed brighter than ever.

She forced herself forward, to take his hand and pretend that she was paying attention. Gideon's emerald green eyes captivated her. Time stopped while she repeated the vows the pastor read to her and then slid the platinum band onto Gideon's finger. He did the same, holding the ring on her finger for seconds too long, as if he still couldn't believe he could touch her. When he kissed her, the world melted away and everything, his embrace, his lips, the sunlight on their faces, the love, made a millennia of waiting, of suffering death, entirely worth it.

Applause. Whistles. The pastor held up their hands and announced them. Gideon ushered her up the aisle and into the reception tent, twirling her into his arms and finding her lips again.

"Well, isn't that the sweetest thing?" Lucifer's voice cut through the air.

She turned to face him. Lucifer leaned up against a post on the other side of the dance floor. Despite the silver and ivory place settings, and the bright flower arrangements, dark shadows clung to him. Lucifer brought his own darkness.

"Leave, Lucifer. You have no place here," Gideon said.

"Don't get your new human undies in a bunch, Mr. Newman," Lucifer said. "You are not why I'm here."

"Then why are you here?" Abigail asked.

"You, Abigail. I thought we had something." He swaggered forward. "You were mine first. You fell for me, remember?"

"Things change. Free will is a bitch, ain't it?" Abigail stepped in front of Gideon and squared her shoulders. She was defenseless except for her will, but she refused to allow Lucifer to have the pleasure of seeing her afraid.

"You are my deepest regret. We could have accomplished so much together, you and I. It was a shame what you did. A bloody shame. I don't deal well with loss." He shook his head.

"Maybe you can find a support group," Abigail said.

Lucifer's eyes blazed. He stepped in closer. Too close. Gideon's hands gripped her shoulders.

"Enough small talk, Abigail. I'm here to let you know that the damage you've done is significant but not impossible to overcome. When I do, you know what they say, payback is hell." His knuckle brushed against her jawline.

The baby hairs on the back of her neck stood at attention. "Don't touch me. You can't do anything to me." Each word was equal parts hope and prayer.

Lucifer tipped his head. "Maybe not today, but I'll be back, Abigail. I always come back." He bared his teeth. "My congratulations to the happy couple. May you have many, many children. Funny thing about kids these days, they always seem to find their own way. Free will's a bitch, ain't it?" He turned on his heel and twisted into shadow, leaving nothing but a faint smell of sulfur behind.

"Was that who I think it was?" Jacob asked from the doorway. Malini hugged tight to his side.

"Unfortunately, yes," Gideon replied.

Jacob pulled a breath spray from his pocket, crossed the dance floor to where Lucifer had been, and spritzed spearmint into the air.

"There. Good as new." He turned back toward Abigail and Gideon. "Looks like the garbage took itself out. Let's get this party started."

Abigail nodded, meeting his eyes. "Thanks, Jacob. Thanks for everything."

Jacob shook his head. "Do you remember the day we met? You scared the bejeezus out of me." He laughed.

"I remember."

"You changed me for the better. I'm so glad you finally got what you wanted."

The sound of Aunt Carolyn's heady laugh brought them back to the present. There was a reception to be had, and Abigail was looking forward to cutting her cake, not to mention her first dance with her husband. She wasn't going to give Lucifer the benefit of even one more minute of her life wasted in worry.

⚜

THREE WEEKS LATER...

The gothic Victorian had never looked better. Abigail had paid a crew to paint it white with light gray trim. She'd redecorated the inside, too, and added a real door to the tower. The interior was now a shrine to neutral tones. Everything about the place screamed cheery rural hideaway. Everything but the stained glass window in her bedroom. She couldn't bring herself to change it but realistically she knew the new owners would probably replace it.

They were turning it into a bed and breakfast.

"All packed up," Gideon said, loading the last trunk into her truck. "Ready to go?"

Abigail slid the SOLD sign into the wire frame in the yard. "I am now."

"Hold it right there, Abigail Newman." John Laudner waved at her from across the street. Aunt Carolyn, Jacob, and Katrina exited the cheery yellow home behind him.

"We were going to stop over to say goodbye," Abigail answered.

"No need. We'll come to you." John reached the driveway. "I just wanted to say, we're going to miss you, Abigail. You've been a terrific neighbor."

"Thanks, John. I feel the same about you."

Carolyn stepped to her husband's side. "I can't believe this house is leaving your family after so many generations. I hope that university you're moving to understands how they've changed this town, luring you away."

"Oh, Carolyn, you're too kind. I'm sure you and the other ladies will find some other topic to keep you busy."

Carolyn laughed. "Oh, hush. You know it was all in good fun."

Katrina stepped forward. "Thanks for everything, both of you." She shook Abigail's hand but her eyes lingered on Gideon.

He returned a knowing nod.

Jacob stepped up last. "Dr. Silva, I mean Newman, working for you was one of the most important experiences of my life. You've meant a lot to me." He shot her a private grin.

Abigail smiled. "The feeling's mutual, Jacob."

They stood for a moment taking each other in.

"Well, Abigail and I have a long drive ahead of us," Gideon said.

"We promise, we'll keep in touch. I plan on visiting Paris often," Abigail added.

"Make sure you look us up," Carolyn chimed in. "You're always welcome."

Abigail nodded and climbed into the passenger side of the truck. Gideon slid behind the wheel.

They backed out of the driveway and drove toward the setting sun. They didn't stop until they reached the delivery entrance of Laudner's Flowers and Gifts.

Lillian had already closed the shop for the night but she let them in the back door. Malini helped load all of their things into the boat in the cavern under the backroom. It took the better part of an hour to move the trunks down the winding staircase.

"Sink it in the lake," Abigail said, handing Lillian the keys to the truck.

"Will do. I'll take the plates off first, just in case."

"Thanks, Lillian."

"I'll see you in Eden."

Gideon nodded. "Classes start next week. I'll make sure the weapons room is ready for you."

"Looking forward to it." Lillian tossed the keys into the air and caught them in the same hand. She gave a little wave goodbye and jogged up the stairs.

Unfolding a pair of sunglasses from her pocket, Malini slid them onto her face and reached for the rope.

"What are those for?" Gideon asked.

Malini shrugged. "Eh, nothing to worry about."

She hoisted the sail.

After a lifetime of magic and sorcery, Abigail didn't think anything could surprise her, but the ball of fire that rolled through the cave had her clutching at Gideon. Gathered into his arms, she screamed as the boat propelled forward, passing through the far wall of the cavern before slowing on a crystalline blue river.

"You could've warned us," Abigail said.

Malini smiled. "Sorry."

She did not sound sorry at all.

Abigail eyed the approaching cherubim, their crossed swords burning. "Are you sure about this, Malini? Are you sure we'll be allowed in? The cherubim were set in place to keep humans and Watchers out. Only Soulkeepers can enter."

"I'm sure. You might say you've become an honorary Soul-keeper. It's all been arranged."

While she heard what Malini was saying, Abigail gripped Gideon's hand tighter as they approached. She thought back on her life, on all of the choices she'd made, good or evil. If she had to weigh her own soul, she wasn't sure which side of the scale would rise. She was sure Gideon's soul would stand up to the test. He'd always been made for good. But if Abigail made it through to the other side, she knew it would be because of grace and mercy.

The moment they passed under the swords the air turned to rubber and the cells of her body felt sifted like sand through a sieve. The boat slowed. For a second, she couldn't breathe. Her body was forced forward, stretching against some unseen force that pressed on her from all sides.

When she thought she could take no more, that she would suffocate for sure, the boat broke past the membrane and floated forward on pristine waters. Colorful birds sang from the trees, calling out a song of joy. The lush jungle welcomed her to Eden.

Abigail tipped her head against Gideon's shoulder, lacing her fingers into his. He kissed the top of her head. With her face tipped toward the sun, and the man she loved at her side, she came home to her new life.

SOUL CATCHER, BOOK FOUR IN THE SOULKEEPERS SERIES is available now. Flip to the next section for a free excerpt.

WOULD YOU LEAVE A REVIEW?

Thank you for reading **Return to Eden**. If you've enjoyed this title, please leave a review at your place of purchase. Reviews are gold to authors.

BOOK CLUB?

Don't miss the discussion questions at the back of this book.

SOUL CATCHER

PLEASE ENJOY THIS EXTENDED EXCERPT OF SOUL CATCHER, BOOK 4 IN THE SOULKEEPERS SERIES.

USA TODAY BESTSELLING AUTHOR

G.P. CHING

THE SOULKEEPERS SERIES BOOK FOUR

SOUL CATCHER

ONE

TAKEN

"Chevy! Come on, time to go." Chevy's father yanked the cord to raise the window shade, his voice holding more than a hint of frustration.

Chevy Kikmongwi tossed an arm across his eyes to shield them from the offending light. He ignored his father's prodding. Why did he need to participate in this stupid ceremony, anyway? Welcome to modern civilization. Time to evolve beyond believing in rain dances, even if he *was* half Native American.

"I'm not leaving, Chevy. You may choose to live with your mother, but until you're eighteen you will respect and participate in Hopi traditions with the rest of the tribe. Now move!"

With no intention of getting out of bed, Chevy flipped to his stomach and pulled the pillow over his head. He should have realized moving back to Flagstaff from Sedona would mean increased visits from his father, but he'd hoped the year away would dull the big man's desire to involve him in tribal affairs. Unfortunately, his dad was not the type to give up

easily or take no for an answer. Robert Kikmongwi was not like
Chevy's mother and did not back down from his fifteen-year-
old son. Without warning the futon flipped on its side, and
Chevy's body crashed to the linoleum.

"Owa! Geez, Dad. What the hell? I could've broken a hip
or something." Slowly, Chevy propped himself on his elbows.

"Next time, be ready, and this will be less painful for both
of us." In a red T-shirt and jeans, his father didn't look any
more Native American than anyone else's dad in Flagstaff, but
looks could be deceiving. A member of the Walpi village, he
bought into all of the Hopi mythology, hook, line, and sinker.
He probably believed the Snake Dance actually brought rain.

No getting out of this. Guess he'd have to get through it. "I
need a minute," Chevy said.

"Yeah, I'd say so. Smells like a brewery in here." Oh, he
was pissed. He was doing that thing where he closed and
opened his fists.

"A couple of the guys came over and, you know."

"Yes, I do. Doesn't your mother have any rules?"

Chevy grunted and ran a hand through his too-long black
hair. "If you got a problem with Mom's rules, go talk to her
about it. Our rules work for us."

"What you mean is, you like having no rules and Shelly
likes not having to worry about parenting you."

The shrug Chevy gave said it all.

His father slapped the doorframe as he exited the room in
a huff. With much effort, Chevy stood, head throbbing in time
with his heartbeat. *Damn.* The bathroom door wavered in his
adjusting vision until he stumbled through to the porcelain
sink. He fished a painkiller out of the medicine cabinet and
tossed it to the back of his throat, rinsing it down with water

from the tap. When he was finished, he spread his eyelids, one side at a time, careful not to tug on his new eyebrow piercing, and dripped some Visine over his chocolate browns. Had to look presentable for the native ladies. A little flirting would go a long way to shorten a slow ceremony. If he was lucky, Raine Nokami might find him in the crowd. She was hot enough to make a day on the reservation worth it.

As he climbed into the shower, the fighting started. Dad must have found Mom, which meant she'd come home last night after all. They'd be rehashing all the ancient history about how she'd promised to raise him the Hopi way. That wasn't going to happen. No way was he going to live in a clay box and farm corn in the desert. And for what? To follow the divine direction of some Great Spirit? Did they even know how people on the outside laughed at their antiquated faith?

Nope, Chevy had bigger plans for himself. Plans to change the world.

Stepping from the shower, he toweled off and tied his hair back into a ponytail. He brushed the taste of stale beer from his mouth and dressed in jeans and a gray T-shirt. Then, as loudly as possible, he exited his room, hoping the stomp of his feet and the slam of the door would shame his parents into giving the argument a rest. The sooner he hit the road, the sooner this would be over with, and he could get back to his real life.

❧

THE RED DIRT OF ROUTE 264 BILLOWED UP AROUND THE tires of his dad's Jeep. The two-and-a-half-hour drive from Flagstaff to the reservation was an exercise in small talk. How was school? Did he have a girlfriend? Like Chevy would share any of his personal thoughts with his parental units. Eventually, the one-word answers and head nods ebbed the flow of questions, and the even hum of the road replaced the forced conversation.

"We'll have to go on foot from here," his dad said as he parked the Jeep in a gravel lot outside the village.

Like Chevy didn't know that. This wasn't his first visit to First Mesa or Walpi, but he held his tongue and obediently followed on the footpath.

"If you were raised here, with the others, it would be time for your coming of age ceremony."

"Yeah?" Chevy internally groaned. Not another ceremony.

"I'd present a challenge, a test of courage, and if you succeeded in overcoming the challenge, you would be invited into the *Kiva* and be part of a ritual. After the ritual, everyone here would consider you an adult."

"Adult enough to decide I never want to come back here?" Chevy snapped.

It was a cruel thing to say. The older man's forehead wrinkled with the grimace that crossed his face, but he didn't say anything to rebuke Chevy's comment. Instead, he raised his proud chin to the pueblos on the top of the mesa, the warmth of the August sun already hot enough to bring a sheen of sweat to the surface of his skin.

This was going to be a majorly long day.

"Cheveyo!" the high voice that called his Hopi name cut through the distance like a bird's caw. Raine. Her straight hair floated behind her, spread like black wings, dwarfing her petite frame as she raced toward him. Dark eyes cut to his soul.

Thankfully, his dad swerved to go talk to a man Chevy

didn't recognize and was out of earshot by the time she reached him. Her brown arms flung around his neck and pulled him into a tight hug before backing to a respectable distance. "I'm glad you came," she said.

"Good to see you too, Raine, but don't call me Cheveyo. My name is Chevy."

"Not here it's not." She smiled and the world stopped turning. "When you were born, your mother held you up to the rising sun right over there." She pointed to the edge of the red-rock crag. "And when the first rays touched you, she named you Cheveyo."

Chevy shook his head and laughed. She always pushed this, every time he visited. "Yeah, and because she was white she didn't realize she'd chosen a bad name. She thought it meant spirit warrior, but it doesn't. Cheveyo is an ogre that steals children in their sleep. If you were named after a monster, you might prefer a nickname too."

"I think it sounds tough. Roll with it." Her eyes flashed and she took a half step closer, tossing her hair over her shoulder. Oh, she smelled good, like sweet spices. "Maybe, you'll become such a great man Hopi will have to change the meaning of the name."

Riiiight. Chevy held his tongue. He didn't want to risk making her angry and losing her company.

His father appeared at his side. "Raine, so good to see you. How'd it go yesterday?"

"Good. I think the spirits helped me."

"Helped you do what?" Chevy asked.

Patting her shoulder proudly, his father answered for her. "Raine was chosen as the Antelope Maid. She told the story yesterday and is going to be part of the ceremony today."

"Wow. Congratulations," Chevy stuttered. "Who had the honor of accompanying you as Snake Youth?" *Please don't say Drew.*

"Drew," Raine whispered as if she could sense Chevy's dread.

"That's cool," Chevy responded too quickly. He nudged his father's elbow. "Hey, we should find Grandma before the ceremony starts."

"Good idea. Nice to see you, Raine."

Close behind his elder, Chevy gave Raine a small wave goodbye as he headed toward the plaza. The frown she wore darted straight into his heart. Hell, it wasn't her fault the tribe had paired her with Drew for the ceremony. But Chevy dreaded the ceremony even more, now. Raine wouldn't be by his side, silently poking fun at the festivities. Instead, she'd be a part of the irrational display. It almost made the experience worse.

He battled with himself all the way into the adobe-walled village. Should he be more supportive of her? Of the tribe? No. No, he couldn't allow himself to be pulled into this. Living the Hopi way was a prison. The reservation was literally land-locked, surrounded by the Navajo. Walpi didn't even have running water for God's sake. This was not the life for him.

His grandmother, Willow, emerged from her pueblo and embraced him in a bone-crushing hug, surprisingly strong for her four-foot-ten-inch frame. "Welcome home," she said. "Come. Let's find a place to observe."

Observe. That was all he could do. He wasn't actually part of all this. Sadly, his father and grandmother wouldn't partici-pate either, even though they probably wanted to. His grandmother was a medicine woman, deeply faithful to the traditions. She would observe and explain to him in some weak effort to make him understand. Everyone tried so hard to bring him along. They would be better off when he turned eighteen. He'd never come back here, and his Hopi relatives would eventually forget about him and go on with their lives. For now, he sat between them on the bench on the edge of the plaza, waiting in the hot Arizona sun, under a cloudless blue sky. The painkiller he'd taken was wearing off, and his head began to throb.

"Over there is the *Kisi*," his father said, pointing at a crude shrine of sticks and animal skins. The focal point was an altar covered in brightly colored sand. "That's where they keep the snakes. The snakes carry the prayers of the faithful to the underworld, and if our dance is acceptable, the spirits will send rain."

Chevy rolled his eyes.

"They come," his grandmother said, stating the obvious. He couldn't have missed the drumbeats. The snake priests and their attendants paraded into the plaza, beating drums and shaking gourd rattles. One by one, the priests reached into the *Kisi*, pulling out whatever snake their fingers wrapped around first. The diamond-shaped head of a rattlesnake poked out from one of the priest's fists. *Damn.* He didn't remember them using poisonous snakes in the past, but then a couple of years had passed since his dad had forced him to attend a Snake Dance. With any luck, he wouldn't have to watch anyone die today.

The priests danced around the plaza, the snakes slithering over and under their hands. For the second lap, the priests held the snakes in their mouths, never missing a beat. At the same time, the attendants tried to distract the snakes from striking with their snake whips.

Chevy wiped his sweaty palms on his jeans.

"They use all the snakes," his father said. "The gatherers will keep them in the plaza as the priests drop them during the dance. See? The feathered wand soothes them and then they throw cornmeal to distract the snake before snatching them by the head."

Either brave or stupid, Chevy thought.

By the time the priests had circled the plaza several times, chanting their prayers, fifty or more snakes wriggled around the gatherers' necks and arms. Then, a snake priest found the *Kisi* empty. With a bowl of cornmeal offered by an attendant, he drew a large ring on the ground. The gatherers released the snakes inside the circle.

Raine, dressed in white, joined the dance and worked to keep the snakes inside the cornmeal boundary. *Holy cow!* Chevy's heart threatened to leap out of his mouth as she leaned over and used her snake whip to turn a rattler back toward the center. The diamond head coiled, ready to strike, and wouldn't you know it, there was Drew, swooping in to save the day. He coaxed the reptile toward the center of the circle, away from Raine. Chevy dug his nails into his thighs.

The whole thing unfolded like a train wreck, terrible and mesmerizing all at the same time. The priests scooped up snakes by the armful, returning them to a different shrine as the gatherers and attendants kept any stragglers from reaching the crowd.

"The snakes are released into the pit to carry the prayers to the underworld," his grandmother whispered.

Chevy didn't even realize he was holding his breath until

the last snake slithered into the shrine. Thankful no one was hurt, he gasped in relief. The priests accepted bowls of liquid from the women of the village. Chevy cringed as they drank, then heaved onto the red dirt near their feet.

"The vomiting cleanses them of the snake charms." His grandmother smiled as if induced vomiting was an ordinary occurrence.

It was all so disturbing: the rhythm, the dancing, the chanting, beautiful Raine in danger, and then the vomiting. Chevy's head throbbed. A war waged within him, his brain telling him the ritual was archaic and ridiculous, but a deep, unused part of him desperately wanting to be part of this, to understand and participate next to Raine. As if those feelings weren't confusing enough, at that moment the previously clear blue sky opened up. Hell if he could explain why, but rain began to pour in sheets over Walpi village. The Hopi people shouted praise and gratitude toward the heavens and the Earth.

Chevy cracked. He leapt up and raced toward the footpath, hurling himself down the mesa.

"Chevy, wait!" his dad called from behind him.

He didn't wait. The rain soaked him to the bone, but he didn't care. He had to get away. If he didn't get a handle on this thing inside of him, this part that wanted to believe, he'd never save his sanity.

Near the car, Chevy stopped short of a grouping of juniper trees, their twisted branches oddly at home in the rain. An enormous winged snake with a white plume of hair stared at him through the leaves. His breath hitched. A *Kachina*, a Hopi spirit! He fell to his knees, quaking.

The snake stepped forward, transforming into a tall redheaded woman in purple stiletto boots that paused in front of his prostrate form. What the hell? Was he hallucinating? Dehydrated from his hangover?

"Well, now this is interesting," the snake woman said in a low, breathy drawl. "You are quite the offender. Kind of kicked the 'honor your ancestors' thing to the curb, didn't you?"

Chevy bowed his head.

"There, there. Take my hand and I'll give you exactly what you deserve." The snake woman extended her long fingers, her sharp tapered nails reminiscent of a bird's talons.

Gaze lifting to her bright green eyes, he extended his hand.

"Cheveyo!" Raine barreled down the mesa, not stopping until her hand gripped his shoulder from behind. She locked eyes with the snake woman. "Who are you? Are you here for the ceremony? You're too late."

Chevy wanted to explain to Raine what the snake woman was, but before he could utter a single syllable, the spirit clasped his wrist violently. A growl emanated from deep within her chest, and her thin lips peeled back from abnormally long, sharp teeth.

Raine cried out and pulled back on his shoulder.

Snake Woman did not release Cheveyo. Her other hand shot out to grip the twisted trunk of the juniper tree beside her.

Everything slowed. For once in his life, Chevy saw things with absolute clarity. The tree bark shingled the snake woman's arm, climbing toward him like a predator. The tree was swallowing the spirit and would eat him too. *Oh no, Raine!* He yanked against the *Kachina's* clutches, but Snake Woman wouldn't let go. Locked around his wrist, the spirit hissed through clenched teeth. Every cell in Chevy's body resisted. Counting to three in his head, he pulled away with everything he had in the opposite direction. The effort paid off. His hand slipped from hers, and he dove into Raine, trying his best to protect her from the bad spirit.

But something was terribly wrong. As he collided with Raine, he entered her skin, sliding inside her body like an overcoat. He blinked twice, staring down at the feminine arms and hands lifted in front of his face.

Then, he gaped in horror as his own body disappeared inside the bark of the juniper tree.

TWO

HARRINGTON ENTERPRISES

Malini straightened her skirt and pressed the button for the elevator. This had to work. She'd been trying to get an audience with Senator Bakewell for weeks, to find the Watcher who was influencing him and take the dark angel out of the equation before the next vote.

"What's the bill called again?" Jacob asked, straightening his tie.

"S. 5109-International Economic Assurance Act. If I read it to you, I'd give you a headache, but the bottom line is the legislation would legalize the employment of slave labor in the United States as long as the slaves were not American citizens."

The elevator doors opened, and the two stepped inside the privacy of the compartment. Jacob grunted. "That would effectively decriminalize human trafficking. Who would ever vote for that?"

"No one with a clear head, but the council and I think

Watchers have been influencing Bakewell for years and possibly a few other representatives. The legislation itself is confusing. Sounds like a boon for the economy to most people. If I wasn't privy to Fatima's loom, I probably wouldn't understand the consequences."

Fatima was Fate, the immortal who lived in the In Between, weaving the destinies of every living soul on the planet into fabric. Malini alone, as the Healer, could read patterns in the fabric and use her gifts to interpret possible futures.

"We might not fully understand the consequences, but the Watchers do. Lucifer's up to something. I can feel it," Jacob said, eyes darkening. The Lord of Illusions always seemed to have a plan B. After the Soulkeepers had forced Lucifer back to Hell that summer, when Abigail botched his human sacrifice, they'd thought they would get a break to regroup. No such luck.

"Yep. I can feel it too."

"So, we end the Watcher and let Senator Bakewell get back to his usual philandering ways?"

Malini giggled. "That's the general idea."

"How are things with the council going, anyway?" Jacob asked.

The new Soulkeepers' council consisted of Malini, because she was the Healer, Abigail and Gideon, as administrators of Eden, Lillian as the head of field operations, and Grace and Master Lee as Helpers. The point of the council was to enhance the communication and coordination of the small team of Soulkeepers. The Watchers outnumbered them. Always would. Even with Mara slowing time in Nod and Hell, the Soulkeepers had to work smarter to thwart the evil Lucifer inflicted on the world.

"Just okay," Malini said honestly. "Sometimes I think the adults don't take me seriously as their leader."

"I thought we'd moved beyond that."

"Me too. But it's still there, Jake, festering under the surface. Some of the things I bring to them are hard to accept. Like when Bonnie and Samantha couldn't return to Nebraska." Her eyes darted down to her tangled fingers. "They lost the restaurant. I thought Grace was going to blow a gasket."

"They're not chained to Eden. If Grace would rather take her chances with the Watchers, she can be my guest. That goes for the twins too."

"Jake!"

"I'm just saying, Malini, they should consider the alternative before taking their frustration out on you."

The elevator stopped, and the doors opened. Malini and Jacob stepped into a vast, pale space, all steel, glass, and ivory sandstone floors. Malini's heels click-clacked as she crossed the foyer to the front desk. Shiny metal letters on the dark wood read *Harrington Enterprises*.

A slender blonde with a French manicure ended the call she was on and fixed them with a hard, green-eyed stare. "Can I help you?"

"We're here to interview Senator Bakewell for our school newspaper. His assistant told us he'd be here meeting with Mr. Harrington and would have a few minutes to talk with us."

"One moment, please." Abruptly, the woman stood and power-walked down the hall.

"That was weird," Jacob said.

"Did you smell her?"

"Yeah. Eau de Watcher with a core of human. Not even masked with illusion. Possessed or influenced?"

"Influenced. Long term by the strength of the aroma." Malini rubbed her nose. "I'm texting Lillian for backup. I'll have her wait in the lobby, just in case." Her fingers flew and then she tucked the phone back into her pocket.

Jacob reached out with his power. If the blonde was influenced, he might need a weapon. "There's a pitcher of water in the conference room to your right, a bathroom down the hall, and a jug of it this way. Maybe some sort of break room," Jacob whispered. "You're covered."

"Let's try to do this without making a scene. She's human. She probably doesn't know what we are. Keep this low profile, less to clean up later."

Jacob nodded.

Click-Clack. The blonde returned, a cardboard smile on her face. "Right this way."

She led them along the windows overlooking the magnificent mile to a door labeled Conference Room D. She rapped lightly.

"Come in," a man's voice drawled.

The woman opened the door. "I have your twelve o'clock. School interview."

"Send them in, Amanda."

Amanda stepped aside, directing them inside with a swing of her arm. A stoic man in a crisp gray suit raised a cup of coffee to his lips before standing to welcome them.

"Senator Bakewell?"

"The one and only." Bakewell's smile lit up the room.

Malini walked around the conference room table and politely extended her hand.

Bakewell stared at her offered handshake and cleared his throat. "Sorry to be rude but I've had a bought of illness recently. Amanda should have explained, I can't touch you. Call me a germaphobe!" He gave a deep laugh. "Truly, it's as much to protect you as me, darlin'."

Malini lowered herself to the chair next to him, flashing Jacob a pensive look. If she couldn't touch the senator, she couldn't heal him of his Watcher influence. Of course, if they didn't find and kill the Watcher responsible, there was no point anyway. He'd be influenced again in no time.

Jacob pulled out a chair across the table and sat down.

"I'm Mandy Witherspoon from St. Scholastica High School. Thank you for agreeing to this interview."

"Always interested in helping the future of America," Bakewell said. "And who are you?" he asked Jacob.

"Oh, I'm Fred." Jacob held the man's stare for a second. "Er, I'm just her ride."

Bakewell laughed. "Behind every successful woman is a man who can parallel park."

Jacob chuckled, but Malini's mouth pressed into a flat line, silencing them both. "Why don't we get started? Your assistant said you only had a few minutes."

"She would know." Bakewell nodded.

Malini pulled a pen from her purse and opened her notebook to a blank page. "How did you get your start in politics?"

"My father was a politician. You could say serving the American people is in my blood. As soon as I'd earned my law degree, I pursued a career in politics. My first position was mayor of the little town of Pointer, Ohio."

Malini cut him off. "I have a history of your career. It's very impressive."

He tilted his head. " I hank you, young lady."

"Can you tell me what legislation you're most excited about right now?"

"Sure. I've sponsored a bill to increase the penalties for illegal drug possession and another to increase our investment research into biological energy alternatives."

"Biological energy alternatives?" Jacob asked.

Malini shot him a sharp look. He shrugged apologetically.

Bakewell chuckled. "The driver speaks! There's a professor at UCLA who thinks he can genetically modify bacteria to produce petroleum. If his research pans out, we could put the little buggers in our landfills where they'd eat our garbage and poop out oil. I think that idea's worth some government funding, don't you?"

Jacob nodded.

"What can you tell us about S. 5109?" Malini asked.

The smile faded from Bakewell's face and his cheek twitched under his left eye. He took another drink of coffee, his eyes rolling in his head as he tilted the cup back. At the same time he set the mug down, he checked his watch.

"I am awfully sorry; it appears we're out of time. I hope you've got enough for your interview. If you want any other information, feel free to ask Amanda at the front desk."

"But I've only asked you three questions!" Malini protested.

Bakewell stood and pushed in his chair.

"I can see you're busy." Malini stood and motioned for Jacob to do the same. She held up a finger and flashed a charming smile. "Please, Senator, one more thing. Your coffee smells delicious. Would it be okay if we grabbed a cup before we go?"

"Of course. Down the hall and to the right." Bakewell gave her a curt nod and rounded the table, holding the door open for the two of them.

"Nice to meet you, Mandy and, uh, Fred." He poked his head into the hall. "Amanda!"

The blonde came click-clacking from the front desk. "Yes, Senator Bakewell?"

"Please show Mandy and Fred to the refreshment area and then show them out. Let Harrington know I'm ready for him."

"Yes, sir." Amanda pointed a hand in the direction she came from. "Right this way."

Malini followed her directions, Jacob sidling up next to her.

"What now, Mandy?" Jacob asked.

"Now, we get a drink," she said.

Amanda stepped ahead of them and opened the door to a small kitchenette area with three vending machines, a microwave, and a coffee pot next to the water cooler. "Help yourself," she said. "Cups are in the cabinet. Let me know if you need anything. I'll be back to check on you in a moment." She took off toward her desk, no doubt to inform Mr. Harrington the senator was waiting.

Malini reached into the cabinet and pulled down a Styrofoam cup. She poured a half cup of coffee.

"Care to share what we're doing in here?" Jacob said.

Raising the cup to her nose, Malini sniffed. "It's in the coffee," she said.

"What's in the coffee?"

"Watcher elixir. Here, smell."

Malini held the cup under Jacob's nose, the scent of cinnamon, sulfur, and spice growing stronger with the movement.

Jacob sniffed, then gagged. "Yep. That's the stuff. Doesn't make sense though. He spends most of his time in Washington, D.C. Do you think the Watcher is here?"

She dumped the coffee down the sink and stared at the wall. "I'm not sure. Amanda has been influenced for quite some time, and she lives here. Bakewell is here regularly but not frequently enough to maintain the type of influence I suspect. The Watcher must be reaching him in D.C. too."

"Huh," Jacob said. He leaned up against the counter and sighed.

Healer or not, trying to think like a Watcher was never easy. With a deep breath, she rinsed the cup out and poured herself some water. She raised the Styrofoam to her lips.

Sniff-sniff. She lowered the cup and stared down into the water. "What business is Harrington Enterprises in, Jacob?"

"I don't know."

"Can you Google it?"

Jacob pulled out his phone and typed the company's name into the search bar. "A bunch of things: pharmaceuticals, energy, water purification."

Malini held the cup under his nose.

Jacob took a deep breath and let it out slowly. "It's in the water."

"Gives new meaning to drinking the Kool-Aid," Malini said.

"Looks like Lucifer is up to his old tricks again."

"Yeah, and there's nothing we can do. The Watcher might not even be here. It's wherever this water is bottled."

They both stared at the water cooler as if it would sprout lips and start giving them answers. Out of the corner of her eye, Malini glimpsed a man in a sharp navy suit pass by the open door to the break room. Something about the way he moved was too graceful, inhuman. She turned her head to get a better look. Dark wavy hair, a smile that could sell toothpaste, and navy blue eyes. He straightened his red tie, and then moved beyond her line of sight. The saccharine sweet, sulfur scent of Watcher hit her full force. Jacob narrowed his eyes at the pull of evil from the doorway.

"He's—"

Jacob was already around the corner. Malini followed, kicking off her heeled shoes and running down the hall at breakneck speed. As she turned the corner into the long stretch of hallway to the atrium, she saw the Watcher tapping the button for the elevator frantically. Unnatural eyes locked onto hers, and a knowing, nervous smile twitched across the demon's face. Without missing a step, Jacob's hand moved toward his ankle, calling the water from his flask. He hadn't counted on Amanda. She leapt around the desk, blocking their target with her body and distracting Jacob.

"Hey, you can't run in here," she said.

He shoved her out of the way in time to see Blue Suit disappear into the stairwell. Malini cruised around Amanda, kicking off the desk to pick up speed and corner into the stairwell. Luckily, bright light filtered through windows lining the small space. Sunlight limited a Watcher's power; they might have a prayer of catching him.

In defiance of gravity, Jacob cartwheeled over the stair rail, dropping to the landing a floor below. The move would be dangerous for an ordinary human, but Soulkeepers developed superhuman agility and strength over time. The Watcher wasn't smiling anymore.

Down, down, she pursued, floors flying by, hot on the

demon's heels. The male frantically tried a doorknob, a gold lion's head ring flashing in the bright sunlight. Locked. Malini smiled. Jacob succeeded in reaching his flask and his broadsword of ice formed in his palm. They had him!

With suicidal resolve, the Watcher dove over the railing, twisting out of reach of Jacob's stabbing blade. Malini watched the demon drop to the landing below, forcing her feet to move faster down the stairs. Only, they'd reached a lower level of the building, and the topography changed. This floor housed a spa with a tranquil atmosphere, partially drawn curtains decorating the stairwell. The Watcher grinned at her one last time before sinking into a sliver of shadow. Navy blue eyes, suit, and golden lion's head ring disappeared in a plume of smoke, leaving behind only a wisp of sulfur stench.

"Damn!" Malini rolled her eyes at the ornate doors to the spa with contempt.

Jacob channeled his sword back into his flask. "Do you think he was the source of contamination?"

"I don't know. The elixir was inside the bottled water. If that was the Watcher responsible, he contaminated the bottle at the source. Senator Bakewell spends most of his time in Washington. If he's influencing him there too, we've got a very busy Watcher on our hands."

"Still, it's possible."

"Yeah, but did you notice his suit? He's posing as an executive. There's something else going on here, Jacob."

"We could go back upstairs and grill Amanda for more info."

"She's influenced too. She won't tell us anything."

"Then what do you suggest?"

"We need to collect ourselves, talk to the council, and do

our homework on Harrington Enterprises. My gut tells me this is bigger than Senator Bakewell."

"Shoes?" Jacob asked, glancing at her bare feet.

She shook her head.

"You're the boss." He led the way toward the atrium to meet Lillian.

"And I can parallel park too," Malini said under her breath.

THREE

THE COUNCIL

T he next day, Malini arrived in Eden alone with two things on her mind: Harrington Enterprises and Cheveyo. She needed to ask Abigail and Gideon for help researching where the infected Harrington water was produced and distributed. Until she understood the connection between Senator Bakewell and Harrington, she was putting out a fire with an eyedropper.

Cheveyo was another story entirely. He'd been missing far too long. With two experienced Helpers on the case, finding him should have been easy, but every lead came up empty. She'd even visited the In Between and searched for his thread. Maybe he'd been taken by the Watchers? She hoped not. They needed every Soulkeeper left alive to stand any chance of keeping Lucifer at bay.

Abigail met her at the door. "No Jacob today?"

"Laudner family brunch."

"Ah yes. How is Aunt Veronica doing?"

"Ninety-six and still gripping to life with both crotchety hands." Malini laughed.

"Same as I remember then." Abigail led the way through the jeweled foyer of The Eden School for Soulkeepers.

"How are things with you and Gideon?" Malini asked.

"Oh ...Uh ... Good, I suppose. Settling in."

"You don't sound thrilled exactly. Is married life not what you expected?" Immediately, Malini regretted the all-too-personal question.

She dipped her head. "Oh, marriage is fine ... perfect actually. Eden, on the other hand..."

"What about Eden?"

"Honestly, sometimes this place feels like a prison. Both Gideon and I would rather be working alongside the other Soulkeepers."

First Grace and the twins, now Abigail. Didn't anyone appreciate the safety of Eden? Malini paused outside the hallway. "I'm sorry, Dr. Silva. It's just too dangerous for you right now."

"Yes, of course. After Lucifer's threat at our wedding, we should be thankful for Eden." She didn't sound thankful.

Malini nodded and let it drop.

"How long do you have today?" Abigail asked.

"A few hours. My family thinks I'm studying at the library. I should be, of course. Senior year, you know."

"That's right! Have you applied anywhere?"

"Your alma mater."

"University of Illinois? They'd be fools not to admit you. What will you study?"

"Journalism."

Abigail turned away but not before Malini caught a flash

of skepticism. Everyone assumed she'd study medicine because she was a Healer, but the idea of having to allow people to die on a regular basis when she had the capability to heal them didn't appeal to her. Life and death were a delicate balance, so easily thrown off by the most benevolent of actions. No, she would be an observer, ferreting out evil and bringing it to light.

At the stairwell, Malini noticed the halls had been conspicuously empty. "Where is everyone, anyway?"

"The rest of the council is waiting for us in the conference room, and the students are studying in the dining hall. We haven't made the curriculum easy."

With a snort, Malini declared her support. "Better hard now than hard later when they're fighting for their lives."

"My sentiments exactly." Abigail hooked right at the top of the stairwell.

"Are Grace and Lee back from Sedona?"

"Not exactly." Abigail flashed a knowing smile and opened the door to the room next to her office.

The conference room consisted of a long wooden table in front of an arched window overlooking the jungle. When Malini walked in, Lillian and Gideon tilted their faces up to greet her. So did Grace and Master Lee, although Malini could see right through their bodies to the chairs they sat in.

"Wha—" she said as her mouth dropped open.

"Warwick's stones," Abigail explained. "We figured out how they worked. They project the image of the person calling to the other stones in the set." She motioned toward the rough, blue gemstone on the table. "Ancient cell phones."

"Handy," Malini said.

Inside the blue tint of his transparent image, Lee's hologram smiled. "Good morning, Malini."

"Good morning," Malini took a seat across from Grace's hologram "Any new clues on Cheveyo's whereabouts?"

Grace spoke up first. "We found an apartment in Sedona with residual traces of Soulkeeper energy. Only, no one lives there anymore. Building manager says a woman and her son moved out over a month ago."

"Did they leave a forwarding address?" Malini asked.

"A place in Flagstaff. The son's name was Chevy."

Gideon shifted in his seat. "Surely a nickname."

"Presumably. We're headed to Flagstaff tomorrow to confirm he's our Soulkeeper."

"Excellent," Malini said. "So, why do you both look so worried?"

Lee sighed. "The residue was faint, Malini. I am an experienced Helper. I've been tracking Soulkeepers for decades. Either he is in transition, or he has never used his power. He is going to be vulnerable."

"Crap. Do you think Lucifer has him?" Malini asked.

Abigail shook her head. "Lucifer may have his name from the list, but if we can't locate him, chances are Lucifer can't either. Something about this boy is making him hard to find, both for us and for the Watchers."

"We need to get to him first," Malini said.

"Obviously." Grace pursed her lips.

What's with the attitude? Malini scowled.

Master Lee made his best attempt to diffuse the tension. "We will find him. Before we leave for Flagstaff, we are visiting his old school and interviewing neighbors. A picture would aid our search efforts."

"Makes sense. Thank you," Malini said.

With nothing left to share, Abigail reached for the stone.

"Thank you for being with us today. I'll keep the stone with me in case you find anything."

Grace nodded, reaching for the sister stone. Her image flickered and then disappeared, along with Master Lee's.

"That was disappointing," Lillian said, turning a paperclip between her fingers.

Malini couldn't argue. Discouragement hung heavy in the air between them. "How are the new Soulkeepers coming along?" she asked, hoping for better news.

"Good. Bonnie and Samantha are tougher than they look, and Jesse was already good as gold after training with Master Lee," Lillian said.

"And Ethan?"

Lillian's eyes flicked to Gideon's. They both made a sound like a soft groan.

"What is it?"

"He's, um, challenging," Lillian said.

"What does that mean?"

"Well, he has trouble following the rules," Gideon said.

Abigail tilted her head in agreement. "He's late for every class, has been caught trying to cheat several times, and is otherwise annoying."

"Annoying?" Malini laughed.

She bit her lip. "He loves to be the center of attention. Yesterday, he burst into song, some obnoxious rap melody, and started grinding against one of the gnomes. We had to give the poor fellow the day off."

As much as she wanted to keep a straight face, Malini couldn't, overcome as she was by a fit of giggles. Soon the others joined in as well.

Lillian shook her head. "He is funny. A joy to have around

most of the time. But can he be disciplined in the field? We're not sure how much we can trust him."

"Hmm. Yes, I can understand why that could be a problem."

Abigail cleared her throat. "He has a past. The night I picked him up I think he was running from the mob. He admitted to stealing some money."

"Ah. Trust is a major issue then."

"Next time you're in the In Between, can you follow his thread?" Abigail asked. "Give us something to go on?"

"Of course." Malini nodded.

"Good." Abigail scribbled a note to herself.

"Well then, Lillian filled us in on yesterday's mission. What is your plan with regard to Harrington Enterprises?" Gideon asked.

"None yet. I need your help with some research. Maybe one of the helpers can bring you resources."

"No need. We have all the resources necessary. Follow me." He gathered his notes and headed for the door.

Confused, Malini said her goodbyes to Lillian and followed Gideon into the hall. Abigail joined them at her side.

"Where are we going?" Malini asked.

Abigail smiled mischievously. "We have something to show you, something I believe you will find quite interesting."

"Interesting like The Huffington Post or interesting like a hive of Watchers trying to decapitate me?"

"The first."

"Excellent!"

Through a door at the end of the hall, Malini followed Abigail into an antechamber.

"I don't remember ever being in here before," Malini said.

"This room wasn't accessible." Abigail pointed toward the door they'd just entered. "That used to be a solid stucco wall."

Malini lowered her chin and raised her eyebrows.

Gideon paused to face her. "I was lamenting the lack of outside information in Eden when Archibald, the good gnome that he is, asked if there was anything he could get for me. I said, 'Yes, a New York Times.' And, without leaving Eden, he brought me one."

"What? How?"

"As we've come to expect here, there's more to this place than meets the eye. Turns out Warwick sealed off this room with magic when he left. I don't blame him. The content is worth protecting."

"Show me." Malini was smiling now. She suspected what might be behind the double doors and crossed her fingers, hoping she was right.

Abigail grasped the carved wooden handle and pulled. Behind the heavy door was a golden, three-story, round room from a fairy tale.

"A library!" Malini said, stepping inside. A winding staircase led to the second and third floor, where curved shelves stretched floor to ceiling, laden with tomes.

"Oh yes, a library. An enchanted library. Come, a demonstration is in order."

"Please!" Malini said excitedly.

"We'll start with the fiction section. What are you in the mood to read?"

Malini grinned. "Romance."

Abigail led her to a shelf of books labeled with a hand-carved plaque in a language Malini didn't know. "Choose a book," she said.

"But the spines have no titles," Malini said, confused. She lifted a leather volume off the shelf and flipped it open. "The pages are blank."

"You didn't tell it what to be," Abigail said. "Close the book again."

Malini did.

"Now concentrate on the book you want to read." Abigail waited. "Open it again."

Delighted, Malini opened the book and read the words that appeared on the page. "'It is a truth universally acknowledged that a single man in possession of good fortune must be in want of a wife.' Holy magical library, this is Jane Austen!" Malini gaped at Abigail, who was laughing as if she still couldn't believe it.

"And that's just the beginning," Gideon's voice boomed from above. He hung over the gold railing on the second floor. "Come check out the Google section."

Malini jogged up the stairs to his side. "Google section?"

"My nickname for this section." He pointed to a row of black tomes. "Ask these books a question—out loud. It seems to work better that way."

Rubbing her hands together, Malini asked the question weighing on her mind. "Where is the Soulkeeper Cheveyo?"

The spines blurred and then filled with print. "Arizona Live Births, the History of Hopi Civilization in America, Flagstaff Arizona visitors' guide. Looks like Grace and Lee are searching in the right place!"

"Incredible, yes? Anything we need is at our fingertips." Gideon lifted the first tome and started flipping to the section labeled "C."

"What does it say?"

"There isn't a Cheveyo listed," Gideon said.

"Figures. But like anything else here, it's a matter of asking the right questions."

Gideon nodded.

"I wonder..." Malini ran her fingers along the spine of a book. "Do you think this place is connected to my power somehow? Where does the information come from?"

Contemplative, Gideon rubbed his chin. "Anything is possible, I suppose, although these books mirror what's available in the outside world and nothing more. They can't predict the future or focus on a specific soul any more than a biography."

"I see."

"I hate to disturb you, Malini," Abigail called from below. "I know there's more you'd like to do here, but the gnomes are expecting to see you before you go, and I think, the students too. It means a lot to them."

Malini nodded. Part of being a leader was being *there* for people. It was something she'd had to get used to, a part of growing up she'd never expected. Her presence, her attention, brought comfort to others. Even on days she didn't believe in herself, she had learned others did with an almost mystic reverence, and it was important that she uphold the responsibilities of her station.

"Gideon, would you mind researching Harrington Enterprises for me? And continuing to dig for more information on Cheveyo?" she asked.

"Of course not. I'd be happy to," he said.

Thank goodness. Malini descended the stairs, straightened her spine, and cleared her head. At Abigail's side, she prepared to give her full attention, her full self, to whoever needed her.

FOUR

STRANGE EXPECTATIONS

In the small town of Paris, Illinois, Dane Michaels adjusted his bright orange tray on the brand-new folding table in the remodeled cafeteria. After the disaster at prom last year, an act of violence the town labeled domestic terrorism, reconstruction had taken an entire summer, but Paris High School was fully operational again.

"Are you guys going to the school dance?" Dane whispered across the table to Jacob and Malini. Not that anyone was listening anyway. The rest of the school had long since decided the three friends, who always sat in the far corner, had nothing interesting to offer. Better they never knew the truth.

Jacob glanced at Malini. "Considering the last dance we went to resulted in Lucifer blowing up the school, I wasn't planning on it. Plus, Malini and I have work to do."

Malini lowered her fork and huffed in his direction. "Jake, yes, okay. There's always work to do. But it's our senior year. We can't miss homecoming just because the devil wants us all dead. I'm not letting him get the best of me."

"Sorry," Jacob said, leaning away from Malini's tantrum. "You wanna go to homecoming?"

"Yes, thanks for asking. I'd love to." She forced a tight smile.

Dane leaned forward in his seat. "Actually, I was talking about the *other* school dance. Although I am on the Paris homecoming committee, and it is going to be fabulous."

His two best friends exchanged glances. Malini raised an eyebrow. "Other school? How have I not heard of this? The Healer should be the first to know." She laughed.

"It's something Ethan's been organizing."

"Ah." Malini poked her baked beans with her fork.

"I guess since there are so few of us, you could just call it a back-to-school get-together," Dane said. Maybe he shouldn't have told Malini. He hoped Ethan wouldn't get in trouble because of him. Dane liked the school in Eden better than Paris. He felt safe there. Unlike Malini and Jacob, he didn't have Soulkeeper powers to protect him if the Watchers returned for a replay of prom night. He was vulnerable to any demon who wanted him dead. Worse, the time he spent in Hell gave Lucifer an imprint of his soul. Outside of Eden, the devil had constant supernatural GPS on his ass and could demand his astral projected presence on a whim. He was a sitting duck.

"You've been spending a lot of time with Ethan, huh?" Jacob said softly.

Malini elbowed him.

"Ow! What the hell? Just making an observation." He rubbed his arm vigorously.

Dane pretended not to catch that Jacob's inference had to do with Ethan's sexual orientation. He didn't want to go there.

"Well, uh, he doesn't have many friends here, you know, and he's not allowed to leave Eden much. He's been helping me on the farm a little. It gives him something to do. Probably boring considering he's from California and used to work in a club, but he doesn't seem to mind." *And he makes me feel safe.*

"Yeah," Malini said. "He needs you, Dane. You've been a great friend. He and the twins are probably going stir crazy. When is this dance?"

"Friday night. After training. Everything's cleared with Abigail." *Damn*, he sounded too excited. He had to remember Eden wasn't *his* school. As lucky as he was to be included, he didn't belong. Not really. When they all graduated, he'd go away to college, hopefully, and then what? He wouldn't be hanging out in Eden every weekend, that's for sure. Or he could do things his dad's way and take over the farm. Not much time for battling evil when there's corn to grow.

A soft brown hand landed on his pale one. How did she know?

"We wouldn't miss it, Dane. We can all go together. Sounds fun. Plus, maybe while we're in Eden, you and I can talk," Malini said.

Warmth infused his arm, and an easy calm settled over him. "Okay." The bell rang, but he couldn't look away from her soothing topaz eyes.

Jacob groaned and swiped her hand from his. "All right, that's enough healing for the time being. Come on, Malini. We'll be late for English." He placed a protective arm around her shoulders and steered her body toward the exit.

Dane followed them from the cafeteria, rolling his eyes at the theatrics. Jacob knew as well as Dane did that he had nothing to worry about when it came to Malini. Those two were destined for each other.

What was his destiny? He frowned as the image of himself dressed in overalls and carrying a pitchfork slid across his mind. Panic shot through his abdomen, and he was reminded of why he needed to concentrate on his studies. Melding into the hallway traffic, he hurried to his next class.

❦

THE HINGES OF THE SCREEN DOOR SCREECHED AS DANE entered the farmhouse, his bulging backpack weighing down his shoulder. Homework in every subject. So much for easing into the school year. Still he'd have to buckle down to get it all done if he wanted his Friday night free to spend in Eden.

"That you, Dane?" his dad called from the family room.

"Yeah. I'm home."

"Good. I need your help in the grain silo. Problem with the blower. Need to get 'er fixed before harvest." The old man rushed into the kitchen with long, quick strides and rubbed his forehead with the back of his thumb. As always, he was in a hurry. A farmer's work was never done.

"Can't today, Pop. I've got tons of homework." Dane eased the backpack off his shoulder and dropped the weighty cargo on the kitchen table for effect.

His dad stopped abruptly, a rarity in the Michaels's household; the man was never still. "Can't you do it tonight, after dark? Only so much daylight left."

"Like I said, I've got hours of homework, and I've got to be awake. All AP classes, remember?"

Plugging his burly hands into his pockets, he shook his

head. "This is ludicrous. There's only so much education a boy needs. You've got responsibilities 'round here!"

"Luke, you heard the boy!" Dane's mother yelled from the hall, a basket of laundry on her hip. The miserable expression on her face said what her words didn't. There'd be hell to pay if his father pushed it.

His father grunted and turned his head away, like he couldn't stand to look at Dane a moment more.

"I can look at the blower on Saturday. I'm sure Ethan would help me if you can wait a couple of days."

"Ethan, huh?" His dad shook his head and stomped through the squeaky screen door. "I'll check if Walter can do it." Dane hoped he'd go easy on his younger brother; his dad was in a mood, again.

Robotically, his mom entered the kitchen, her thin lips pursed. She'd aged this year. New wrinkles carved out the path her frown took on her face, and her hair was gray at the roots. "You haven't helped 'round here much since you've been home," she said, her voice heavy with disappointment.

"I help when I can."

"Which ain't often."

"It's not what I want to do." The words were out before Dane could consider the implications of the admission.

His mom scooted the basket off her hip and onto the table near his backpack. She started forcibly folding the laundry. "Sometimes a thing grows on a body once they try it."

"I spent the first seventeen years of my life trying it," Dane murmured, then immediately regretted it. Tears gathered in his mom's eyes. He hated to hurt her. None of this was her fault, and he'd put her through so much this summer when he disappeared.

Of course, it wasn't *his* fault either. He'd been captured and held prisoner by Lucifer. But he couldn't tell his parents the truth about what happened. Instead, he'd said he didn't remember anything, and the town assumed his fate was the same as Stephanie Westcott's, who also couldn't remember anything. Dane was told he was abducted, drugged, and kept in a warehouse, a victim of a human trafficking ring. He was freed, just in time, by an FBI sting operation. While a good story, there wasn't a grain of truth to it. Nevertheless, his family welcomed him home and eventually stopped asking questions.

Things hadn't been the same since, because Dane wasn't the same. Not only was he still a bit thinner, his mind was constantly elsewhere. He couldn't force himself to pretend anymore that he wanted anything to do with the farm.

Now his mother stared at him with dull eyes as if she didn't know who he was anymore. "You may not remember anything about your abduction, but I do. You left a gaping hole in our family. It broke my heart."

"I'm sorry—"

She held up one bony hand. "You're eighteen, a legal adult, and I suppose you'll do what you want to do. But we need you, Dane. Whatever happened to you was traumatic. Your father and I've let you do your own thing for a while so you could recover. But I'm beginning to think this isn't about recovering. Don't you want to be part of this family anymore?"

"Mom." Dane shook his head. "I *do* want to be part of this family. But why does that always mean corn and soybeans? Isn't it enough I'm here, and I'm healthy? I'm not the only one who can work the farm. You've got Walter and Jenny."

"Walter's only fourteen and doesn't have half the brains

for business you do. You know that. And Jenny will never be able to handle the physical demands."

"You underestimate both of them. Give them a few years." Cracking his neck, Dane shuffled to the cabinet to pull down a mason jar. He opened the fridge and reached for the lemonade.

"We may not have a few years," his mom said from behind him.

He abandoned his quest for a beverage and turned back toward her. "What is that supposed to mean?"

"Your father isn't well."

Dane closed the refrigerator door.

"He's had some tingling in his toes for a year or so now. It's advanced recently. Sometimes he can't feel his leg at all. Now it's started in his fingers. Doc doesn't know what it is. After harvest, he's got to see a doctor at Mayo clinic for more tests. Of course, he should go now, but he won't. Not with a full field."

Suddenly nauseous, Dane swallowed hard and pressed a hand to his stomach. His father, sick? He'd always thought his dad was practically invincible. Nothing ever slowed the man down. An ongoing joke in their family was how his dad was back in the field the same day Dane was born. He'd never spent a morning in bed his entire life. What if it were true? If his father needed him, genuinely needed him, he'd have to help, at least until Walter was old enough to take over. That meant no college, no Eden. Not for a long, long time.

"So, after harvest? In December? That's when he goes to Mayo?"

"Yes." His mother's face paled.

"Give me until then. I need time. I'll start in the spring, if he's not better, if he really needs me. I'll help out more."

For the first time in what seemed like forever, his mother smiled.

Continue the story—>Soul Catcher, Book 4 in the Soulkeepers Series. Visit https://gpching.com/books/soul-catcher to learn more.

ABOUT THE AUTHOR

G.P. Ching is a USA Today bestselling author of science
fiction and fantasy novels for young adults and not-so-young
adults. She bakes wicked cookies, is commonly believed to be
raised by wolves, and thinks both the ocean and the North
Woods hold magical healing powers. G.P.'s idea of the perfect
day involves several cups of coffee and a heavy dose of nature.
She splits her time between central Illinois and Hilton Head
Island with her husband, two children, and a Brittany spaniel
named Jack, who is always ready for the next adventure.

www.gpching.com
genevieve@gpching.com

f facebook.com/450457555307350

y twitter.com/gpching

◉ instagram.com/authorgpching

BB bookbub.com/authors/g-p-ching

BOOKS BY G.P. CHING

The Soulkeepers Series

The Soulkeepers, Book 1

Weaving Destiny, Book 2

Return to Eden, Book 3

Soul Catcher, Book 4

Lost Eden, Book 5

The Last Soulkeeper, Book 6

Soulkeepers Reborn

Wager's Price, Book 1

Hope's Promise, Book 2

Lucifer's Pride, Book 3

The Grounded Trilogy

Grounded, Book 1

Charged, Book 2

Wired, Book 3

BOOK CLUB DISCUSSION QUESTIONS

1. In Return to Eden, Abigail tries to be something more than she is. Do you believe people can truly change? Or are we born what we are?

2. Have you ever been tempted in a way that you felt was impossible to deny?

3. The immortals in the In Between sometimes break the rules in order to maintain the balance between good and evil. Are there circumstances in real life when the moral choice is to take action that in other circumstances would be considered immoral? Is there such thing as a "white" lie?

4. Mara learns that she can create her own reality in the In Between. If you could create your own reality, what would you change first?

5. With her transition to the In Between, Mara loses her power. Later, she rises to the challenge presented to her. What do you think motivates Mara's character to accept the challenge in spite of her new vulnerability? Would you do the same?

6. In Return to Eden, God appears as the best version of the person viewing him/her. What do you think of this depiction? Do you think we see ourselves in God?

7. During the battle scene, Abigail and Gideon get what they want at the worst possible time. Have you ever received a blessing at a time that makes it feel like a curse?

8. In many young adult novels, the main character changes from being human to a supernatural being. In Return to Eden, the change is in the opposite direction. How did this make you feel? Do you think becoming human is a worthy goal for a supernatural character?

9. When characters in The Soulkeepers Series use the red stone, they enter a reality that helps them interpret their experiences. Why do you think Gideon's mind chose a 1950s diner?

10. Return to Eden introduces a new Soulkeeper who is openly homosexual. Did this surprise you? Discuss.

ACKNOWLEDGMENTS

Return to Eden was a difficult book to write. I've always related to Abigail and writing this story sometimes left me in tears. She irrevocably changes. Saying goodbye is never easy. I couldn't have finished this book without the following people.

Special thanks to Karly Kirkpatrick and Angela Carlie for your help, support, and friendship. You made Return to Eden possible. Thanks to Deranged Doctor for the cover art and to all of the Indelible authors for your support. Thanks to Dani Crabtree for help editing the series. Finally, thank you to my family for tolerating my absence when it seemed I'd never come out of the editing cave.

Printed in Great Britain
by Amazon